DAYS OF
VENGEANCE

Books by Harry Mark Petrakis

Novels

LION AT MY HEART
THE ODYSSEY OF KOSTAS VOLAKIS
A DREAM OF KINGS
IN THE LAND OF MORNING
THE HOUR OF THE BELL
NICK THE GREEK
DAYS OF VENGEANCE

Short Stories

PERICLES ON 31ST STREET
THE WAVES OF NIGHT
A PETRAKIS READER—TWENTY-SEVEN STORIES

Autobiography

STELMARK

DAYS OF
VENGEANCE

Harry Mark Petrakis

DOUBLEDAY & COMPANY, INC.
GARDEN CITY, NEW YORK   1983

Library of Congress Cataloging in Publication Data
Petrakis, Harry Mark.
Days of vengeance.
I. Title.
PS3566.E78D3   1983   813'.54
ISBN: 0-385-04921-8
Library of Congress Catalog Card Number: 82–45364

For my wife Diana's parents
John and Lambrini Perparos

Would God my passion drove me to slaughter
you and eat you raw . . .
You'll have no bed of death, nor will you be
laid out and mourned by her who gave you
birth. Dogs and birds will have you, every
scrap.

> Akhilleus to Hektor

Vengeance is mine; I will repay, saith the Lord.

> Romans 12:19

CRETE
1909

‖‹‹❖

CHAPTER ONE

Manolis

That glowing day in autumn gave no warning of being different from many other days Manolis and Aleko had shared. They worked on the mountain, trimming fruit trees of branches shattered in a storm the night before. Above them loomed the rugged peaks and high cliffs that sheltered the valleys from the morning and evening winds. Below them was the winding road that ran across the mountains from the seaport town of Rethymnon to the villages that included their own Vilandredou.

Shielded from the sun by the shade of the trees, at midday they put aside their shears and ate some fruit and nuts. Then they sprawled side by side on the ground to rest.

For a while, the shrill cries of the starlings swooping down the sheer rock cliffs kept them awake. After the birds fell silent, Manolis slept. When he woke and roused Aleko, the sky had turned crimson, the trunks of trees obscured in a hazy, scarlet mist.

Emerging from beneath the trees, Manolis saw the dust of moving wheels on the road below. When the wagon crossed the ridge, caught by the sun, it glowed as if it were a chariot of fire.

"That's Leontis and Spiro returning from Rethymnon," he called to his brother.

Aleko leaped to the crest of a boulder and raised his hands to wave. His voice bellowed down the slope like a clap of thunder. The wagon stopped and both men on it stood up, waving in an animated response.

"They seem delighted to see us," Aleko laughed. "All right, boys, you've proved your friendship. We'll see you later."

Leontis and Spiro continued to gesture wildly.

"I think they want us to come down," Manolis said.

"If they've been drinking and this is some joke," Aleko said grimly, "I'll raise lumps on their lopsided heads."

He started down the slope with Manolis close behind him. After a few strides, Aleko stopped.

"It doesn't make sense for both of us to go down," he said. "By the time we climb back up here, we won't be able to finish the trimming before dark. The old man will want our heads. You go down, Manolis, and see what they want."

Manolis continued down the slope, the stalks of weeds crackling beneath his boots, his heels kicking loose a small slide of stones. The closer he came to the road, the more frantically the men on the wagon waved. As if to hasten their meeting, both Leontis and Spiro leaped down from the wagon and began climbing toward him.

"Alekooooooo!" Leontis bawled up the mountain. "Alekoooo!" He motioned at Manolis in agitation. "Why didn't he come down? Can't he see us waving like madmen?"

"Stop howling and tell me what you want!"

"He's going to America!" Leontis shouted. Spiro grinned and nodded.

Manolis stared at him in bewilderment. "Who's going to America?"

"Who do you think, you boob! Your brother, Aleko, is going to America!"

"And I'm going to Constantinople to see the Patriarch!" Manolis said in disgust. "You're lucky I came down instead of Aleko to hear your nonsense!"

"You wet-eared pup, it's the truth!" Leontis roared. "The steamship agent in Rethymnon found us in the marketplace and gave us the message for him! His years of prayers have been answered! Your uncle Agrios, in America, has sent him a steerage ticket and some money for the journey! Do you understand? Aleko's going to America!"

As the impact of the words burst against Manolis, he felt a dreadful loss. Then that selfish emotion was swept aside in jubilation for Aleko and he began to shout.

"He's hacking at the trees and can't hear us!" Leontis cried impatiently. "Let's holler together!"

The three of them joined their voices. "Alekooooooooo! Alekooooooooo!"

Aleko appeared from beneath the trees, his white-shirted figure outlined against the blood-red sky that rimmed the mountain.

"Now he'll think the three of us have gone crazy!" Manolis said, and he waved vigorously with the others. Suddenly Aleko started down the slope. He walked rapidly at first and then broke into a run, leaping over the clumps of heather and thyme, sprinting across the distance that separated them as swiftly as a racing wolf.

"He'll break his neck!" Spiro said.

"No he won't," Manolis said. He heard the mountain rumbling in celebration for Aleko. There were goat bells and the bells of distant churches and the crack of faraway guns. "He's been waiting for this dream to come true all of his life," Manolis said. "He won't break his neck now."

The four of them rode home in the wagon through the twilight, shouting and singing, their wild voices echoing across

the mountain. In barnyards, chickens cackled, and several
dogs ran barking at their wheels. Before their house Aleko
jumped down and rushed inside with Leontis and Spiro to
break the news to his mother and his sisters Coula and Eleni.

While the girls shrieked and hugged their brother, Manolis
saw his mother staring mutely at Aleko. He understood the
things she felt as she walked slowly to kneel before the cluster
of small icons and votive candles. She whispered her prayers
and made her cross. Afterward she sent Eleni to carry word
to their father, who was still working in the fields.

"Let's go down to the coffeehouse and break the news!"
Leontis laughed. "I can't wait to see the faces of some of
those old goats!"

They scrambled back into the wagon and rode to the village square. Before the coffeehouse they jumped down and
stamped into the smoky and crowded room. Aleko, flushed
and elated, made his announcement. His news was met with
shouts of approval and best wishes. Panfelio, the wiry old
owner of the coffeehouse, bought a round of raki and several
men vacated one of the corner tables so Aleko, Manolis,
Leontis and Spiro could sit down.

While the villagers listened eagerly, the story had to be
repeated in greater detail, beginning with the steamship agent
finding Leontis and Spiro in the marketplace and giving them
the message from Uncle Agrios. How they were anxiously
carrying the good news back to the village when they recognized Aleko's voice shouting down to them. And throughout
the recital, bottles kept tilting, glasses were refilled, raki
flowed. Manolis felt his senses reeling with the fumes of liquor,
cigars and black coffee.

When their married sister's husband, Gus Klouvakis, entered the coffeehouse, the stories were repeated to him. He listened in astonishment.

"A ticket and money for the trip to America!" he said.

"Can these really be waiting for Aleko in Rethymnon or is it some hoax?"

"I saw the ticket myself!" Leontis cried balefully. "Do you count me a fool? It was blue and white, with a picture of a steamship on one side! Beautiful-looking document, like a marriage or a baptismal certificate!"

"Perhaps it looked like the citation I got from the king when I was wounded in Macedonia in '97," Xilakis said earnestly. "You saw my honor, Leontis. Did you think the ticket resembled it?"

"Now that you remind me, Cleon"—Leontis winked at the others—"it did resemble your honor from the king."

Gerakaris spoke to Gus Klouvakis. "Several fellows who can't afford it have bought drinks for this joyous occasion, Gus," he said gravely. "Since you're the wealthiest man in the village as well as the only moneylender, you should buy a double round."

Manolis smiled at Aleko. Both of them knew that any disbursing of money for which he wouldn't receive interest caused Gus Klouvakis severe pain. Everyone in the coffeehouse enjoyed his agonized struggle. Finally, family pride overwhelmed his natural stinginess.

"Bring out a couple of bottles, Panfelio"; Gus tried to speak heartily. A few of the men accorded him a modest cheer. That rare accolade for the most disliked man in the village brought tears to his eyes.

As the vapors of drink and the swirls of smoke grew thicker, the men began debating the merits of the trip.

"Even if someone sent me a ticket, I wouldn't go," a dour-faced baker named Spetakis said. He was jeered, but he waved the objections aside and pulled a worn, crumpled envelope from his pocket. "Here, Manolis," he said. "You read better than any of us. Read this letter from my cousin

Menelaus, in Peets-burg, America. You don't have to read it
all, since everyone has heard it. Just the last paragraph will
do."

Manolis pulled the frayed letter from the envelope and read
the final paragraph:

> All day we sell candy from a basket tied around our
> necks and they call us beggars and swine and by
> other names that we do not understand but that we
> know are insulting. I think sometimes of killing one
> of them to let them understand they cannot treat a
> Cretan this way, but then I would rot in jail and not
> be able to return home to the village, which I pray
> to do as soon as I have saved enough money.

"That is the way all your relatives whine, Spetakis!" Or-
fanos shouted. "Your clan finish up beggars and malcontents,
wherever they go. Listen to what my nephew Gorgios writes
from America." He pulled a letter as stained and tattered as
the one displayed by Spetakis and handed it to Manolis to
read as well:

> Here the people work regularly and get paid on time
> and eat well and rest all day Sunday and, some-
> times, even Saturday, too. This day I am writing
> you is Saturday. I took a bath in hot water with
> scented soap, had two glasses of milk, and will pass
> my day at leisure. Where did I ever know life so
> contented? I wish you could come here, Uncle, and
> we would prosper and live this good life together.

"That's more like it, eh, Aleko?" Leontis exclaimed. "That's
what's waiting for you over there!"

Through the toasts and drinking, the banter, excitement
and reading of the letters, Aleko's mood had grown quieter.
He sat with them in the coffeehouse, and yet Manolis under-

stood his thoughts were far beyond the village, tracing the pattern of his journey.

When Manolis considered how empty his life would be without his brother, an iron fist squeezed his heart. From childhood they had been linked by ties of love more binding than blood. There was a saying among the villagers that God's eye looked upon Aleko with approval.

At twenty-five, six years older than Manolis, Aleko was taller, more vigorous and handsomer than any Cretan within the range of a dozen villages. Dressed in his finery for a festival or a wedding, wearing a beaded shirt, silver-festooned vest, gleaming boots and a dark band about his raven-black hair, he exuded the bold, majestic demeanor of a brigand chieftain.

Manolis had grown up under his brother's tutelage. Aleko had taught him how to mend his boots, shoot a musket and a pistol, hunt, wrestle and run. Aleko had helped him understand his sexual awakenings during the nights they spent in the sheepfold on the mountain talking of life, dreams and love.

Even as their bonds grew stronger, Manolis was always aware that one day his brother would have to leave the village. Like their uncle Agrios, who had gone to America and had volunteered in that country's war against Spain, Aleko's life was guided by a star like a glowing sentinel.

As for Manolis, his dreams were more modest. He wanted to remain under the stars and mountains of Crete, wanted to marry and raise his children on his own land. That was an ordinary dream, but he had long before accepted that he was an ordinary man.

Aleko looked across the table and smiled at Manolis.

"I think it's time to go, brother," he said. "The old man will be back from the fields and I have to get ready to leave."

At that moment the door of the coffeehouse banged open

and Stellios Trombakis stalked in, followed closely by his brother, Mitsos. Manolis felt a chilled, unsettling wind sweep the room.

Stellios was a villager about Aleko's age, a violent, acrimonious man who lived from impulse to impulse. They were nearly matched in size and strength, and for years Stellios fought Aleko in a rivalry that Aleko won whether the contest involved hunting, running or dancing. The mordantly proud Stellios brooded about these defeats and for a long time a virulent tension had grown between them.

A few weeks earlier a new hostility had been added with a rumor that Aleko was interested in Stellios' sister, Froso. The girl, who was lean, timid and unattractive, must have been overcome with delight and, for two Sundays, attired in her best clothing, waited for Aleko to call on her family.

Aleko had never shown any interest in the girl and knew nothing of the rumor, which might have been started by one of the men Stellios had mistreated. When he learned of the incident, Aleko made an effort to explain to Stellios, who remained convinced that Aleko had made sport of his sister. Each time he and Aleko were together, a confrontation threatened.

Stellios started walking toward them. At each table he passed, the voices and revelry were muffled, until by the time he reached Aleko, the room was snared in a total silence.

"I'm glad you came, Stellios." Aleko tried to speak sociably. "Have you heard? I'm leaving for America. Join us for a drink."

"I'm not here to drink with you," Stellios said, his voice as cold and stony as his face. He motioned to his brother. Mitsos pulled open the coffeehouse door to reveal their sister, Froso, standing on the threshold. In the light of the paraffin lamps the girl was wearing the finery she might have worn to a cele-

bration. But there was only wretchedness and shame in her
face. As the stern, silent men stared at her, she cringed and
began to tremble.

Stellios pointed his finger like a knife at Aleko. "Before all
these witnesses now, Aleko Manousakis, I demand that you
honor your obligation to my sister!"

His words struck like thunder through the silence. Several
men coughed nervously and Leontis started angrily to his
feet, but Aleko caught his arm, staring with pity at the
forlorn figure of the girl in the doorway. Manolis saw that all
rejoicing had been driven mercilessly from his face.

"How could you do this to your sister, Stellios?" Aleko
asked in a shocked voice. "How could you bring her here and
shame her like this? Come to your senses, man, and take her
home."

"Never mind my senses!" Stellios said hoarsely. "I call on
every man here to witness my accusation! My father isn't
alive and so I am here as head of my family to demand you
fulfill your pledge to my sister!"

A few men muttered in disapproval. Stellios swept them
with a glare that silenced them. Aleko rose and slowly walked
around the table to face Stellios. Both men were the same
towering height, with muscled shoulders and arms.

"I haven't offended your sister or your family," Aleko said
quietly. "I've told you that already, Stellios, and now before
these witnesses, I swear it again."

"You made a pledge for Froso!" Mitsos cried from the
door. Manolis knew him as a craven young man whose spirit
and courage depended upon his older brother.

"Aleko could have any girl in the village!" Leontis said
sharply. "Why in hell would he choose your sister?"

"This is between Aleko and me!" Stellios said to Leontis.
He spoke again to Aleko, the words hissing from his lips.

"I warn you, Aleko, don't try and leave Crete without fulfilling your obligation . . ."

Sparks of anger flew from Aleko's eyes. "Damn you, Stellios! I haven't made any advances to your sister in word or thought! That's God's truth and Froso knows it's the truth! Now, leave me alone and take the poor girl home!"

Stellios lunged and grabbed Aleko around the throat. Froso shrieked and Manolis leaped to his feet, tangling with the men scrambling from their chairs. As Aleko and Stellios grappled and pushed, the muscles in their arms and shoulders strained against their shirts.

Still trying to avoid a fight, Aleko shoved Stellios roughly away. The enraged Stellios charged back to butt Aleko in the chest, battering him against the wall. He twisted aside just in time to avoid a kick Stellios launched at his groin.

When Stellios charged again, Aleko drove a hard, stinging blow to his chest that rocked Stellios back on his heels.

"Finish the bastard, Aleko!" Leontis cried harshly.

Aleko raised his hand to Stellios in appeal. "In God's name I don't want to fight you!"

"Whoreson!" Stellios spit the obscene word. "Coward!"

His own rage bursting then, Aleko leaped forward to hammer his fists into Stellios. With one and then another savage blow, he slammed Stellios back. Struggling to keep his feet, a trickle of blood running from his mouth, Stellios braced to attack again.

"Stop this madness now!" Panfelio cried to the crowd. "They'll kill each other! Stop them!"

A dozen men hurried to form a barrier between them and hold them both in check. Stellios flung several men aside until by sheer weight of numbers they held him. Manolis had never seen Aleko angrier, his face so dark with rage. Leontis, Spiro and he had all they could do to hold him from hurling himself upon Stellios again.

The men pulled and dragged Stellios to the door. They let him go there, forming a barrier lest he try to return to the fight.

For a raging moment he stared at Aleko, black eyes burning with his hate. Then he turned and stamped into the night. Mitsos followed him, dragging his whimpering, moaning sister by the arm into the darkness.

Leontis and Spiro drove them back to their house in the wagon. Their father had returned and had been told about the ticket to America. When he heard about the fight with Stellios, he bristled with anger.

"You let him off too easy!" he said to Aleko. "You should have broken every tooth in his dirty mouth!"

"If they hadn't stopped the fight, Aleko would have knocked him senseless," Manolis said.

"Just as well they stopped it, then," his mother said. "That Trombakis family has always been long-winded on words like honor and short-breathed on words like sense. Those sons are snakes and deserve what they get, but I pity that poor, miserable girl. How could they think Aleko would have anything to do with her? Her only suitor will be some old, sick man who needs a nursemaid to fetch and carry."

"To hell with that family," his father said grimly. "If they want trouble with us, I'll see them all in hell!"

"Is that the way to talk before your daughters and sons?" his mother said sharply. She turned to Aleko. "In a few days you'll be gone, so stay away from Trombakis until then."

"I'll go anywhere in the village I want to go, Mama," Aleko said. He paused and reached out to clasp her hand. "Mama, listen," he went on gently. "I won't be staying here a couple more days. I want to leave for Rethymnon in the morning. Manolis can drive me and bring back the cart."

"So soon!" his mother gasped, and Coula and Eleni echoed

her distress. "Wait a few more days, my son! Stay at least until Sunday, so we can go to church together one last time."

"You know how long I've been waiting for this day, Mama," Aleko said. "Every time one of my friends left the village for America, part of my soul went with him. Now that my turn has come, I can't bear to wait another day."

"But you must pack and get ready!" his mother pleaded. "You can't do all that tonight!"

"What will I take with me to America?" Aleko asked pensively. "My shoes caked with manure? The pants I wear to work in the fields? My riches and my jewels? Mama, the reason I want to go to America is because I have nothing." He stroked her fingers and smiled. "I'll wear my good jacket, breeches and boots," he said, "and pack a small parcel with underclothes and socks and the Bible you gave me when I took my first communion. There isn't anything else I need."

For a moment, no one spoke. His father turned away and his mother made an effort to compose herself.

"Well, at least you will have a bath," she said. "Eleni, bring water from the shed and some more wood for the fire. My son will leave my house soaked and scrubbed clean."

While Aleko bathed in a tub behind a sheet hanging across a corner of the room, Manolis polished his boots briskly, rubbing the leather to a glossy shine. When he finished, he could see his face reflected in their luster.

"Be sure you keep them that way in America," he said to Aleko.

As the fire burned lower, Aleko and Manolis climbed to their bed in the loft. They lay with their feet and shoulders touching, both of them silent.

"America . . ." Aleko whispered the word in wonder. "After so many years of waiting, so many disappointments. America . . . God bless Uncle Agrios!" He turned on his side, speaking in a whisper so they wouldn't disturb the family sleeping below. "No more chopping down and hauling trees, no more digging away stumps and dragging boulders, no more cleaning the press, loading the grain, working like a bloody donkey."

"You're not expecting to find gold in the streets over there, are you?"

"Not gold," Aleko said, "but a chance to work hard for myself, and to do more than I ever could have done here."

"You'll miss a few things here," Manolis said. "No more dressing up and kicking your boots in a *Pendozali*. No more strutting and swaggering before the admiring village girls. No more—"

"All right! I'll miss a few things," Aleko laughed, "and I'll miss you and Mama and the girls and Leontis and the white-crowned mountains and the smell of the orchards in the spring. But that's all I'll miss." He sighed. "God bless Uncle Agrios."

"You blessed him before."

"I'll keep blessing him for as long as I live!" Aleko gave him a light shove. "Now, listen to my final instructions."

"I know what I have to do," Manolis said. "You've told me enough times."

"Then, listen to me again," Aleko said. "Don't forget the kilos of honey Stavros promised us for helping him with his harvest. Watch out in the spring, when the snows melt, that you reinforce the dam we built. Look out for Coula and Eleni and Mama and keep your mouth shut around Stellios Trombakis. His quarrel is with me, not you, but if he tries to provoke you, let Papa or Leontis handle him."

"I'm not afraid of him."

"I know you aren't afraid, brother," Aleko said. "And I know you can take care of yourself. But just do what I say anyway." He shifted restlessly, as if impatient for the night to pass. "Uncle Agrios must have a good job for me. That's probably why he took so long to send for me. I'll work hard and save money to send back here for the girls' dowries. Then I'll send you a ticket so you can come and visit me in America. Who knows? You may want to stay with me once you see what life there is like."

"By the time you can afford to send me a ticket," Manolis said, "I'll be married with children and with acres of my own land."

"I'll still send you a ticket! You can come work with me for a while and then we'll make a visit back to the village. We'll jingle gold pieces in our pockets and dress like those dandies from Paris or Trieste whose pictures we saw in the French newspaper. The villagers will greet us like returning heroes! Here come the wealthy, successful Manousakis brothers!"

"Keep dreaming," Manolis laughed. "Mama will brew you some camomile tea for the gas."

In spite of making fun of his brother's vision, Manolis mustered the spirit for that epic dream. With Aleko, nothing was impossible.

They grew quiet and Aleko turned his face to the wall. After a moment his voice drifted drowsily across the darkness. "America . . ." he whispered. "America . . ."

Long after Aleko had fallen asleep, his breathing even and tranquil, Manolis lay awake, unwilling to give up the last hours they'd have together. The night around the house grew still and, in that stillness, from the corner of the room below the loft, he heard his mother crying.

When he opened his eyes the loft was still dark, not a trace of light yet visible between the shutters. He knew dawn was near, because the cicadas were hushed in that breathless interval before the night gave way to the day.

He stretched his foot and touched Aleko's leg. His brother

answered with pressure of his own. Neither of them spoke, and he felt Aleko storing the day's beginning against all the mornings he would wake alone in a strange land.

The hungry hens gathered outside the house, their cluckings echoing crisply in the fall air. He heard his mother rising, always the first one up, into the chill and darkness, to stir the fire and put on the kettle.

Knowing how grieved she was at Aleko's leaving, Manolis listened for some change in her ritual, but every movement seemed the same as it was each morning. He heard her drawing the long bone comb through her thick hair, the rustle of woolen cloth as she dressed. She moved through the darkness past the loom, around the wooden table, pausing to whisper her prayer before the icons with their flickering tapers. Perhaps the prayer was longer than usual. Then she passed under the strings of onions and garlic that dangled from the arch, around the donkey saddle and bridle. She knelt at the hearth scraping through the ashes to fuel the embers, adding some wood. In a moment a flame leaped through the darkness to light the beams of the loft. Manolis turned to look at his brother's face. Aleko nodded and smiled.

As his mother roused his sisters, his father's heavy tread resounded through the house. When he opened the door, the noise of the hens became a clamor, a few scurrying inside the house. His father stepped outside and pissed on the ground, not bothering to walk to the thatch-roofed latrine.

His mother came to the foot of the ladder, the firelight casting her shadow into the loft.

"We're awake, Mama," Manolis said.

"All right, then," she said, and he heard the tremor in her voice.

To dispel his own melancholy, Manolis punched Aleko roughly in the shoulder. "That's so you won't forget me when you're over in America!"

"I'll give your sassy head something to remember!" Aleko shouted.

Manolis scrambled from the bed to escape the swing of his brother's big hand.

They gathered around the wooden table, as they ate together every morning, but this morning was different. Aleko was dressed in his best jacket and breeches, his black, unruly hair carefully brushed, his dark eyes gleaming with excitement. In addition, the table held an unusually bounteous breakfast of eggs, some chunks of cheese his mother had sizzled and browned over the fire, and even a few sausages she had been saving for Christmas.

"There is too much food here for a poor family," his father grumbled. "Twenty people could eat at this table."

"There aren't twenty people here to eat," his mother said grimly. "But there is one son we may never see in our lifetime again. Let him remember this meal and forget all the others when he rose hungry from this table."

In the silence that followed her words, his father bent his head and mumbled a grace. As they began eating, Aleko made an effort to banish their gloom.

"I'll be the best-dressed Cretan ever to land in America!" he said. "When I get off the ship in that place New York, a delegation of officials will greet me and marvel at my splendid jacket, breeches and high-glossed boots!"

"You won't be dressed fancy, but you'll be neat and clean," his mother said. "I'd be ashamed to send you from my house any other way."

"Your uncle Agrios wrote us that people dress properly in America," his father said gruffly. "They're not ragpickers over there like some blockheads back here. Keep yourself neat and clean and don't make us ashamed."

"I won't, Papa!" Aleko smiled. "I promise you and Mama

I'll mend my ways in America and become a respectable citizen!"

Eleni giggled and Manolis suppressed his own laughter. Aleko gave them a wink.

"Heaven help that country when you get there," his mother said to Aleko, but she spoke each word as if it were a caress.

While Aleko said his farewells to the family, Manolis went to the shed and harnessed the donkey to the cart. He rode it back before the house as his parents, sisters and brother emerged, their figures shrouded in the dawn light.

Aleko placed his canvas bag in the rear of the cart and swung up on the seat beside Manolis. Coula and Eleni called up their last, tearful goodbyes. His father raised his arm and waved slowly, his fingers catching the glimmers of the light. His mother remained motionless until the cart began to move, and then she walked quickly alongside and reached up to Aleko. She clasped his hand tightly. Manolis halted the cart for fear of hurting her.

"Lambrini," his father said quietly.

She shook her head mutely.

His father made an awkward effort to draw her away. She shook him off, still clutching Aleko's hand, not saying a word.

His father motioned to Manolis, who flicked the reins at the donkey, and the wheels of the cart began to roll. For an instant longer his mother gripped Aleko's hand and then their fingers were wrenched apart. When they both turned to look back at her they saw her standing alone, the others behind her. Then all of them were obscured in the mist.

The donkey trudged over the mountain road toward the port town of Rethymnon. The cart lurched from side to side, the wheels rattling on the stones.

They rode in silence, while Aleko stared about him, absorbing sights, sounds and smells.

As if to provide him a treasure for his memories, the day rose with an adorning beauty. The sun crested the mountains, sweeping the road with a golden light. The dew sparkled on the foliage of junipers and pines. A rank of cypresses loomed like plumed sentinels bidding Aleko farewell, while the remnants of the night took refuge in dark crevices between the boulders.

After traveling about two hours, they entered a terrain with the boulders massed thickly along the slope. Manolis pointed ahead to an obstruction blocking the road.

"Some rocks and debris from a slide," Aleko said. "We'll get the cart across."

Manolis drove nearer to the rubble. He held the donkey's reins while Aleko swung off the seat to the ground.

"I think we can clear a path—" His voice snapped off and he stared sharply up the slope. He turned to warn Manolis at the instant two men leaped from behind a boulder and came running swiftly down the slope. They sprang into the road before the cart and Manolis recognized Stellios and Mitsos Trombakis. He saw the pistols in their hands and screamed for Aleko to flee.

His brother never had a chance. Only a few feet from where he stood, both men fired their guns at him. The donkey reared and shrieked, its squall joining the thunder of the gunshots that echoed from the canyons, muffling any cry Aleko made as he tumbled to the road. Manolis leaped from the cart while Stellios and Mitsos fled up the road.

When he crouched over his brother, Manolis saw Aleko's great, stunned eyes staring at the sky. A trickle of blood ran from his lips, and his mouth trembled as he tried to speak.

"Aleko, hold on!" Manolis pleaded. "In God's name, hold on!"

He looked for the cart and saw it far down the road, where the donkey had bolted. He knew it was useless to shout for the animal.

Heaving and crying, he dragged his brother's big, strong frame from the road onto the softer slope, his gleaming black boots bumping along the rocks. He sat down and cradled Aleko's head in his arms. He prayed silently and cried, feeling his spirit torn with despair.

He didn't know how long he sat there, hugging Aleko, whispering to him not to die. His brother's shocked eyes were still open, and from time to time his teeth chattered, his fingers flexed, one of his booted feet jerked.

The sun grew brighter, washing the slopes and road in a strange, sulphurous glow. The earth grew warmer, and the smells of gunsmoke and blood were dispersed into the scents of olives and grapes, and the woolly smell of the flocks carried to them on the wind.

Later in the morning some shepherds found them, men from another village leading their flock to a higher grazing ground. The donkey had returned and stood by the rocks, still hitched to its cart. When the shepherds first bent to look at Aleko, Manolis warned them fiercely away. After one of them spoke soothingly to him, he let them lift Aleko carefully into the rear of the cart. Manolis climbed in beside him, hugging his brother again, cushioning his body against the jolting of the cart as the shepherds took them back home.

CHAPTER TWO

Father Basil

When he received the message that the Bishop of Rethymnon wished to see him, Father Basil left his church and started for the bishopric, walking on the street above the harbor and breathing in the splendor of the autumn day. The sea was olive green, with the sun's reflections skipping like gulls across the water. A few fleecy white clouds were visible on the horizon.

From the shipyard at the harbor's end he heard the clatter of carpenters hacking away with their adzes at the timbers and sternposts of skeleton hulls. In another part of the yard some calkers sang as they worked.

The singing was a favorable augury, the priest thought, a sign that conditions were improving. The oppressive Turkish troops that had occupied the island for centuries had finally been banished by the Great Powers. Within a few more years —God willing that their intrepid premier, Venizelos, would make France, England and Russia fulfill their pledges—Crete would finally be joined to Greece.

In addition to the general optimism about the future, his own life was flourishing. Cristina, his wife for sixteen years, since their marriage in 1893, continued to be a loving, devoted spouse. His daughters, Alexandra and Soula, were growing into lovely young women, and his son, Andreas, the last of their children, was healthy and bright.

Things at his parish could not be better. He had a fine church and his parishioners seemed pleased with his service. Several of the elders had told him that for a young man, not yet forty, he showed remarkable capability and judgment. They indicated their intention to relay their satisfaction to the Bishop, and perhaps that was the reason His Grace had summoned him.

On the street of the foreign consulates, he walked up the steps of the bishopric of Rethymnon. He opened the large, paneled door and stepped into the damp, shadowed foyer. In a moment the Bishop's deacon, a fair-faced young man with a sparse blond beard, appeared. They greeted one another with an embrace and a blessing.

"His Grace will be pleased you have come so promptly, Father," the deacon said, "but he has had a harried morning with the Russian consul, which delayed his rest. Would you be kind enough to wait in the sitting room until he wakes?"

He followed the deacon into an adjoining room. A small charcoal fire barely flickered in the brazier and the room was cold.

"That wicked boy has left the fire burn down again!" the deacon said in exasperation, and he hiked up his cassock and squatted to poke the flame. He added a few more coals, smiled wanly at the priest, and left the room.

Father Basil went to stand before the brazier. In the shadowed, silent room his earlier confidence passed and he wondered nervously if the Bishop had summoned him for a reprimand. He couldn't imagine what he might have done wrong. Perhaps it had something to do with his wife. Some of the sour viragos of his parish thought her habit of speaking her mind, unbecoming. If that was the reason for his summons, he would defend her vigorously and appeal to the Bishop's fairness.

He became so lost in his reveries and in the fire that he didn't hear the room door open. Not until his superior's vibrant voice spoke his name did he turn around to see Bishop Donos standing there, imposing in his high, dark ecclesiastical hat.

Father Basil bent quickly to kiss his hand. "I'm sorry, Your Grace, I didn't hear you enter."

The Bishop waved his apology aside. "How is your good *Papadia* and your lovely children, Father?"

"Papadia is fine, Your Grace, and the children are a delight. We had Alexandra's name day last week. She's our eldest child and already fifteen now. I can't imagine where the years have gone."

"Time will pass even more quickly as you become older," the Bishop sighed.

Bishop Donos was a sturdy man in his sixties with piercing eyes that cannily appraised people. His background, Father Basil knew, wasn't that of an ethereal cleric who had spent his youth in the cloisters. He had labored in the stone quarries and had also been a fisherman. Now he walked to the brazier and rubbed his fingers together slowly.

"The afternoons are growing chillier," he said.

"Yes, Your Grace," Father Basil said, thinking uneasily the Bishop hadn't brought him to the bishopric to discuss the autumn weather.

He waited until the Bishop was seated, and then he sat down in a nearby chair, smoothing his cassock across his knees. They rested in silence for a moment, and then, from the tower of the Ramat Mosque, they heard the chant of the muezzin calling the Muslim faithful to their prayers.

"I asked to see you, Father Basil," the Bishop began slowly, "on a matter of critical importance for our church

. . . and for me. I won't expect an answer at once. Go and talk to your Papadia and make your decision together."

Father Basil waited for him to go on, an almost unbearable tension sharpening the uneasiness he had felt earlier.

"I am asking you, Father," the Bishop said gravely, "to take your wife and your children and become spiritual father to a new parish in the United States of America."

Father Basil stared at the Bishop in shock. He tried bewilderingly to encompass the immensity of such a journey. America . . . thousands upon thousands of miles away, across a vast, bottomless and menacing ocean! America! . . . God help him!

"Your Grace!"—his voice came shrilly from his lips—"are you sending me away because I've failed you here? Have you some grievance with me?"

"Not at all, Father!" The Bishop spoke earnestly. "It is because I regard you so highly that you've been chosen for this momentous challenge." He reached between the folds of his cassock and pulled out a letter.

Father Basil stared at the envelope as if the fragment of paper were a summons to death.

"This letter arrived from America a week ago," the Bishop said, "from one of the states in the heartland of that immense country, a place called Utah. It will be the fourth letter a church committee there has written to me in the past nine months. I have meanwhile confirmed that what they are telling me is the truth. Now, I won't bother to read you the letter, but it speaks of the many young Cretans who have left our island in the past few years to emigrate to their region, a place called Carbon County. There are almost five hundred Cretans working in the coal mines in this town of Snowmass, Utah. They have built themselves a fine church, but they have no priest except a circuit-riding cleric who visits once a month. They plead for a regular priest . . ." He stopped as if he had suddenly become conscious of the priest's disorder. "You still seem shocked, Father," he said with concern. "I'm sorry. Shall we wait a few moments so you can compose your thoughts?"

"I understand what you're saying to me, Your Grace," Father Basil said, "but my first thought is, Why have I been chosen? Why should Papadia Cristina and our children be asked to undertake such a long, hazardous journey? There must be other, young priests who are newly married and do not yet have families. Why, if you'll forgive me, Your Grace, choose us?"

"I haven't chosen you at random, Father," Bishop Donos said gravely, "but because it is crucial that the priest we send to this Carbon County be the right one. He shouldn't be too young, for then he may not be able to make judgments based on experience. Neither must he be so old that he isn't able to understand and accept change, crossing an ocean to repeat the habit of old, parochial conflicts. As for your Papadia and the children . . . why, any priest in such a parish of young men should have a fine Cretan wife and Cretan children as an example for those lonely men who might be tempted to turn to foreign women for matrimony. Believe me, Father, I have thought long and carefully and prayed devotedly for the guidance of the Lord to help me find the right man. Just the other day, several members of your church council called on me to affirm their high regard for you. They validated my earlier consideration of you, and that is why you've been chosen."

The deacon entered the room, bringing them little dishes of candied orange slices and glasses of water. Father Basil held the dish weakly on his lap, struggling to overcome his distress and dismay. He waited to speak again until the deacon had left.

"I understand what you're saying, Your Grace," he said,

"but forgive me for also reminding you that we're settled here in a good parish with people who care for us. My children are happy. My girls are on the threshold of young womanhood. To uproot them for such a long, dangerous journey . . . into a strange, unknown land . . . why, it doesn't seem just."

Bishop Donos placed his dish carefully on the table beside his chair and sighed.

"The questions about justice, Father, have not been properly answered since Job. All I ask you to remember is that our calling resembles that of fishermen. Some put boldly out to sea, battling the currents and storms, seeking a greater challenge, a more abundant catch. The timid fishermen sail back and forth along a familiar coast. Their challenge is less satisfying, their catch thinner and more meager. What I am asking you to do, Father, is to join those fishermen who put boldly out to sea."

The Bishop spoke in a low, somber voice, his words assembling the firmament of their faith, the suffering and sacrifice of all the pilgrims and martyrs. Father Basil felt ashamed of his faint heart.

"Go and think about it, now, Father," the Bishop said. "If you and Papadia Cristina decide not to go, I will respect your decision. But if you do agree to make the journey, then you will both become missionaries for our church, not among the heathens but among our own fine young men who have left their land and their homes. If we don't heed their pleas and prayers, we leave them without a single caring soul to console them in their loneliness. And when they grow ill, die as some of them must, they will not even have a priest to hear their confession, to offer them a final prayer before they are interred forever in the earth of a strange land."

He rose and Father Basil rose. The Bishop crossed the short span between them and pulled Father Basil into his arms, for an instant embracing him tightly. With their faces close together, the priest saw the tears in the Bishop's eyes.

When Father Basil emerged into the foyer of the bishopric, he found the young granddaughter of Cleon Gavalas waiting for him. Gavalas was an aged parishioner who was dying, and although the priest had already given him communion, his wife requested it a second time. Father Basil sent the girl to his house to bring the small satchel with his chalice and wine to her grandfather's. He left the bishopric, walking slowly through the streets, not thinking of the dying old man but of his own turmoil.

Away from the magnetism of the Bishop's presence, he began to perceive the monstrous sacrifice being asked of his family. He had seen letters written by men who had made the crossing, letters that described in distressing detail the suffering and hardship of the journey. Some had even died in passage, their friends writing back the sorrowful tidings. The whole idea was madness! He should have been courteous to His Grace but explicit in his refusal!

At that moment he made up his mind. After he had given Gavalas communion, he'd return to Bishop Donos and inform him that, regretfully, he couldn't possibly go to America. They'd just have to find another priest.

The courtyard of the Gavalas house was unkempt and littered with scraps, the garden overgrown with weeds. Aspasia Gavalas, an acerbic-tongued old lady with warts on her cheeks, met him at the door of the house.

"Good afternoon, Kyra Aspasia."

"Not much good about it, Father," she said peevishly. "My granddaughter just brought your things and the old man is waiting."

He followed her through a narrow corridor.

"He's growing weaker and nearer to dying," the old woman grumbled, "but that doesn't make him penitent, or humble toward his Maker. Not him! He's mean as a lizard!"

"Patience, Kyra Aspasia," Father Basil murmured. "Later on you will feel grateful for having made his final hours as comfortable as you could."

The priest entered the shadowed sickroom and was assailed by the odors of incontinence and decay. He walked slowly to the iron bed, where the skeletal head of old Cleon Gavalas lay still within the folds of blanket.

"Cleon, it's Father Basil."

"I didn't think it was the Archbishop come to see me off," the old man said loudly.

"See what I mean, Father?" his wife snapped from the doorway. "Irreverent to his last breath. Oh, the devil will be waiting for him!" She stamped off through the corridor.

Father Basil sat down on a stool beside the bed. He watched the old man for a moment in silence, experiencing no special bond beyond the simple pity one might feel for any human being whose life was ending.

"She's right," Gavalas said.

"About what?"

"About the devil waiting for me."

"She wasn't serious, Cleon," Father Basil spoke hastily to reassure him.

"But I'm serious!" Gavalas said. "The devil will be waiting for me. He'll ask for news about his sister that I married!" He erupted in a cackle of laughter.

Father Basil had witnessed the final hours of a number of his parishioners. Some were fearful or remorseful, repentant or resigned. Still others were angry at what they felt to be their misdirected, premature fate. But old Gavalas demonstrated a jocularity the priest hadn't seen before in someone dying.

"Your color is better today, Cleon."

"Your eyesight is worse, Father."

"But your voice seems stronger."

"That's because I'm closer to the big leap now, Father," the old man said zestfully. "I've been impatient for weeks and, finally, my wretched carcass has caught up to my ambition."

A silence settled over them and the priest struggled for something to say. The odors of the sickbed were clammy and oppressive and he was anxious for sunlight and air. He rehearsed the firm words he'd speak to Bishop Donos when he returned to the bishopric. When Gavalas coughed suddenly, he felt remorse at his selfishness and reached forward to clasp the tendinous hand above the blanket.

"Shall we pray together, Cleon?"

"If you like, Father, you can hear my final confession, which, I promise, will be short and sweet. I have been a wicked, merry man and I do not regret my life."

The priest waited for him to go on.

"That's all there is," Gavalas said.

The priest reached into the satchel and drew out the chalice. He poured wine from the flask into the bowl and murmured a prayer and then held the cloth beneath the old man's chin. Gavalas swallowed the thimble of wine and smacked his toothless gums.

"I could stand a quart more!" he said fervently, and his ravaged face seemed to glow. "I tell you, Father, you see only the wreck of what I appear to be now. But, God's truth, I feel young, on the edge of a great adventure, and bearing the joy of a bridegroom about to raise his new wife's veil!"

When Father Basil emerged from the Gavalas house, twilight had mantled the streets. From a nearby garden he caught the piquant aroma of lemon trees. That familiar scent produced a surge of nostalgia. He recalled his excitement as a boy when he had climbed the ramparts of the castle and stared across the steeples and minarets that resembled some fabled city in the old tales. He remembered the bazaars teeming with people, the merchants and buyers haggling, the street musicians playing their flutes and tambourines. He remembered strolling with Cristina in the park, a glowing moon visible through the filament of trees. He remembered the lazy summer afternoons when his children were still infants, playing at the water's edge, their shrieks blending with the chanteys of the fishermen sorting their nets upon the beach. He remembered his church in the stillness of a Sunday daybreak, while he tolled the bell to bring his congregation to their prayers.

Dispersing these warm memories, he remembered, finally, the dying Gavalas. Thinking of the way the old man had girded himself for death with more courage than the priest could now muster to meet new life made him decide to postpone returning to Bishop Donos until the following day.

At home that night, sitting with Cristina before the fire after their daughters and son were in bed, Father Basil told her about the long, uncertain journey they were being asked to make. Her first reaction was one of shock and fear. They sat up most of the night reflecting on all the valid excuses they might use to refuse the Bishop's request: They couldn't endanger their children in such an adventure. They owed a responsibility to their aging parents, who would be brokenhearted if they left. There were friends and parishioners who had come to depend upon them.

In the stillest, deepest hours of the night, words and arguments failed them, and they fell wearily silent. They felt themselves suddenly at the edge of the world, the abyss of an unknown future looming before them.

What reconciled them, finally, was the knowledge that wherever on earth they traveled, the heavens would remain above them and they would still be visible to God's eye. He wouldn't allow them to perish.

As the first light of dawn appeared between the shutters, they prayed together and accepted that they would have to go to America. Through the long hours of the night, they had come to understand that, once offered such a challenge, to reject it would make of their lives a hollow retreat.

Later that morning, sitting around the table at breakfast with their family, Father Basil told the children of their decision. For a startled, silent interval, their daughters and son stared at them. Anxiously awaiting their reaction, Father Basil couldn't resist an intemperate pride in their comeliness and brightness. Young as they were, their characters had begun to form, certain traits suggesting what they would be like as adults. Alexandra had a strong will, her great dark eyes containing defiance and purpose. Her younger sister, Soula, was gentle and graceful, at a time when other girls her age were awkward. She was the most sensitive and empathetic, the child quickest to understand a problem or sense a distress. Finally there was Andreas, the boy raised between the Herculean pillars of older sisters, fighting to assert himself against them. He was the first to speak.

"I'm not afraid to make this trip!" he said loudly.

Alexandra raked him with a derisive look. "Papa isn't talking about a sail along the shore," she said. "He's talking about crossing the world. Do you know how big the world is?"

"I know about the world!"

Alexandra turned from him and stared somberly at her father. "Will we ever come home?" she asked.

"We might, someday," he said gently, "but it would be best not to expect that return journey for many years."

"Do you think I'm afraid?" Andreas asked Alexandra defiantly.

"What is this town in Utah like?" Alexandra asked.

"We don't know much about it," Cristina said. "All we know is that there are many young Cretans there and they have built a church. So we will have our own people around us."

"I've read about America in school," Andreas said. "They have red-skinned savages there who cut off people's heads." He smirked at his sisters.

"Not their heads, their hair," Alexandra said. "So your skimpy stubble wouldn't be worth the trouble."

Throughout their exchange, Soula remained silent. Thinking he saw tears in her eyes, Father Basil rose and knelt beside her chair. He hugged her tightly.

"Don't cry, my love!" he said earnestly. "Whatever is ahead for us, we'll all be together and look after each other."

"I'm not afraid," Soula said quietly. She stared pensively through the window toward the shed that housed their donkey. "I am thinking of Mirabella . . . what will become of her if we have to leave?"

"We'll find her a good home," her mother said. "A family that will love her and care for her as you have done. We'll promise you that."

The children rose and left for school. Father Basil and Cristina watched them through the window as they walked into the courtyard. While Alexandra and Andreas continued arguing, Soula lingered behind them, pausing to enter the shed.

"She's gone to visit Mirabella," Cristina said softly.

Father Basil waited at the window until Soula emerged. He watched her run to catch up to her brother and sister. The last glimpse he had of his three beloved children was of their receding figures crossing a rise.

Within a few days of their decision, Cristina was sternly deciding which possessions they would take and which ones they'd have to leave. Father Basil had never admired her

more than he did when, without complaint, she consigned the
fine furniture from her dowry to her sister's safekeeping.

He wished he could have been as resolute in his own prepa-
rations. At odd times during the day, he felt his heart pounding with anxiety. He considered several times returning to tell
Bishop Donos that he had changed his mind, but shame made
him resist that temptation.

Although he had never been troubled with sleeplessness, he
began to suffer insomnia. Lying beside Cristina in their old
wooden bed (another cherished possession they would leave
behind) he tried not to let his restlessness disturb her. Yet,
seeing her sleeping so placidly sharpened his own distress.

There was a night when she suddenly seemed restless as
well. Several hours after they had gone to bed, he heard her
breathing fitfully.

"Basil, are you asleep?"

"No."

"I thought I heard one of the children."

He strained to hear a sound, but there was only the wind
rattling the shutters. Cristina fumbled beneath the blanket for
his hand.

"There is something I want to confess to you, Basil," she
said in a low, shaken voice. "You'll be ashamed of me, I
know, but I am terrified about this journey."

"My darling, you seem so composed! Everyone has been
marveling at your courage and spirit!"

"That's a charade to reassure the children," she said. "In
my hours alone, I think of the ship sinking and our bones
bleaching at the bottom of the sea. I want to run and hide in
a cupboard the way I did when I was a child."

He drew her tenderly into the circle of his arm. Her confession of fear emboldened him and he spoke with confidence.
"Thousands of others have made this journey safely, my darling!" he said. "We'll meet the challenges as well, and build a

good life in America. You'll see, Cristina, that I will care for you and the children."

"I am a coward," she sighed, "but as long as I have you I will find the courage I need. You make me brave with your bravery." She was silent for a few moments and then murmured sleepily. "I love you, Basil."

As if calmed and reassured, she fell asleep in his arms. He was grateful that he had been able to console her, even though he could still not sleep. He lay awake brooding over his bold and valiant promises.

In the final week before their departure from Rethymnon, Father Basil became aware of how many Greeks and Cretans were emigrating to America. The newspapers of Piraeus and Athens that arrived in Rethymnon a week late reported that hundreds of applicants were gathering daily at embarkation points in Patras, Piraeus, Kalamata and Zante for passage on Greek, Italian or English ships to America.

With the numbers growing so rapidly, the restrictions had become more stringent. Several physical examinations were required, and every applicant had to prove that he had a sponsor and a job waiting for him in America.

Father Basil and his family were spared all but a single physical examination conducted by a doctor at the bishopric. Their applications and passports were arranged through the British and American consuls. Their tickets, paid for by the parish in Utah, were cabin class, an accommodation much better than those provided to the men in steerage.

Because he was grateful for these privileges accorded his family and himself, Father Basil spent hours each day in the assembly hall at the port of Rethymnon, helping the young Cretans through the processing by the inspectors and steamship agents.

The young men came from scores of mountain hamlets in

the interior of Crete. Their lives were marked by poverty, physical hardship and ignorance of what the world outside the village was like. Their codes of blood and family made them sensitive to any slight or affront, and the result might be murder. These killings were rarely reported to the authorities, because the years of Turkish occupation had taught the villagers to be secretive and suspicious of police.

They were also antagonistic to any authority, and the bureaucratic tangle and regulations of the processing center caused eruptions of anger. The obdurate young Cretans couldn't understand what business it was of the agents to verify how much money they carried (often sewn into the lining of their jackets) or whom they would be staying with in America. Another common argument resulted when the agents sought to confiscate baggage so it might be disinfected and stored until the ship's departure.

As the time came closer for their ship to leave for Piraeus, the arguments in the processing center grew more acrimonious. On an afternoon several days before their departure, Father Basil found himself caught once more in a tangle of disputes.

"My mother packed my best clothing in that bag!" a young man said angrily. "She made me swear an oath not to allow it out of my hands!"

"You'll get your bag back, my son," Father Basil said.

"I'm carrying a gift for my uncle in America!" another young man said. "If anything happens to it, the shame will kill me!"

"He'll receive the gift from your hands," the priest reassured him. "Everyone's baggage, including gifts, will be returned before we board the ship."

An older villager came to tug at the sleeve of his cassock. "There's a boy over there in serious trouble, Father." He pointed to an agent at a desk some distance away.

Father Basil walked to the desk occupied by an officious agent he knew as Mr. Lazaros. Across from him stood a tall Cretan youth about nineteen or twenty years of age with a handsome bronzed face and a work-hardened body. He had black hair and dark eyes that glowed now in agitation as he confronted the agent, who kept shaking his head in vehement refusal.

"Can I be of some help here, Mr. Lazaros?" the priest asked.

"Nothing I say seems to be getting through this fellow's head," the agent snapped. "We're holding a ticket and some money for his brother. He says his brother's dead and his uncle wants him to use the ticket and money instead."

The young man looked entreatingly at the priest. Father Basil was caught by a pride and fidelity in his face.

"Do you have proof of who you are and that your brother's dead, my son?"

"I brought a letter with that information signed by my father and the schoolmaster."

"The letter might be a forgery!" the agent said shrilly. "We'll be in a fine mess if his brother turns up later asking for his ticket and the money!"

"I told you he's dead!" the young man's eyes flashed. "Do you think I've crossed the mountains for a lie?"

"What's the name of your village?" the priest asked.

"Vilandredou."

"Did your brother die of some illness?"

The young man stared silently at the priest.

"He was killed in an accident . . . on the mountain," he said in a low voice.

Father Basil peered closely at him, trying to unmask any deception. As he spoke of his brother he saw the youth's face marked with so raw and pervasive a sorrow he couldn't believe the young man was lying.

"I'm sorry," Father Basil said.

"We can't accept this fellow's word and a paper with signatures that are unknown to us!" the agent said. "A confirmation must be obtained! A police official must visit the village and make the proper inquiries and obtain the word of witnesses!"

"All that might take weeks," the priest said. "But I believe this young man is telling the truth. As long as his brother's dead, why shouldn't he take his place?"

"That isn't proper procedure!" the agent cried. "His story must be confirmed!"

"I'll vouch for him, Mr. Lazaros." The priest spoke in a quiet, reassuring voice. "If you feel my pledge isn't enough, then let's take the matter to the Director, Mr. Vassiliades."

The agent cast a quick, craven glance toward the glassed enclosure of the Director's office. Vassiliades was a Lasithian with the short temper of a maddened Turk, and every agent and inspector twisted fervently to avoid incurring his wrath. His cheeks grimacing with frustration, the agent jerked the young man's papers closer. He raised his stamp and struck them several times so hard the noise resounded like hammer blows through the noisy hall.

"The responsibility is on your cassock, then!" he snapped at the priest. He threw the papers at the young man and gestured brusquely for him to step aside. "Next!" he shouted. "Next!"

The young man stepped away from the desk, clutching the papers. He stared mutely at Father Basil for a moment and then bent to grasp and kiss the priest's hand.

"God bless you, my son," the priest asked. "What's your name?"

"Manolis Manousakis."

"Well, Manolis, if you have further problems, ask for Father Basil, of St. Constantine's Church, in Rethymnon. How soon are you leaving?"

"In two or three days, I think, Father," Manolis said. "The overnight boat for Piraeus and then the *Moraites* to America."

"That's our ship too!" the priest said excitedly. "My Papadia and family will be with me on that ship! We'll make the crossing together!"

"He's not on the ship yet!" the agent snarled. "There are further examinations and other questions! Others may not be as lenient as I've been!"

The priest shook his head. "The man's a fanatic," he murmured to Manolis and then started away.

"Father?" Manolis called after him.

The priest turned back.

"Two brothers named Trombakis, Father," Manolis said quietly. "Stellios and Mitsos Trombakis. They were going to America too. They might have passed through here about ten days ago."

The priest tried to untangle the scores of young men he had met and spoken to in the past weeks.

"I cannot remember men by that name," he said, "but then, hundreds pass through here each week. I could have missed them. Are you sure they were leaving from here?"

Manolis shook his head.

"Then, they might have left from Iraklion or Canea," the priest said.

Manolis nodded in farewell and turned away. The priest watched him walking to another line. A fine, decent young man, he thought, a model for what my own son, Andreas, might be like in ten years. He felt a surge of affection for the youth and was grateful that he'd been able to help him.

He suddenly considered asking the young man home to

share the evening meal with Cristina and his family. At that instant he was distracted by another argument that broke out between an agent and a passenger over the baggage, and he hurried to resolve the problem. When he had soothed the young villager and looked around to find Manolis, he couldn't see him anywhere.

In those last few days, a steady procession of his parishioners came to see him and to receive communion from him for the last time. Many embraced him with tears in their eyes, and he felt his heart warmed by their affection.

One of the last services he held in the church was the funeral for old Gavalas, who had finally relinquished his fierce grasp on life. Looking down at the old man's still, cold face in his pine coffin, raw with an undefeatable power even in death, he prayed to inherit a measure of his strength.

On Thursday of that last week, two days before they were to leave Rethymnon, the Bishop loaned them his carriage so they might drive to say goodbye to Cristina's parents and to his mother and sister, who lived near them. The day was one of the most mournful he had ever experienced. His sister wept all through the meal, and his poor mother offered a catechism of warnings. Cristina's parents alternated between sighs of sorrow and outrage that he was taking their daughter and grandchildren away from them. He sympathized with their lament and loss and promised that they'd all write home often.

Friday night, with their departure scheduled for the following afternoon, none of them could sleep. The girls and Andreas talked in their beds for hours, while he and Cristina sat silently on the dark terrace, listening to the trilling of crickets and to the wind rustling the leaves of the trees in their garden. At dawn he went to groom Mirabella for the final time, setting her stall in order, changing water in her pail. He had sold her for less money than she was worth and placed her with a kind master he was sure wouldn't abuse her. Now the sturdy animal with her sleek coat, well-rounded quarters and alert eyes looked at him with what he felt was reproach.

"I will miss you too, my beauty." He stroked her glossy coat. "And I will never forget you."

As his eyes grew moist he shook his head in exasperation and looked toward heaven. "Oh, Lord," he said, "I'm not certain what use I'll be to you in the new land if I cannot even part from my donkey without breaking into tears."

Their ship's departure, scheduled for late afternoon, brought a crowd of townspeople to the port. Even those who didn't have a relative or friend leaving came to share the tearful farewells. People brought small gifts and gave them to strangers, crying as they embraced them for a final time.

Father Basil, Cristina, and the children, their cheeks wet with the tears of friends as well as their own tears, stood at the railing of the ship, waving down with as much cheer as they could muster. Almost fifty of his parishioners had come to see them off, including Pericles Androulakis, the best man at their wedding, who had brought his entire clan of twenty-eight relatives including his great-grandmother Electra. Perched like a gloomy ship's figurehead on a bale of cargo, from time to time the nearly blind old lady, who was some years beyond a hundred, raised her arm in a sepulchral farewell. That dolorous salute, waved at the town behind her or, again, in the direction of the open sea, set off another funereal chorus.

The ship's horn sounded, so drawn-out and piercing a shriek that it cowed the crowd on the dock to silence. For a few minutes an eerie hush prevailed, and then a ship's bell clanged and a seaman's hoarse cry whirled across the bow.

The rumble of the engines grew louder and the deck trembled beneath their feet.

As they watched the ship receding, the crowd below raised their voices again, a dolorous wail that swept up like a wind and scattered like a benediction into the setting sun.

The port grew smaller. The houses of the town loomed in tiers of crimson and gold, from which mosques and churches extended flaming steeples and minarets into the sky. The mountains beyond the town darkened like mourners.

Through the mist that swirled across the water, Father Basil could still see the crowd on the dock herded together as if for consolation and warmth. Even after the port and the whole beloved town disappeared as if they had suddenly plummeted into the sea from which he would never witness them rise again, he could hear that lamentation, that dirge of separation and loss uttered by men and women since the beginning of time.

CHAPTER THREE

Stellios

After dragging down brush and rocks to block the road Aleko would travel on his way to Rethymnon, Stellios Trombakis and his brother, Mitsos, had waited through the night. Mitsos dozed fitfully, but Stellios couldn't sleep. Although he had hunted wolves among the crags, he had never waited to kill a man before.

The night was full of strange omens. With barely any wind, the peaks of cypress trees lashed the air as if caught in a gale. Then he swore he could hear bells tolling from a monastery or a church, infernal bells he knew shouldn't be ringing at that hour of the night.

When dawn rimmed the peaks of the mountains, he walked down the slope to check their horses, tethered out of sight up the road. Once he'd decided to kill Aleko, they had made plans to ride to Canea and board a ferry for Naples. From that city they'd catch a ship to America.

He returned to shake Mitsos roughly awake. They ate a melon, slicing it apart with their knives. The juices should have been sweet but left a sour aftertaste in his mouth. Afterward they waited, while the road below them slowly became visible.

"If Manolis is with Aleko, will we kill him, too?" Mitsos asked nervously.

"Our quarrel is with Aleko," Stellios said. "When he's dead, the stain on our honor will be erased."

"Do you think their kinsmen will come after us?"

"Keep worrying and you'll travel with wet breeches!" Stellios said scornfully. "Even if they do come after us, they'll have to wait until Aleko is buried, and besides, they'll never figure we'd leave from an Italian port. We'll be in America before they put to sea."

Mitsos fell silent, but Stellios could smell the sweat of his panic. That confirmed that his brother was a coward, not to be trusted in any bold action. Stellios would have left him behind if it had not been for his mother.

"Kill Aleko Manousakis if you feel your honor blemished!" she told him savagely. "But, afterward, I never want to see your face in the village again! That man is idolized here and his family and friends will try to avenge him. You must leave and cross the ocean and take Mitsos with you, because they'll murder him." She spit in disdain. "They won't harm your sister or me. We're poor, common women and not worthy of male vengeance!"

So he had taken Mitsos with him and would haul him along to America, as well. His mother would have leveled a curse on him if he had refused. Many villagers thought she was a witch, and seeing her crouched before the fire at night, a scarlet glow on her face, he suspected those whispers were true. He was afraid of her, believing that the demon in her must have driven his father to death when Stellios was still a child.

"Tell me again what we should do when he comes, Stellios," Mitsos pleaded. "I want to be sure to do it right."

"When the wagon reaches the barricade, we'll run down," Stellios said. "Don't panic and shoot hastily. Don't try for his head, which would be a smaller target, but for his chest.

Shoot to kill him. If he's only wounded and recovers, the bastard would follow us not only to America but to hell."

In the silence broken only by the cries of birds, they heard the creaking of wagon wheels on the stony road. The creaking became a rumble and they saw the donkey appear from the mist. Mitsos started to his feet, fumbling at his gun, and Stellios jerked him down. By squinting he made out the figures of two men on the rattling, swaying cart. When it stopped before the barricade, he recognized the tall figure of Aleko swing down from the seat.

Stellios sprang to his feet and ran down the slope, his boots kicking loose a flurry of stones. As if in a frenzy not to be left behind, Mitsos came racing at his heels.

Aleko stared at them in shock. He must have understood they were going to kill him, and yet he didn't run or plead for his life. That angered Stellios and he aimed carefully at Aleko's chest and fired. Mitsos fired an instant later. The shots exploded in thunder across the mountains, and flocks of terrified birds burst from the rocks and trees.

Aleko sprawled on the ground, one arm flung out with his fingers extended as if he were grasping for something just out of reach. Stellios saw the dark-red stain of blood spread across his jacket.

He had almost forgotten Manolis until he leaped down from the cart. Stellios braced for an attack, but Manolis ran to his brother's body. Mitsos was running toward their horses, and Stellios followed him with an unhurried walk, slipping the gun into his belt to be thrown away before they reached Canea. By the time he reached the horses, Mitsos had mounted.

"Hurry, Stellios! For God's sake, hurry!"

Stellios gripped the pommel and swung his body into the saddle. He turned to look back toward the barricade and saw

Manolis, crouched over his brother's body, staring after them.
With a chill knifing through his blood, Stellios was suddenly
sorry they hadn't killed the younger brother as well.

They rode across the mountain, and at the crossroads
turned away from Rethymnon and started for Canea. That
night, they rested in a grove of lemon trees. After dark,
Mitsos grew more nervous, trembling with every sound.

"You're a jackass!" Stellios cried. "They won't even have
had his wake yet!"

Arriving in Canea during the afternoon of the second day,
they sold their horses in the marketplace, taking less than the
animals were worth for a quick exchange in cash. Early the
next morning, they boarded a ferry for Naples. In that city
they located a Greek steamship agent whose name Stellios
had obtained from a friend. With a bribe of some silver the
agent assisted them through their examinations and booked
steerage passage for them on a ship to America.

They had to wait three days for the ship's departure, and
they spent that time in a port tavern teeming with sailors and
whores. Mitsos drank himself into a stupor while Stellios
drank and remained sober and morose. He watched the
whores, their fleshy bodies in skimpy dresses inflaming him.
But he was supicious of them and of the sailors who pawed
them, babbling in a language he couldn't understand. Not
until one of the dark-haired harlots, her swollen tits overflow-
ing her spangled bodice, sat down at his table to tease him in
broken Greek, did his desire suspend his distrust. She led him
up a flight of stairs into a dim corridor with numerous doors
through which he could hear the gruntings of rutting men.

He followed the whore into a dingy stall stinking of wine
and the spillings of sex, containing only a basin of water and
a stained pallet on the floor. The door didn't have a lock and,
wary that thugs might burst in and rob him, Stellios un-

buckled his breeches. When the whore stretched out on her back on the pallet, tugging her skirts above her naked thighs, he dropped his breeches and crouched between her legs. Prying her thighs apart, he pounded into her roughly, ignoring her shrieks and thrashings until he had drained off his sacs. Then he swung quickly off her body. She rubbed her tits and moaned.

"Animal!" she cried.

"Just a real man, you whore," Stellios grinned. He threw a copper at her, buckled his breeches, and swaggered down the stairs.

When the agent came for them the morning of their ship's departure, Stellios and Mitsos drenched their heads under a fountain and followed him to the docks. They passed their final physical examinations and boarded the ship, securing adjoining bunks in the dismal steerage.

Those first days and nights at sea, locked away from the sky and sun he had freely possessed all his life, were the most wretched and unhappy Stellios had ever known. Staring for hours at the weaving lanterns with their flickering lights, he couldn't separate night from day. He slept and woke and slept again, stumbling from his bunk to void in one of the buckets or to eat some lukewarm soup, lumps of stringy dried beef and chunks of black bread. As the stink of excrement and vomit grew worse, bedeviled by the bites of lice, the doughy-faced Italians in the bunks around him began to moan like children. Although he suffered with them, Stellios forced himself to endure the misery in silence. He threatened to gag Mitsos if he didn't stop sniveling.

"We are Cretans!" he railed at his brother. "Let them whine like cowards! We'll hold ourselves together like men!"

To pass the endless, dreary hours, he recalled the sights of the village. He thought of a pear tree with ripened fruit ready to be plucked; of dark ambrosial honey seeping into the pockets of his cheeks. He remembered sitting under the shade of an olive tree on a hot day, drinking raki and cracking almonds. Finally, he called up the celebrations he had shared, the feast days and weddings, the glow of the blooming, virginal girls and the strutting bucks in braided vests, silk sashes and gleaming boots.

These memories weren't without danger. He also saw Aleko at the celebrations, not dressed in finery as the others, but dancing as a grisly apparition from the grave. Stellios could clearly see his festered cheeks and temples, his eyes fed upon by worms so only the bony sockets remained. Aleko extended a skeletal hand to Stellios, seeking to draw him into an embrace and drag him down to his grave.

To dispel that nightmare, Stellios tried to reject the memories as desperately as he had once recalled them. He also reproached himself for not having mutilated Aleko's body after he had shot him. If he had severed one of his enemy's hands, he would have prevented the dead man's becoming an evil spirit able to roam from his grave in pursuit of the men who had killed him. Stellios feared that unholy stalking more than any retribution from living men.

At the end of what Stellios reckoned was their second week at sea, a dreadful storm battered the ship. The men in steerage clung to their bunks, screaming and praying, the wind and water tearing at their ship. With all his pride and courage stripped away, Stellios shouted his own frantic prayers into the din. Convinced he would drown, his body sinking fathoms into the ocean, he was more terrified than he had ever been in his life.

But the dreadful storm passed, the ship remained afloat and, miraculously, he survived. In gratitude for having been saved, he whispered his confession to God. He admitted that he had not killed Aleko for the affront to his sister. He had never believed that peerless man, who could have chosen any of the most beautiful girls in the village, would have bothered with a stringy, titless prune like Froso.

The problem had been his envy at Aleko's supremacy. From the time they were boys, whether running, wrestling or hunting, he could never be more than second best. Even as they grew older, in athletic feats and at the festivals where men competed at dancing and improvising the ballad, Aleko vanquished him. The man's unreachable superiority, continuing year after year, frustrated Stellios and finally fashioned in him a rage to murder.

When some vagrant rumor prompted his foolish sister into believing Aleko would come to court her, Stellios encouraged the illusion, grasping it as the excuse he wanted to vent his bitterness. One step led to another and, after Aleko had beaten him in the coffeehouse, he knew he had to kill him. Yet the price he paid for the killing was having to forsake the village. He was amazed that he hadn't considered the consequences of his action. If he had only waited for Aleko to leave for America, Stellios could have assumed his rightful place of leadership among the village men.

When the ship finally entered the harbor of the Upper Bay, at New York, the men crowded on deck, carrying their battered suitcases, wicker baskets and parcels. Along with the others, Stellios stared with shock at the statue of the colossal woman. She loomed over his head like some kind of vengeful deity and, for a fearful moment, he wondered if her magic allowed her to see into the hearts of the men seeking entrance to America.

A ferry came alongside their ship and they were transferred to it, jamming every portion of space. When the ferry moored at the port, he descended the gangplank, Mitsos close behind

him. Stepping on the ground, he seemed to feel it still swaying
under his feet.

In the midst of men dragging their baggage, he and Mitsos
moved from the pier in a long, ragged line that wound slowly
into an immense domed building filled with a huge and noisy
throng. People stood in lines before the desks of inspectors or
huddled on wooden benches, babbling at one another, pleading with the officials.

Joined to the mob, Stellios felt himself different because he
was Cretan. He wished he could communicate that unique-
ness to the uniformed men in charge. He was motioned
into a cubicle and told to strip to the waist. For an instant he
was embarrassed at exposing his body to strangers, but as the
doctor looked with admiration at his muscular arms and
powerful shoulders, he felt a prodding of pride. From that
moment he moved through the lines with greater confidence.
The only thing he regretted was that the weeks of the voyage
had caked his boots with dirt and grime that resisted any of
his efforts to wipe them clean.

They were examined and questioned, and when he showed
them that he and Mitsos weren't paupers, their papers were
stamped. They moved inside a wire enclosure, waiting for the
ferry to carry them to the mainland. Within several hours the
enclosure grew crowded, men filling the benches while a few
women with children huddled in silent groups on the floor.

After a while, an attendant pushed a cart loaded with small
brown paper sacks into the enclosure. He distributed a sack
to each immigrant. Men and women ripped them open eagerly and took out a chunk of bread and some dried beef.
When the attendant handed one of the sacks to Stellios, he refused it, and, by his glare, warned Mitsos to follow his example.

"But why, Stellios?" Mitsos asked unhappily when the man

had moved away. "My belly is sticking to my ribs with hunger. Why shouldn't we take some food too?"

Stellios gestured scornfully at the men and women around them. "Because we aren't like the rest," he said. "We don't take what we haven't paid for."

Someone shouted that the ferry had returned, and people rose from the benches and floor, pushing toward the gate. Stellios and Mitsos joined them.

On board the ferry they claimed a section of deck beside a bulkhead and sat down. In a few minutes Stellios heard Mitsos snoring. He was hungry himself, tired and uncertain of what lay before them.

A man suddenly appeared beside him. In the dim light of the lamp, Stellios recognized him as a man he had seen earlier talking to a group of the Italians in the compound. He was surprised when the man, who was slim and short, spoke to him in Greek.

"May I sit down with you for a minute, my friend?"

"I don't own the ship," Stellios said. "Just don't sit too close."

The man squatted down, being careful to keep his distance. He smiled and Stellios caught a glimpse of sparkling gold teeth.

"You're from Crete, aren't you?" the man said. He motioned at the sleeping Mitsos. "You look like brothers, although you're bigger." Without waiting for Stellios to answer, he went on. "One can always pick out the Cretans. They're taller and more manly-looking."

"We're from Crete," Stellios said. "Where are you from?"

"I'm bred from the four winds," the man laughed. "My father was from Tripoli, my mother from Smyrna, my grandfather from Russia." He paused. "Are you going to relatives in America?"

"Even if you're only part Greek," Stellios said sharply, "you know it's unwise to ask too many questions."

"You're absolutely right!" the man said quickly. "I just wanted to see if there wasn't some way I might help you. I could tell you were different from the others. When you refused the food in the waiting room, I said to myself, Kalingas, there's a proud Cretan."

"We take nothing we haven't paid for."

"I admire you for it!" Kalingas said earnestly.

They sat in silence for a few moments. Mitsos snored more loudly and Stellios jabbed him with his elbow.

"Why would you want to help us?" Stellios asked finally, warily.

"A few years ago I was an immigrant myself," Kalingas said. "I know what it is to land in a strange country, without work or a friend. I've made some good contacts here, and now I try to help special fellows like yourself and your brother by bringing them together with employers who need good workers. The work is too hard for any but the strongest men, so I have to pick and choose carefully."

"What kind of work?"

"Good, healthy work on the railroad in the western part of this country where there are mountains like the ranges of Crete. The work out in the sun and air all day is hard, but the wages are good."

"We aren't afraid of hard work."

"That's why I picked you! When I saw you refuse that food, I said to myself, Kalingas, this proud Cretan will be one of the best workers you've ever found. By the way, what's your name?"

"Stellios."

"I tell you, Stellios, I put some other Cretans to work out there a few years ago and they've blessed me ever since. Of course, to be fair, a big, strong fellow like you would find work anyway. But this is special work that takes a special quality of man."

"Were you talking to the Italians earlier about work?"

Kalingas nodded.

"That work of yours can't be so special if you'd hire them to do it," Stellios said contemptuously. "They whine like babies and don't have the courage to kick a donkey's ass."

"But you're right!" Kalingas spoke in a low, astonished voice. "That was my appraisal after talking to them for a while. I decided they'd be good only for some inferior labor. But you spotted them at once! You aren't only strong but brain-loaded too! Is your brother the same way?"

"My brother is my brother and comes with me."

"Of course," Kalingas said quickly, "I'd be delighted to have both of you. All we'll need to do when we dock is to sign some papers, a work agreement listing the wages you'll be paid and other benefits like food and housing the company gives you."

"What does the company give you for finding workers?"

"I receive a small commission."

"I didn't think you were doing it for nothing," Stellios said.

"Believe me, Stellios, it is barely enough to make my expenses!" Kalingas said earnestly. "But I don't care, because it provides me a chance to help my own people."

"I'll think about it."

"Of course, I understand," Kalingas said. "You're the kind of man who doesn't jump into anything before examining it carefully. I admire that quality. Well, Stellios, I'll be in the port area all morning. If you and your brother decide to join us, we'll sign the papers and get you both on a train going West. I'll take care of everything for you. After you've spent even a few hours in one of these noisy, crowded cities, you'll yearn for the clear air of the mountains again."

After Kalingas had risen and moved back into the shadows,

Stellios stared across the dark water at the lights of the city.
Despite his posture of confidence before the agent, he was ap-
prehensive of what lay ahead of them. Their money wouldn't
last forever. While he didn't really trust the gold-toothed
juggler of compliments, the man seemed to understand the
worth of Cretans.

Stellios bent and shook Mitsos awake to tell him what they
were going to do. With the decision made, he felt better. Perhaps God had been pleased at his confession and had sent the
agent to them as a reward. He suddenly recalled the golden
fringe of the altar cloth in the sanctuary of their church in
Vilandredou. That link to the agent's gilded teeth seemed a
bright augury that reassured Stellios.

They debarked from the ferry in a gray dawn, the figures of
men and women shrouded in an eerie mist. A child separated
from its parents began to wail, and then its frightened voice
was lost in the noise and confusion of the port. Uniformed
officials shouted and directed groups of people into areas
where trains waited. When Mitsos exclaimed about the trains
and tall buildings they could see beyond the port, Stellios
reproved him.

"You're not back in the village now," he said scornfully.
"This is America. What did you expect?"

But as they were pushed and prodded along with the
crowd, Stellios was grateful he had made the decision to align
himself with Kalingas. Recognizing several of the Italian immigrants off their ship entering a large shed at the side of the
dock, Stellios and Mitsos followed them into the building.

They found Kalingas in the center of a circle of about
twenty men. He flashed his teeth in pleasure when he saw
them.

"Here are our Cretan friends to join our happy little band!"

he cried. "Welcome! I'm just passing around the contracts! You're just in time!"

Most of the group in the shed were Italians, but there were a few other Greeks, who had apparently come off another ship. Stellios stared at them warily, but they looked to be an ordinary clump of farmers. Alternating swiftly from Italian to Greek, Kalingas distributed one of the contracts to each man.

"But I can't read what is written here," a grizzled Greek farmer a little older than the others said.

"The contracts are written in English, because that is the language of this country," Kalingas said. "They merely record that you will work for a period of two years in those places specified for your employment by Mr. Leonidas G. Skliris . . ."

"Who is this Skliris?" Stellios asked.

"Who is Mr. Skliris?" Kalingas stared at Stellios in amazement. "Mr. Skliris is the padrone, a man of immense influence and power and your benefactor. The newspapers in the West call him 'Czar of the Greeks.' He is the employment representative for the Denver, Rio Grande and Western Pacific railroads, the Utah Copper Company and coal mines in Carbon County, Utah. He also supplies workers for the Union Pacific and Oregon Short Line railroads, the Pueblo steel mills and the Nevada metal mines!" When Kalingas paused for breath, his teeth sparkled. "Does that answer your question, my friend?"

Feeling humiliated at having his ignorance about so famous a man exposed, Stellios nodded somberly.

"I've heard about him," he said in a low voice.

"All right, now, back to the contracts," Kalingas said. "You'll remain committed to Mr. Skliris for two years. During this term of whatever employment he finds for you, from your wages, which will be twenty, twenty-five, even thirty dol-

lars a month, you'll pay only one dollar a month to Mr.
Skliris. That's all the good Christian man asks, because he understands you'll want to save money you earn here to send
home."

"I have three unmarried sisters back home," a young Greek
said dolefully. "They are wonderful girls and fine home-
makers but they're not beauties. I'll need a bundle of money
for their dowries."

"Exactly!" Kalingas said. "Mr. Skliris understands such
problems!" He nodded vigorously and then, turning to the
Italians, he delivered a rapid, reassuring speech to them. Afterward he turned back to the Greeks.

"Is that all this paper says?" the older farmer asked him.
"All this writing and it says only that we will work for Mr.
Skliris for two years and give him a dollar from our wages
each month. What's all the rest of this writing about?"

"What's your name?" Kalingas asked, his voice sounding
impatient for the first time.

"Nikolaos Hatsos, from the village of Mikroelata, sir." The
farmer spoke in a low, respectful voice.

"All right, Nikolaos," Kalingas said brusquely. "That is all
the paper says. The rest is the language of lawyers and means
nothing to you. Now, we have spent enough time on explana-
tions. If you miss your train, Mr. Skliris will be displeased
with all of us."

The men continued looking uneasily at one another, their
distrust of documents and their ignorance of the language
making them nervous and hesitant.

Finally, one of the younger Greeks asked, "Where is Mr.
Skliris from in Greece?"

"He's from Sparta," Kalingas said.

"Sparta!" another Greek said excitedly. "So important a
man and he comes from a town less than ten miles from my
village! I was in Sparta once!" He reached out for one of the

pens. "A man from Sparta can always be trusted! I'm ready to sign!"

He bent over the contract and, pressing the pen hard upon the paper, he slowly signed his name. The other Greeks followed him, each of them signing or making a cross on the contract. Stellios motioned to Mitsos and they signed as well.

Fearing that the Greeks were wresting their employment away from them, the Italians surged forward to sign their own contracts.

Afterward the men, clutching their parcels and bags, followed Kalingas from the shed across a ramp to a railroad siding. Beyond several pairs of tracks, a train was loading passengers into a string of gleaming cars with numerous windows.

"There's our train!" a Greek said eagerly.

The Italians also pointed to the train, waving their hands excitedly and smiling. Kalingas gestured curtly for the men to keep moving. With the contracts signed, Stellios noticed grimly, the agent's amiable manner had changed to one more harsh.

They followed him away from the station and down an embankment alongside a track with railroad cars that resembled immense, windowless boxes. Pausing before one of the cars, Kalingas stretched on his toes to peer into the open door. A barrel-shouldered man with the powerful frame of a wrestler appeared from the dark interior. He was short, his eyes slanted and his face glinting with a yellow sheen unlike any man Stellios had ever seen before.

"This is Mishima." Kalingas spoke first to the Greeks and then to the Italians. "He's the work boss who'll be in charge of your journey West. You must obey him."

Several men stepped forward to peer into the bleak, dingy boxcar.

"Is this the train we're riding in, Mr. Kalingas?" Nikolaos asked.

"Do you think I'm conducting you on a tour of the railroad facilities?" Kalingas said shortly. "Of course you'll ride in there! Each man will have a blanket and there's straw on the floor. You'll be comfortable as hens in a nest."

"But there aren't any windows," Nikolaos said.

"Did you have windows in steerage?" Kalingas snapped.

"Forgive me, Mr. Kalingas," Nikolaos went on. "We had no choice there. But now we are in America and we shouldn't be penned in like sheep."

When several other men joined his complaint, muttering in disapproval, Kalingas cut them sharply to silence.

"If any man here prefers to travel in one of the regular passenger cars, I'll show him where to go and buy a ticket!" the agent said angrily. "That would cost about fifteen American dollars. Some padrones would have made each of you pay for your own passage to the West, but Mr. Skliris has arranged to transport you free of charge! How disappointed he would be if he heard you grumbling and complaining! Well, if you're so unhappy, come on, then! Who wants to go and pay for his ticket?"

The men fell silent, staring nervously at the irate agent. Stellios thought suddenly of grasping the little weasel by his throat and turning him upside down. But he had no wish to pay the fifteen dollars and he remained silent. After a moment of indecision, several men raised their parcels and bags onto the car and hoisted themselves up. Other men hurried to follow them.

When a man didn't climb into the car quickly enough to please the work boss, Mishima grabbed him by the jacket or breeches and jerked him roughly into the car. As Mitsos climbed up, Mishima grabbed him and shoved him into the interior. When Stellios hoisted himself up, the work boss grabbed for him but Stellios swiftly shoved him away. Taken by surprise, the work boss stumbled and then, with a quick bunching of his limbs, recovered his balance. He whirled toward Stellios, who braced himself for an attack.

Kalingas cried loudly to the work boss. Mishima hissed a curse at Stellios, gesturing angrily at the men still on the ground to resume their ascent.

"You had best not be so gandy-tempered here, Cretan," the agent spoke harshly to Stellios. "This isn't a wretched backwoods hamlet where you're king of chickens and goats. This is America. We have strong jails here for men who don't respect authority, jails where you can rot for the rest of your life!"

Stellios started to tell Kalingas that he'd die before he'd let them put him behind bars, and then he decided to curb his tongue. With a scornful and defiant look at the agent, he turned and walked into the interior of the car.

The Italians occupied one section of the car, the Greeks settled in another. Nikolaos motioned for Stellios and Mitsos to join them, but Stellios took a section near the door. He picked up one of the coarse blankets and sat down on the scraps of straw. Mitsos sat beside him.

When the last of the men were in the car, Kalingas stretched up on his toes again and gave them a final, jaunty wave.

"All right, my friends," he said. "Mishima will see you are fed and, when the train stops, will allow you out to stretch your limbs. You see that Mr. Skliris and I have your welfare at heart."

"You're not traveling on the train, Mr. Kalingas?" Nikolaos asked.

"Unfortunately, no," Kalingas said. "Mr. Skliris depends on me to meet the ships as they arrive. But Mishima will be traveling on the train and will look after you like a father or an older brother."

"Does he speak Greek?"

"No, he doesn't speak Greek or Italian," Kalingas smirked. "I must admit he's poorly educated."

"How will he understand us if we want to tell him something?"

Speaking in a strange, shrill tongue that sounded to Stellios like the cackling of chickens, Kalingas relayed the question to Mishima. The work boss laughed hoarsely.

"Don't worry, my friend," Kalingas said to Nikolaos. "What is important on this journey is that you all understand him."

He stepped away as Mishima, bracing his stocky body against the frame, dragged the heavy door closed. For an instant Stellios thought he'd remain with them in the car, but when only a small opening remained, Mishima leaped through it to the ground. From there he finished closing the door. The weighted, wooden panel banged against the frame and they were plunged into darkness. An instant later a metal bolt was rammed into place.

For a little while there were only the sounds of men breathing nervously, coughing hoarsely, clearing their throats. One of the Italians began to pray in a low, plaintive voice.

The car lurched forward and then rocked back. Several men cried out in panic.

"Easy, easy, now . . ." Nikolaos spoke so quietly and soothingly that even the Italians, who could not understand his words, seemed reassured. "They're moving the car to hook us to the train."

For what seemed a long time, the car rocked and bumped along the tracks. Then the noise and clash of car against car subsided. From somewhere ahead of them sounded the peal of a bell. Finally, they began rolling forward, slowly at first and then gathering more speed. The whistling from the iron wheels rose to a shriek. A draft of cold air swept down from the vents in the roof of the car.

Stellios shivered and drew his blanket about his shoulders. He felt Mitsos groping nearer, hesitantly, as if fearing Stellios might shove him away. After another moment Mitsos shifted closer, drawing his blanket up across both their legs.

For the first time in his life, Stellios felt grateful for the closeness of another human being.

CHAPTER FOUR

Manolis

During the crossing from Rethymnon to Piraeus, Manolis stood at the ship's stern watching the huge globe of the moon reflecting across the backwash of water. Along the rail on either side of him, men stared silently back toward Crete, the red tips of their cigarettes flickering like beacons in the dark. Some of them had found places to sleep on deck, curled up beside coils of rope and canvas, or beneath the suspended lifeboats.

The wind from the sea giving him a light-headed sense of flight, Manolis tracked the moon across the water to his island, imagining it glowing upon his house. He followed it over the sleeping village, crossing the deserted square, passing the church and, finally, illuminating the cemetery. Even over the miles of water and land separating him from that enclosure of markers and tombstones, he felt the moonlight mourning at Aleko's grave.

Aleko had lived for three days following the shooting. He couldn't speak, and only his frantic eyes revealed his fierce struggle to live. A coven of old women like a rank of black crows prayed beside his bed. The village priest, white-haired

Father Harilaos, came to give Aleko communion, forcing the tiny golden spoon between his frozen lips.

Unable to endure the hours of watching and waiting, Manolis would leave the house to walk in the fields. When he'd return, he'd find his mother still sitting at Aleko's bedside, her gaze never leaving her son's face. When his father entered the house, he stood mutely in the shadows of a corner. Outside the house, groups of villagers kept vigil with lighted candles.

At dawn of the fourth day, Manolis, who had been dozing before the fire, was wakened by his mother's scream. He ran to the bed and saw his brother's torn face. Aleko's breath bubbled in his throat and his lips spit a final heartbeat of blood. Then, as if every candle in the village had suddenly been extinguished, his face grew dark and cold.

His mother bent over Aleko's body and gently touched the blood at his lips. She smeared her fingers and then rubbed his blood on her own cheeks. As the old women began to wail, Manolis fled from the house.

There had never been a death in the village mourned more by the villagers. All day and all night they walked slowly through the house to view Aleko's body. He had died unmarried and was garlanded like a bridegroom, a nuptial ring on his finger, a crown of wedding flowers set in his dark, thick hair. Even in death, Manolis thought with awe, there was a majesty about him, his strong body and stone-chiseled face resembling the corpse of some hero in legend.

On the day of the funeral, every man, woman and child in Vilandredou joined the procession carrying the long pine box with Aleko's body from the house to the church. The procession shuffled through the village, the pallbearers breathing heavily under the load, the women keening, the sun sowing

light everywhere except in the black pools of shade beneath
the coffin.

After the service in the church, the crowd pushed into the
cemetery, tramping across the tablets and markers. In the
final moments, as the coffin was lowered by ropes into the
grave, the keening women rioted in grief, tearing at their clothing and hair. Froso Trombakis, her face swollen and dis-
figured by weeping, had to be dragged back from hurling herself into the grave.

Manolis stood wedged between his mother and sisters in the
forefront of the crowd. Eleni and Coula had cried for hours,
but his mother remained exhausted and mute during the funeral. Only when the gravediggers began shoveling dirt and
clay into the grave did she begin to moan. As the dirt struck
the pine box, she shuddered as if the earth were striking her
flesh, as well.

His father, who hadn't cried since Aleko died, stood, still
silent, at the head of the grave. He held a packet of flowers
from which he clumsily tugged off petals that he tossed into
the grave. As soon as those petals were covered by the dirt,
he flung in others, finally tearing apart and hurling in the
stems and leaves. They formed, Manolis thought gratefully, a
chain of blossoms from Aleko's coffin to the surface of the
earth.

The day after the funeral, in spite of her mother's threats
and curses on her daughter for speaking, Froso told everyone
that her brothers had planned to confront Aleko even before
they learned of his departure. If he rejected them, they had
schemed to kill him and, afterward, flee to America. As she
confessed, she cursed her brothers, vowing she never wanted
to see them alive again.

Since the murderers were known, everyone in Vilandredou
expected that Aleko's kin would undertake the quest for ven-

geance. That was the way it had always been in the villages on Crete. When a murder had been committed, the ancient code required that it be answered with murder. In the victim's family, a shirt or scarf stained with the murdered man's blood was displayed in the house. Men would let their beards grow as a sign they understood and accepted the obligation of revenge. In the old days, the windows of houses would be shuttered, sometimes even sealed with bricks and stones, the family living in darkness until the murder had been atoned.

Manolis remembered the tales of vendettas he had heard as a child and of the calamities that befell families that ignored the summons for vengeance. Besides suffering the scorn of other villagers, they faced reprisal from their own slain kin. If the dead were unappeased, their spirits became vindictive.

He couldn't believe that Aleko would willfully harm any one of their family, but he wasn't certain about the ways death might change a man. Things were clear and tangible in the sunlight, but the grave was an endless darkness that might make a man bitter and vengeful, extending his curse to his kinsmen as well as his enemies if he wasn't allowed to rest in peace.

As soon as word could be carried to them, from across all of Crete their kinsmen gathered in Vilandredou for a council of retribution. There were a dozen of Manolis' cousins and his uncle Seferis and his great-grandfather Odysseus, a still lean and wiry warrior in his nineties. He had fought in the island's rebellions against the Turks during their long occupation of Crete. As a younger man he had also known several vendettas. His youngest son had been killed in such a feud. Manolis remembered his father telling him that his great-grandfather had repaid that murder by gouging out the eyes of his son's murderer before killing him, so that the last thing on earth the man would see was his avenger's face.

The family held a day-long meeting to weigh the means and method of vengeance. Uncle Agrios was already in America, and it was decided he would lead the family's pursuit of the murderers. Since Manolis could identify the brothers, it was also unanimously agreed that he would travel to Chicago to join Uncle Agrios and help avenge his brother's death.

"We place this sacred responsibility in your hands, boy," his great-grandfather told him gravely. "Your father and I are too old to make this journey. Your cousins are not linked as closely to Aleko as you are by blood. So go and join your uncle Agrios and together erase this grievous wound against our family." He fell silent for a moment, staring at Manolis with his fierce, relentless eyes. "Don't let me die, boy, and have to face the wrath of Aleko when I meet him in death's pasture still unavenged."

Only his mother sought to dissuade him from leaving. She tried to make Manolis understand that his quest for retribution would only deepen her sorrow and pain.

"Forget the rantings of that savage old man!" she said about his great-grandfather. "He has spent so many years at war with Turks and with his neighbors that his eyes and spirit are bloodthirsty!"

"Someone must go to punish those murderers, Mama," Manolis said. "I'm proud that the family has chosen me."

"You have been chosen by madmen for madness," she said bitterly. "If I lose another son, how does that make up for the agony of losing Aleko?"

"I won't be lost."

"If you follow this spoor of vengeance, you will be lost!" his mother said. "You'll be killed or end up in some foreign jail. God have mercy on us, for your family you will be lost!"

She turned toward the corner of the room, where his father

sat silently smoking his pipe. The fire glittered across his impassive face.

"Janco, tell the boy not to go," his mother said.

"Mama!"

She waved Manolis to silence, looking beseechingly at his father.

"Do you hear me?" his mother asked. "Janco, he will listen to you. Tell the boy not to go."

"He'll do what he must do," his father said.

"Have mercy on me!" his mother pleaded. "Since the day we married I have never asked you for anything! I have labored for you, borne your children, suffered by your side! I have lost one son, let me keep the other! I beg you now if you hold a shred of love or mercy for me in your heart, tell our son not to go!"

"His brother has been murdered," his father said quietly. "He'll do what he must do."

When Manolis examined his own heart, he found it empty of anger or any urge for vengeance. Perhaps that numbness came because he wasn't able to believe his brother was dead. He had witnessed Aleko's funeral and seen the box holding his body lowered into the ground. Yet they had spent so many years together, laughing, working, sleeping side by side, that Aleko remained an earthbound presence. A dozen times a day Manolis swore he heard his brother's voice, saw him waving from the end of a village street, caught strains of his laughter on the wind.

Only when he woke from a fitful sleep at night and quickly stretched out his hand to the pallet beside him did he understand his brother was gone. In those dark and solitary hours, the quilt absorbing his tears, he began mourning Aleko for the first time. He thought then of his own dying with a curious anticipation, because that would unite their spirits again.

He knew he couldn't remain in the village. With every passing day, he endured the stern faces of the villagers, the accusing silence of the men in the coffeehouse, who couldn't understand why he hadn't already begun the pursuit.

The hardest part about leaving was losing Sofia Souris. Although he and the bootmaker's lovely daughter had never confirmed any betrothal between their families, he had always sensed her special feeling for him. In their few, spare conversations at church and during family gatherings, her dark eyes made pledges her lips dared not speak. A day would have come soon when he would have asked his parents to speak to her father. He felt Sofia loved him and, like his mother, wouldn't want him to leave.

For several days, he was assailed by rash thoughts. He'd ask permission to marry Sofia Souris and then take her to America. That fantasy was banished when he remembered grimly that his purpose in undertaking the long journey wasn't to build a home and family in the new land but to exact vengeance.

Finally, about a week after Aleko's funeral, obtaining a written confirmation of his brother's death in an accident, and a letter of identity from Father Sotiris and his schoolteacher, so he could use Aleko's ticket, he prepared to leave. He packed a few belongings in the same canvas bag Aleko had packed for his journey and asked Leontis to drive him in the wagon over the mountain to Rethymnon.

On his last night at home, as he started up to bed in the loft, his younger sister, Eleni, hugged him tightly for a final time. When she left his embrace, he found a solitary chrysanthemum and a small, folded slip of paper in his hand. The fragrance of the flower quickened his pulse and he hurried up the ladder to the loft and lit a candle. In the wavering light he read the few words in the note: "I will wait for you." There wasn't any signature, but he knew at once it came from his beloved Sofia. He blew out the candle, undressed quickly and slipped into bed. He slept that last night in the village with the flower and the note pressed against his heart.

Their ship docked at the port of Piraeus shortly after daylight. Carrying his suitcase in the crush of other passengers, Manolis descended the gangplank into the teeming confusion of the port. Strident-voiced peddlers hawked fruit, currants and smoked meat for the travelers, while, beyond them, in the narrow streets running from the docks, he saw more carts and wagons than he'd ever seen in his life.

Pushing through the peddlers who pulled and clutched at his clothing, Manolis joined a group of the men from his ship and went to the steamship office.

"We'll start the final checking and boarding in a few hours, so don't wander," an agent warned them. "The *Moraites* will depart later this afternoon."

Manolis moved away from the office to return and wait at the dock.

"Manolis!"

Startled to hear his name, he turned and saw the cassocked figure of the tall priest who had helped him in the steamship office in Rethymnon. He stood in the doorway of a small cafe, and Manolis walked to greet him. As he bent to kiss the priest's fingers, Father Basil gently rejected the gesture of respect.

"We aren't in church now but travelers together," the priest said. "You can't keep bobbing up and down." He smiled and motioned to the cafe. "My family and I are having a snack. Come and join us."

Manolis followed the priest into the cafe to a circular table occupied by a slender, bright-eyed woman, two dark-haired, pretty girls and a young boy. The three of them stared up at him with unblinking intensity.

"What are you staring at?" the priest said briskly. "Haven't you seen a young Cretan before?" He smiled. "This is my Papadia Cristina," he said, "and this is Alexandra, Soula and Andreas."

The girls were lovely replicas of the handsome mother, with great dark eyes and glowing cheeks. The delicate, sensitive face of the younger daughter, Soula, reminded him of his sister Eleni.

"This is Manolis . . ." The priest paused ruefully.

"Manousakis," Manolis said.

"Join us for some cheese and fruit, Manolis," the Papadia said, in a soft, pleasing voice.

"I'm not really hungry . . ."

"Of course you are!" the priest insisted. "We've been together on the ship all night and I'm sure you haven't eaten."

Manolis nodded sheepishly and moved to join them. Soula flashed him a smile and moved her chair to make room. He sat down between the girls, pressing his knees together, wary of his elbows and arms.

The waiter brought him a plate, and Papadia Cristina served him some crisp bread and thinly sliced oranges with cheese. In a moment he had overcome his awkwardness and ate hungrily.

"Manolis said he wasn't hungry," Andreas said. "Now he's swallowing his food without chewing it."

The Papadia smiled and Soula glared at her brother.

"That's the way we always eat in our village," Manolis said gravely. "No one ever chews their food."

"They don't?" Andreas asked in disbelief.

"Of course not," Manolis said, "and once you get used to it, swallowing isn't hard with slices of fruit and cheese but it is more difficult with a loaf of bread and a chicken . . ."

"You're fooling me!" Andreas cried. Everyone laughed and Manolis joined them. The loosening of the rigid lines about his mouth felt strange, and he recalled he hadn't laughed since Aleko's death. He was suddenly grateful for being allowed to share the warmth of the family.

"Father tells us you'll be with us on the ship," Papadia Cristina said, and he saw the shadow of fear in her eyes. "We have such a long journey ahead of us."

"I'm not scared of the crossing!" Andreas said. "Are you scared, Manolis?"

"Yes, I'm a little scared," Manolis said. "But many others have made this journey safely. We'll make it too."

"Of course we will!" Father Basil said earnestly. "God has plans for all of us in that new land!"

An uneasy silence followed his words. Manolis thanked them for the lunch and rose to leave. The Papadia stood up, and he was surprised at how small she was. She stretched on her toes and embraced him lightly. With a tremor he remembered his own mother.

"We'll see you on the ship, Manolis," Father Basil said.

Manolis left the cafe. He stood outside on the street a moment and saw that Soula had left the table and come to stand in the window. She stared at him through the glass, and it was as if their fingertips had brushed in passing. There was something unchildlike about her, he thought, a sensibility that grasped and understood his secrets.

He waved at her a final time and saw her slim hand raised in response. She turned then and walked back to join her family. After she had gone, he had the warm feeling that her glance and wave had nested like a pair of small, downy birds in his spirit.

Later that afternoon, after passing a final inspection, Manolis joined the line of men filing up the gangplank of the huge ship. Several agents and a ship's officer waited on deck to check the numbers imprinted in ink on each passenger's wrist, matching it with the numbers on his papers. Before going below, Manolis looked vainly for sight of Father Basil and his family, but then realized they would be traveling in cabin class and not in steerage.

He left the deck and descended into the murky, cavernous belly of the ship. When his eyes grew accustomed to the shadows, he saw the tiers of narrow bunks and was reminded of the maze of a beehive. Around him men noisily claimed bunks, a few arguments breaking out and threats hurled back and forth.

Unable to find an unoccupied lower bunk, Manolis tossed his suitcase into an upper tier. The pale-faced farmer in the lower bunk watched him.

"Better shake that pallet before you lay down up there," a man in the adjoining lower bunk growled.

"Why?"

"That will dislodge the more sickly bugs," the man said. "The sturdy ones will hang on no matter what you do."

"There shouldn't be any bugs here!" the farmer below Manolis protested.

"Explain that to them when they bite your ass," the other man said. He untangled himself from his bunk and swung his legs into the narrow aisle. When he stood up, Manolis saw a burly giant with unruly hair and a beard.

"Of course," the man went on amiably, "after a week down here with a couple of hundred other bumpkins, the bugs won't bother you. The stink of vomit and shit will occupy your thoughts."

"How do you know what it's like?" the farmer cried.

"Friends of mine made the trip and wrote me."

"What else did they write you?" the farmer asked nervously.

"How they boarded the ship as innocent as virgins but learned fast enough about dysentery, ship's fever, poor food," the giant answered. "And when a poor devil died, over the side with his body to feed the bloody sharks."

The farmer stared up at the giant with consternation. He leaped from the bunk, grabbed his parcels and staggered away to find another bunk. Manolis reached for his bag and placed it on the vacated lower bunk.

"Aren't you afraid too?" the man asked Manolis in a mocking voice.

"Yes, I'm afraid," Manolis said, "but if the ship makes it to America, I will make it too."

"You're a strapping young buck and probably will," the giant said. "What's your name? Just the first, since we don't have time for formalities."

"Manolis."

"I'm Starkas." They shook hands and the giant returned to his bunk. Manolis climbed into his own bunk and lay there listening to the men dragging suitcases and parcels through the cramped aisle. After a while, a tense, brooding silence settled over the hold.

Manolis stared at the underside of the bunk above him. On both sides of him, other bunks hemmed him in. He thought of the confinement of a grave. With a rush of longing, he recalled the limitless horizons of the fields and mountains of home. Now, in the dismal pit of the steerage, he drew desperately on that memory of space and light that would have to sustain him during the weeks of the voyage.

As long as he lived, he'd never be able to clear his nostrils of the reek of vomit, urine, shit and sweat. He'd forever hear the muttering, moaning and babbling of the men in the bunks around him. And no matter how often he bathed later, he'd never rid himself of the grime and grease on his body. "Steerage armor," Starkas called it, a maggoty crust a man couldn't ever scrub away.

There were other moments of the voyage he'd never forget: when, during the deepest hours of night, he heard men softly cry the names of sweethearts or wives. Sometimes, hearing their gasps and grunts, he understood they were using their bodies to relieve their loneliness and despair.

That carnality roused his own longings, and he spent hours in ruttish fantasies. He tried not to involve his beloved Sofia, fearing his lust would desecrate her purity. Since he had never seen a naked woman, the visions he called up were disembodied fragments of statues he had seen in a field excavated by men from another country. There were granite trunks and torsos, stone thighs and marble breasts. He fitted them into naked, symmetric bodies. About the heads he placed garlands of fresh flowers and he gave their faces the soft eyes of birds. Into them he breathed his passion so they came to life, responding to his caresses. And when he achieved a frenzied release, he didn't care that he moaned as wretchedly as the other men.

He brooded for hours at a time, as well, about Stellios and Mitsos Trombakis. In those moments he saw himself as if he were another man lying motionless in his bunk. He saw his face, the hollows of his eyes, the shadow across his cheeks. He considered the murder, the despoiling of his brother's life. Because of the killers, his mother, father and sisters had become mourners. Because of the assassins, he had become an exile, his bond to his land and to Sofia broken. His anger grew and nourished his hate, providing him the strength to endure the misery and privation.

Each day for a little while they were allowed to go on deck, to breath the fresh sea air, and to wash their hands and faces in buckets of cold, salty water. Looking up toward the cabin-class deck, from time to time Manolis caught a glimpse of Papadia Cristina and the girls. Soula waved excitedly when she saw him. The other cabin-class passengers stared down at the steerage travelers as if they were watching a herd of animals.

The priest came to the steerage daily to say a prayer. He was always pursued by a swarm of men, pulling at his cassock, begging him to listen to their laments. He tried to spend a few moments talking to Manolis but was quickly tugged away by others.

In an effort to break the hours of tedium and apathy, Starkas started to teach a group of the men English. He directed these sessions sternly.

"Not fok-tar, you clod," he snapped at Limberis during one lesson. "Fak-to-ree. Say it slowly. Fak-to-ree."

"That's just what I'm saying, Starkas," Limberis protested. "Fok-tar!"

"Hung-ree . . . hung-ree," Starkas said to Panayotis, who had difficulty untangling his tongue around the h's and r's.

"Would it be all right if I just rubbed my belly and groaned like I'm starving?" Panayotis asked.

"If you want them to throw you in a madhouse and probe your fat head," Starkas said.

"How do you ask an American girl to lay down and spread her legs?" a young, good-looking farmer smirked.

"Go find her father and show him your cock," Starkas snapped. The men burst into laughter, but Starkas never smiled.

"You morons think we're playing games!" he said grimly. "If you don't learn the language of America, you'll dig ditches and wash dishes for years. And there are other dangers. I knew a Greek laborer on the railroad who couldn't speak a word of English and who was slammed into jail for being drunk and pissing on the street. That night, a mad mob broke into the jail looking for some prisoner who had molested a child. They dragged the poor shrieking Greek to a tree and set a noose around his neck. No one could under-

stand his howls of innocence. He was saved at the last minute
by a deputy who showed up to explain he had transferred the
child molester to another jail. If he had been a few moments
later, the poor devil's family back in Greece would have got-
ten the news that the boob was hanged in America for taking
a public piss!"

Despite that warning, most of the men wearied of the struggle and the nagging of Starkas. Manolis continued to press
him for help. He knew any pursuit of the Trombakis brothers
was futile if he couldn't speak English. In the first two weeks
they were at sea, he learned to understand bare sentences and,
in simple phrases, make himself understood as well.

As the days went on, a number of the men in steerage became ill with fever. They lay shivering in their bunks, moaning as the sea scraped and battered the hull. Their companions tried to help them, but little could be done to relieve
their ailments. Some grew better, while others became sicker.

There was a night Manolis was wakened by Starkas to join
several other men in carrying a sack holding the body of a
man who had died. They gathered on deck under a bright
moon whose light crested the dark, turbulent waves. Starkas
loomed above the group, which included the ship's captain
and a detail of seamen.

Someone went to fetch the priest and, in a few moments,
Father Basil and Papadia Cristina joined them.

"Who is it?" the priest whispered to Manolis.

"Kostas Ligarakis."

"I saw him just a few hours ago!" the priest said in a
shocked voice. "He seemed better then."

"All right, Father," the captain said sharply. "Let's get this
over with."

"Can't we wait for a funeral service until daylight, Cap-

tain?" Father Basil asked. "Some of the other men might wish
to be present. Why do we have to bury this poor man in the
middle of the night?"

"The dead begin to stink and rot fast in the salt and mois-
ture," the captain said. "We usually read a prayer and heave
the corpse overboard. But since we have a man of the cloth
on board, these fellows thought you should pray. So let's get
on with it . . ."

Father Basil stepped closer to the misshapen sack on the
deck. Papadia Cristina came to stand beside Manolis, reaching out to clasp his hand. He felt her fingers trembling. The
men formed a tighter circle and the priest began a soft,
shaken prayer.

"Our beloved brother, Kostas . . . may he rest in peace
. . . may his spirit dwell in the bounty of the Lord's love and
mercy and forgiveness . . ."

Even as the priest spoke the words he must have uttered so
many times on land, Manolis felt the strangeness of the moment. The moon gleamed like God's eye weeping for a man
whose dreams were now confined for eternity in a coarse sack
soon to settle on the bed of the fathomless ocean.

When Father Basil finished his prayer, the seamen stepped
forward to hoist the sack.

"Hold off there," Starkas said somberly. "He's our man and
we'll dispatch him ourselves."

Without waiting for the captain's consent, Starkas bent and
firmly grasped one end of the sack. Manolis and the other
Cretans joined him. They lifted the sack to the rail and, at a
muttered command from Starkas, heaved it over the side. The
body struck the water with a loud splash.

The captain motioned brusquely for the gathering to dis-
perse. The seamen moved away, but the priest, the Papadia
and the men from steerage lingered in a mournful assembly.

"Poor man," Papadia Cristina whispered. "We must write to his family."

"He was the first, but he won't be the last," Starkas said. "Say another prayer for the living now, Father, for those wretches who may join Ligarakis in his grave before this voyage is over."

Starkas was right. As if the cycle of fever and crisis ran a similar course, in the next three days two more men died, both buried, like Ligarakis, at sea. A brief service for them was held under a cloudless, sun-bright sky that made Manolis yearn for darkness, because out in the water he could see the fins of sharks stalking the ship.

On the final afternoon before the day they were to arrive in the harbor of Ellis Island, the land of America visible on the horizon, a celebration took place. Every man contributed whatever provisions he had left, a few even sharing the last of their carefully hoarded wine. Other spirits were added by seamen who slipped among the revelers to sell them beakers of a potent rum. Several men brought out shepherd's flutes and one of the seamen joined them with his accordion. They devised a makeshift band and, in a few moments, the shrill, bracing melody of a mountain dance rang across the ship. A circle was quickly cleared and a dozen men formed a line to dance, clasping arms and kicking and leaping with abandon. The passengers in cabin class crowded the railing of the upper deck to watch them.

Manolis drank a little wine but remained aloof from the celebration. When darkness fell, he moved away from the revelers to stand alone at the rail. He watched the moonlight shimmering across the waves, and stared toward the new land hidden in darkness and mist. When he turned back to the festivities, he saw the silhouette of the dancers still circling and leaping. The spirited figure of the agile leader reminded

Manolis of the animated, graceful way Aleko had danced. The memory stung his eyes with tears.

The following morning, with billows of mist crossing the deck, Father Basil said a final mass of thanksgiving. He was surrounded by a throng of men holding their caps and hats. His resonant voice sounded clearly in the stillness that was broken only by the cries of gulls.

As they neared the bay, the restrictions on passengers were eased and Papadia Cristina and her family joined Manolis and Father Basil on the lower deck.

When they saw the colossus of the giant woman lifting her torch into the sky, the girls and Andreas let out expressions of wonder and awe. A number of the men clustered around them made their cross and a few cried.

"Is she really welcoming us, Papa?" Andreas asked.

"Yes, yes, she is!" Father Basil said earnestly. "For years now she's been greeting hundreds of thousands of immigrants from countries all over the world. She is welcoming us now too! Wave to her!"

Andreas began to wave vigorously. Laughing a little, Soula began to wave. When she looked excitedly at Manolis, buoyed by her delight and her faith, he started waving to the statue as well.

A short while later a cutter pulled alongside their ship. Two men in uniform came aboard and pushed their way quickly through the steerage passengers crowded on deck and up to the cabin areas. A brief examination was made of each of them, and the cabin passengers left the ship for the cutter. The priest and his family had to say their farewells swiftly.

"When you're settled with your uncle, write us in Utah, Manolis," Father Basil said. "Let's not lose touch."

"I'll write," Manolis said.

Soula moved closer to him and spoke in a whisper. "Promise to write to me alone, Manolis, and I'll answer right away."

He nodded his promise. She stared at him out of her deep, dark eyes, and once again he had the disquieting feeling that the young girl could see what wasn't visible to others. When he hesitated before embracing her, she stretched up and kissed him on the cheek.

Starkas and a contingent of men escorted the priest and his family to the gangplank. Men touched his cassock as he passed, murmuring fervent farewells to the Papadia and the children. They descended into the cutter with the other cabin passengers, standing in the midst of the baggage that was piled in a small mountain at the stern of the boat.

"All right, Cretans!" Starkas shouted. "Let our Cretan priest and his family hear our affection and our thanks!"

The men delivered a thunderous farewell. Father Basil and the Papadia, a small, slender figure beside him, waved back.

As the cutter chugged away from the ship, their figures grew smaller. The final glimpse Manolis had of the beloved family was of the priest's tall, cassocked frame disappearing into the reflection of the sunlight on the water.

Later in the day, when the ship docked, the men carried their luggage down the gangplank. The luckier ones, like Manolis, had a single bag, but less fortunate men struggled with several. They filed along the pier through roped enclosures until they entered a huge building with floors of concrete, iron railings, cages of iron, and wire netting.

The uniformed guards, shouting and gesturing, drove them along toward the cubicles occupied by doctors and inspectors. When they were ordered to strip to the waist, Manolis took off his jacket and shirt. Starkas pulled off his shirt to reveal his muscled arms and powerful, barrel chest covered by a tangle of hair.

"By God, Starkas," Limberis said in awe. "They'll take you for one of those gorillas from Africa."

"If they need proof, I'll tell them we're related," Starkas snapped. But there was an unusual nervousness in his face, and Manolis noticed the labored way he breathed.

When Manolis' turn came to enter the examining room, a short, stout doctor gestured brusquely for him to open his mouth. The doctor swiftly checked his teeth, peered into his eyes and ears. He was told to raise his arms, flex his legs, to bend and squat and balance on one foot. His neck was probed and his back thumped.

He was passed and told to leave. He hurried gratefully from the cubicle and saw Starkas emerging from an adjoining room. In another cubicle they saw a doctor fussing over skinny Gorgios from their ship, his ribs protruding against the sheath of his flesh.

As he and Starkas slipped on their shirts and jackets, the doctor with Gorgios called to a guard. The officer brought Gorgios out. He looked stunned, his naked shoulders trembling, and he dragged his bag and jacket along the floor. As the guard led him away, Gorgios looked back at them in panic.

"They're going to send me home!" he cried. "Help me, Starkas, in God's name, speak to them!"

Every man who heard his anguished cries stood watching in fear as Gorgios passed along the lines. Some men shrank away from him as if afraid that the cause of his rejection might contaminate them. Even the doctors ceased their examinations until the weeping, pleading man disappeared.

"You know the language so well, Starkas," Manolis said in a low, shaken voice. "Couldn't you have spoken up for him?"

"They probably found the poor devil with consumption," Starkas said shortly. "I couldn't have helped him by speaking." He stared somberly at Manolis. "Look out for others if you can, Manolis," he said, "but if you're going to survive in this savage land, you must first look out for yourself."

For the next few hours they moved slowly through the great hall. They were separated for a while and then reunited in another enclosure, from which they walked onto a ferry bound for the mainland. As twilight darkened the sky above the cold, stark buildings of the island, Starkas and Manolis found a place along a section of rail.

"When we land, we'll go directly to the railroad yards," Starkas said. "We may have to wait for a day or so until we can catch a freight train heading West. I'll drop you off in the yards in Chicago and then keep going myself for Colorado."

"What will you do in Colorado?"

For a few moments Starkas didn't answer. Somewhere in the darkness, not far from them, a group of young men talked in loud voices as if to bolster their spirits. Then the human sounds were muffled as the engines of the ferry began rumbling.

"I've come to regard you as a friend, Manolis," Starkas said quietly. "We'll separate soon and friends should not part with secrets. You must have wondered how I knew what the voyage would be like, how I had learned this land's language, and why I was so tense today."

"You don't have to explain anything to me, Starkas."

"I want to tell you, Manolis," Starkas said. "I trust you and, besides, there will be a relief in sharing what I've carried alone. By God, they almost had me back there, the whole journey blasted by one inspector with a bloody good memory to recall that he'd seen my oversized carcass before. I had to talk fast and explain, through the interpreter, of course, that my village was famous for its hulks. I told him he must have seen another of my villagers who resembled me. For a few moments I nearly expired, but he seemed appeased. I looked and sounded like a clod and that satisfied him."

As the ferry moved farther away from the lights of Ellis Island, stars became visible in the darker sky. A breeze carried the smells of the land. Manolis waited for Starkas to go on.

"So now you know I've been to America before," Starkas said in a low voice. "I first came five years ago, traveling West to find work in the coal mines of Colorado. There isn't any way to explain to a farmer what a coal mine is like except to say it's an underworld of never-ending darkness where the devil is king. Men labor in that domain for twelve, fourteen, or more hours, chipping at the seams with axes, the only light coming from lanterns and tiny gas flames on their caps. I tell you we had the Turks in Crete but this labor was a harsh slavery too." A bitterness entered his voice. "Men are killed and maimed in explosions and cave-ins and all to make money for the bloated owners. Well, men can only be pushed so far. We organized a federation of miners and we called a strike."

"What is a strike?" Manolis asked.

"A strike is when the workers protest the conditions and the pay of their labor. They refuse to work until those conditions and pay are improved." He paused. "Well, the strike went on for months. They beat up our men and we assaulted some of their goons and company police. They tried to bring in a trainload of strikebreakers, and while that train sat in the depot at Cripple Creek, an explosion tore it apart. Fourteen of the scabs were killed, while the arms, legs and torsos of other men were scattered around like fragments of lightning-shattered trees." Starkas stared silently at the water. "I had nothing to do with that bombing, Manolis, I swear that's the truth. But some of our men might have been guilty. That massacre broke the strike and broke the union. The Army was called in, and those of us who were leaders were threatened with hanging. A carcass my size would have required a double noose and I was more scared than I'd ever been in my life. Hiding by day and riding the freights by night, I got back East and caught a ship returning to Greece. I planned to marry, raise a family, to hell forever with miners and mines."

He expelled a harsh gust of breath.

"But it's hard to alter the course of a life," he said. "I found a girl who loved me and we planned to marry. But I couldn't forget my friends and comrades, the hopeless faces of the men who went down in the cages every day. I began to feel I'd abandoned them and that I'd never know any peace in my life. So I said goodbye to that girl, we both cried, I took a different name and I've come to America again. I'll make my way back to Colorado and join that fight again. A different battle now but the same bloody war."

Manolis was grateful and moved that Starkas had taken him into his confidence. He tried to find words to reassure him of his friendship. "I never met that other man," he said finally. "You'll always be Starkas to me."

Starkas turned from staring at the water to look at Manolis. "I knew you'd feel that way," he said quietly, "or I wouldn't have put my life in your hands." He paused. "Now, my friend, you've learned something about me. I haven't yet learned what demon lurks within you. If ever I saw a man who should have remained on the land, it is you. That lament for home was in your face each time I caught you staring back across the ocean at blessed Crete. Tell me now, a secret I'll keep as you keep mine, what whips you to this journey you don't wish to make?"

Drawn by the bond he felt to Starkas, Manolis told him then about Aleko, the jubilant summons from Uncle Agrios, his brother's thwarted destiny. His voice gathering emotion as he spoke, he described Aleko's murder and his own vow of vengeance that brought him in pursuit of the murderers.

After he had finished, Starkas was silent for a while. He spoke, finally, in a solemn voice.

"The man who swears a vow," Starkas said, "makes an appointment with himself at some unknown time and place. Whether the appointment is met, you'll have to decide. I won't tell you that one way is right or wrong. But I know this new land will either embitter you and sharpen the vow or provide you peace so you abandon the vendetta. Meanwhile, Manolis, you'll live your days under a storm, and see gloomy visions in your dreams."

He looked around at the shaded figures of the other immigrants traveling on the ferry.

"I wonder how many others there are here," he said grimly, "with their real purpose for this journey locked inside themselves. We look at other men with eyes we think are open and clear, but even if we gain the wisdom of the old sages, we'll forever remain blind to what hides in a solitary human heart."

AMERICA
1909

CHAPTER FIVE

Stellios

During the day, the sun beating on the roof of the freight car overheated the interior, so Stellios rode soaked in sweat. At night, when the cold wind whistled through the transom, he huddled beneath his blanket, wishing he had the labor agent, Kalingas, in the car so he might strangle him.

"We are blind and helpless animals in here," the farmer Nikolaos said gloomily on their second day.

That was true, Stellios thought bitterly—they were blind, helpless animals in a locked box, crossing an invisible land. Although he couldn't see that land, traces of earth and sky filtered in to him. He smelled the foliage of trees, the freshness of rain and the aromas of burning wood and brush.

Stellios claimed a place near the door for Mitsos and himself that no other man in the car challenged. Although the other Greeks tried to involve them in conversation, they remained aloof. Stellios passed his hours listening to the rumbling wheels forming certain words. Sometimes the word the wheels repeated, over and over, was "Crete." Then he recalled blue skies and lofty mountains of his island. He remembered the freedom of the orchards and the fields and resting at twilight in a bower of fruit trees, men bantering and smoking.

Another word hurled up to him by the wheels was "woman." That recalled all the female thighs and tits he had conquered. As a beardless, ignorant boy there had been the little girl Melissa, whose slim, barely budded form was the first naked girl's body he saw. He touched her mysterious slits and soft hollows and thought her tiny tits were all the bulblets any woman developed. But, at fifteen, with a group of randy youths, he visited an encampment of gypsies and saw the whores with their dark and pendulous globes, the nipples hard as daggers. For the first time then he discovered the force and power in his body and how making love was like war.

When he grew tired and could no longer control his reveries, the wheels rumbled the name of "Aleko." As if in a nightmare, he was returned to the morning when he and Mitsos waited on the mountain. He recalled racing down the slope, felt the gun recoil in his hand and saw Aleko fall. To dispel the dark memory, Stellios pressed his palms tightly against his ears, trying to mute the rumble of the wheels.

The train made several stops during each day. At each of them, the door of their car was unbolted and dragged open by the work boss, Mishima. The Italians and Greeks would scramble to their feet and rush to the doorway to draw in breaths of air, being careful not to violate the space held by Stellios and Mitsos. Despite the pleas of the men to descend, Mishima allowed only several of them out to haul down the slop buckets to be washed. Afterward these men would lift in the boxes with their daily ration of food no better than the fare on the ship.

Angered by the confinement and the way he was being treated, Stellios considered making an effort to escape during one of the stops. As if Nikolaos understood what he planned, he whispered a warning to Stellios.

"This is my business," Stellios said brusquely. "I'll do what I want to do."

"Forgive me for interfering," Nikolaos said quietly, "but you don't know the country or the language. They'll capture you and lock you away. Wait, my friend . . . a better time and place may come later."

Even as his temper and anger urged him to violent action, Stellios understood the farmer was right. At the following stop, when the door was dragged open and Stellios caught sight of sky and open fields beyond the station, his muscles tensed to leap and run. But he hesitated and the door was dragged closed and bolted again. He cursed Nikolaos as they were once more imprisoned in darkness.

By the end of their second day, Stellios had begun to recognize the voices of some of the Greeks. Nikolaos was the leader, cautious as an old hen, soothing their grumbles and complaints. All in all, they seemed little better than the whining, jabbering Italians at the other end of the car.

One of the Greeks was a man named Buzis, who talked more than anyone else. He babbled to others when they'd listen, but often spoke to himself. The more nervous and frightened he became, the faster the words flew from his lips. "Poor Buzis!" he cried. "Poor, miserable wretch! If his dear mother had only known what he would have to endure on his journey to America, she'd have drowned him as a tyke! Everyone would have said, Good riddance, and he'd not be here to bother his good comrades with his laments!"

"All you need to do is shut up!" Antonis called harshly.

Buzis would make an effort to oblige, remaining silent for a while. Then, impelled by renewed anxiety or fear, the words rushed from him once more. "That slant-eyed jailer who

opens our cage each day resembles a jaundiced bull!" he said
earnestly. "But, wait! A bull is too noble an animal! Shall we
try, perhaps, a pig? But, wait! We must be careful not to
offend a real pig, who is a worthy, useful animal! So we might
call him a bloated imitation of a pig! Yes, yes, that is right!
For the feat of identifying him precisely, Buzis should be re-
warded with a bucket all his own! See how little he requires
for true joy?"

Some of the men laughed at his babblings, but others became impatient and threatened him with slaps or kicks.
Nikolaos defended him.

"Let the man talk," Nikolaos said. "His chatter helps us
pass the time."

"Barba Nikolaos, I thank you!" Buzis cried gratefully. "My
beloved father—bless his hallowed bones—would be consoled to hear your commendation! He would often say, My
boy, your mouth will be your undoing! But see now, Barba
Nikolaos has proclaimed that the chatter of Buzis helps pass
the time! Miracle of miracles, nothing under God's sky is
wasted! Shit and mouth each serves a purpose! One fertilizes
the earth and the other helps pass the time!"

During one of the stops when the door was opened and
men swarmed forward for air, Stellios saw that Buzis was a
skinny runt with a thin face and the twitchings of a frantic
rabbit. He scrambled forward with the rest each time for air
and each time was jostled and shoved back by bigger, stronger
men. He tried vainly to claw and wriggle his way through the
mass of bodies.

At the following stop, Stellios watched his futile struggle
begin again. On an impulse he rose and caught Buzis by the
arm. Using his big, powerful body as a ram, he split the pack
of men and dragged Buzis to the open doorway. For the first

time then, the little babbler seemed speechless, staring up at Stellios with moist, adoring eyes.

On the afternoon of the fourth (perhaps it was the fifth) day the train made another stop. In a few moments Mishima dragged open the door. Thinking it was another lull in which to empty the buckets and bring in food, a group of men rushed the doorway. Standing on the ground, jabbering in the shrill tongue no one understood, Mishima gestured for them to jump down. Realizing they had reached their destination, the men rushed back into the car for their belongings. In a few moments the car became a mass of scrambling, pushing men.

Stellios and Mitsos were among the first off the car, and they climbed into one of the wagons waiting beside the switch tower. The other Greeks followed them and the wagon was quickly filled, while the Italians climbed into the other wagon.

One of the last men out of the freight car was Buzis. Mishima caught him by the scruff of his jacket and shoved him toward the wagon with the Italians. Buzis ran instead for the wagon that held Stellios. Grasping the tailgate, he tried desperately to hoist himself off the ground.

Mishima called harshly for Buzis to get in the other wagon. When Buzis ignored his shouts, Mishima ran toward him. Buzis let out a shriek of terror and lost his balance. He would have tumbled to the ground at Mishima's mercy if Stellios hadn't stretched from the wagon and grasped him by the arms. He hauled him swiftly over the tailgate and into the wagon.

The men in the wagon burst into laughter. They hushed as Mishima stared balefully up at them. He glared at Stellios with a storm of hate in his face. Then he stamped angrily to the other wagon and swung his stocky, muscled body into the

seat beside the driver. The drivers prodded their horses and
the wagons lurched forward.

"That was a merciful action, Stellios," Nikolaos said. "But
be careful of that devil. He'd like to drink your blood."

"Stellios doesn't have to fear the pig." Buzis tried to speak
defiantly despite a voice that still trembled at the closeness of
his encounter. "Buzis will protect him. You can be sure of
that."

The men around him burst into raucous laughter.

"You pipsqueak!" Mitsos snickered. "How can a goat's fart
like you protect a giant like Stellios?"

Squeezing between Mitsos and Nikolaos to get close to
Stellios, Buzis waited patiently until the jeers and laughter
had ceased.

"Buzis sounds absurd to all of you," he said quietly, "but,
my friends, you must know life is also absurd. No man can
foretell his destiny and, in that mystery, a pipsqueak may
prove the equal of a giant."

After traveling for several hours through a rough plain
rimmed by mountains, the wagons came to a sprawling settlement of shacks and sheds. There was a fenced enclosure with
donkeys and horses, a blacksmith's forge, and railroad engines linked to a string of flatcars.

The wagons bounced and clattered over the rocky roadway
to the camp entrance. At the gate they passed men holding
rifles who stared up at them with grim, hostile faces.

"They look friendly as Turks," Buzis whispered. "God help
us."

Stellios stared beyond the camp at the setting sun, which
crested the peaks with scarlet. The sight of mountains had
renewed his confidence and faith. He inhaled deeply, vowing
he'd endure any misery as long as he wasn't denied the sun
and ranges he had always owned in Crete.

That first night in the railroad camp, they were assembled in a large shed and directed to strip. Then, in a swiftly moving column of naked men, they passed through a cold shower, drying off with rags. Afterward they were sprayed with a pungent powder that coated their bodies with a chalky film. Men grumbled and complained, but a snarling Mishima and several other foremen bullied them to silence.

Stellios was angrier than any of the others, but he noticed Mishima watching him as if hoping he'd cause trouble. Remembering the warnings about jail, he restrained his temper.

They were assigned cotton shirts, pants, socks and ragged jackets. Their ration of food for that first night was a grainy, lukewarm stew, some chunks of bread, and coffee. But the men ate hungrily, soaking up the last morsels of tasteless gravy with their bread.

They were assigned to shacks in groups of four. Buzis tagged closely behind Stellios and was housed in his shack with Mitsos and a stocky farmer named Gravas.

"Why the hell does the runt have to be with us?" Mitsos protested.

"Be fair, Mitsos," Buzis pleaded. "Buzis belongs with you because he is Cretan too."

"A shrimp like you?" Mitsos said sharply. "You're lying."

"He's from Crete," Gravas said. "I've seen his papers."

"If the runt is Cretan, let him stay with us," Stellios said.

"Thank you, Stellios!" Buzis exclaimed, hurrying to keep up with his longer stride. "Buzis pledges you will not be sorry!"

"I'm sorry already," Stellios muttered.

Their shack was a drafty hovel, built from odd-sized planks with heavy rolls of tar paper covering roof and walls. Each shack was furnished with narrow plank beds bearing thin pallets of straw. Wind whistled through cracks in the tar paper and almost extinguished the cabbage-headed candle Mitsos lit.

"My animals back home lived better than this," Gravas said, and cursed.

Stellios didn't say anything but threw his bag on one of the beds. Buzis moved quickly to take the pallet closest to him.

"There are ways to make a place more homelike!" he said earnestly. "Buzis will scrounge for whatever materials he can find. He'll make this shack the most comfortable in the camp!"

"You can't make it any worse." Gravas shrugged and flopped on another bed.

When Stellios left the shack, Buzis followed closely. A bonfire was burning a short distance away, and Stellios sat down beside it. Buzis sat down a few feet from him, extending his hands to warm them. Across the fire from them several men whispered back and forth. Buzis shifted closer to Stellios and spoke in a low voice.

"Thank you for permitting Buzis in the shack with you, Stellios," he said fervently. "He'll make it warmer and keep it clean . . . you won't be sorry."

"If you're going to sit here, quit babbling."

Buzis murmured an apology and fell silent. From one of the shacks, men's voices rose in a heated quarrel. Other men shouted for them to shut up. When their voices had been stilled, a donkey brayed loudly, the shrill sound lingering in the night.

Buzis fumbled at the collar of his jacket and tugged out a small pouch on a cord.

"Buzis has a treasure here, Stellios," he whispered. "Do you want to know what it is?"

Stellios didn't answer. Buzis mustered his courage and went on.

"It is a leathern pouch with Cretan earth he has carried all the way from his village," he said in a low, trembling voice. "All through the voyage he kept the pouch near his heart. He was consoled by knowing that even if he were to sink through the water to the floor of the ocean, this fragment of Cretan earth would remain bound to him forever."

From another shack the plaintive strains of a flute floated across the darkness.

"The pouch has magic, too, Stellios." Buzis spoke in a low, earnest voice. "By holding it to his cheek, Buzis can smell the mushrooms of home, the mulberries and saffron leaves, the thick, dark honey from his uncle's hives, the cucumbers from his mother's garden, the pine needles and the morning dew."

He waited vainly for Stellios to respond.

"Buzis isn't speaking nonsense, Stellios," he said nervously. "Throughout the hard, terrible journey, he would have given up and died many times without its magical power."

"Believe what the devil you want," Stellios said. "Just quit chattering. I want some peace."

"Just one minute, please!" Buzis pleaded. He reached to his throat and worked hastily until he snapped the cord free. He extended the pouch to Stellios.

"Take it, Stellios," he spoke in a shaken voice. "It will keep Crete near you and will keep you safe from harm . . . you'll see I'm right . . ."

His voice trailed away. Stellios stared at him in silence. He was perplexed why Buzis had offered him the pouch. He might ask money for it later or, perhaps, he was trying to buy his protection. Then, something naked and trusting in the man's face and voice, made him uneasy.

"You carried it across the ocean," he said. "It belongs to you."

"Buzis wants you to have it! You're his dearest friend and he wants you safe! What happens to him isn't important! But your destiny, Stellios, will be like those of the heroes in the stories told to us by our grandfathers! Buzis understands now that he has carried this pouch across the ocean for you!"

For a moment Stellios wavered, tempted to accept the pouch. Perhaps it did contain those fragments of home and it might also have sorcerous elements that would protect him. But he also realized quickly that if the magic of the pouch were true, Buzis was making an astonishing and generous gesture. That angered him.

"You must think I'm a Cretan without pride!" he said harshly. "The damned pouch belongs to you! If I had wanted a pouch of earth from home, don't you think I could have brought one for myself? Now, for the last time, I'm tired of your sniveling about amulets and smells! Close your mouth or get the hell away from me!"

Buzis stumbled to his feet, his fingers trembling as he slipped the pouch into his jacket. He hurried away from the fire and entered the shack. In the dark he must have bumped one of the beds, for the angry voice of Mitsos cursed him. Then there was silence.

Before daylight each morning, the work foremen paced the streets between the shacks, blowing their whistles loudly. If the men weren't dressed and out quickly enough, the foremen banged their short clubs against the doors.

They stumbled from the shacks into the darkness, shivering in the raw cold. In the cookshack each man was handed a ration of thick oatmeal, sourdough bread and tea. With only a few minutes to eat, they were harried to the flatcars. When they had climbed on board, the steaming locomotive carried them along several miles of track to the day's work area. Once again the foremen prodded them off the flatcars as the first streaks of daylight uncovered the peaks of the mountains.

They labored at replacing narrow-gauge tracks with standard rails, of a wider dimension. The first team of laborers heaved and strained with long steel rods to pry up and dislodge the rails. As soon as the sections of track were carried to the side, other teams brought up new lengths of rail. At the end came the drillers, special workers wielding the heavy sledgehammers to hammer in the iron spikes that fastened the rails to the ties.

Driven by the shouts of the foremen, men who had never worked except as solitary farmers were now commanded to join teams and grip and carry the rails in unison. That first day, men fell over one another's feet, stumbled and slipped on the tracks, sustained bruises and sprains.

By early afternoon they were allowed to rest and given a ration of soup and hardtack. Stellios felt they must have covered a dozen miles but when he looked back to the point where the day's work had begun he was dismayed to discover how short a distance it was.

During a brief rest period the Greeks segregated themselves again in the shelter of a rocky overhang. Stellios, Mitsos and an exhausted Buzis sat a short distance away.

"But this isn't labor," a Greek said gloomily. "This is slavery for donkeys and oxen, not men."

"My back is broken," another man said. "I swear that Italian bastard behind me wasn't lifting at all."

"God burn those foremen!" Antonis said. "I can't understand them, but I know they're cursing us! Are we animals to be driven by curses?"

"If we have to work like this every day," a fourth man lamented, "we won't last to collect our first pay."

"What kind of Greeks are you?" Stellios called to them sharply. "On board ship you whined, in the freight car you wailed, and now that you're finally working, you groan and snivel like children!"

The men looked silently and shamefacedly at one another.

"All well and good for you to talk, Stellios," Antonis said quietly. "You're the biggest, strongest man here. You can handle any labor."

"A man should be able to handle any labor or he isn't a man!" Stellios said. "The work is harder than work we have done in the past, but we are working under the open sky! These mountains are like the mountains at home! Stand up, then, like Greeks, and show these foreigners that you're different from the rest of them!"

"Stellios is right," Nikolaos said. "We've been cramped up for weeks, first in steerage and then locked in the train. Our muscles are still stiff. But we will get used to the work and, when we're paid, we'll be given more money than any of us saw back home in a year!"

The mood of the men lightened and they bantered with one another. When the foremen shouted for them to return to work, they rose quickly and moved to the tracks.

Buzis groaned as he pushed himself wearily to his feet.

"Buzis doesn't wish to disgrace his friends," he said weakly. "Others may get used to the work but Buzis will not. His wretched ass is near total collapse."

"Maybe we can ask for some lighter work for you," Nikolaos said. "An assignment in camp with the cooking crew."

"Cretans don't ask for special favors!" Stellios said. "He'll do his share like the rest!"

"Stellios is right!" Buzis said quickly. "Buzis pledges to his friends he'll do his share!"

"Well, at least stay close to the crew that works with me," Nikolaos said. "I'll make certain that strong men work on either side of you."

"God bless you, Barba Nikolaos!" Buzis said fervently. In spite of his weariness he made an effort to walk briskly toward the tracks. Stellios and Nikolaos followed him.

"The men needed to hear the things you said today, Stellios," Nikolaos murmured. "If we're going to survive here we'll need pride as well as strength. The men see that pride in you and look to you as a leader."

"I lead only myself."

"Leadership isn't something a man chooses," Nikolaos said. "It's something that men give to the one among them who can inspire and lead them. It's as simple as that . . ."

When they first began working on the line, the trees along the slopes of the mountains still held a late-autumn shade of russet and gold. In the space of a few weeks, that color had faded into the gray hue of winter apples with mottled skin. The shrubs around the tracks became dry, thin stalks that rustled in the wind.

The first snow of winter fell and the men labored in a mist of thick flakes. The snow covered their hoods and jackets and glazed the tracks, making the rails slick and hazardous to grasp and carry.

Whatever the weather, the driving forward of the track went on, mile after punishing mile. All day long there sounded the clanging of the iron rails, the pounding of the sledgehammers, the hoarse shouts of the foremen. The railroad crews were like a ragtail army, Stellios thought, invading a tranquil land, disturbing the jackrabbits and gophers, agitating the ravens and crows, which trailed down shrill, fretful cries.

To relieve the drudgery and monotony of the work, the Greek workers converted one of the larger shacks into a makeshift coffeehouse. They set up tables built from barrels and used boxes as chairs. They brewed a black, syrupy coffee and blended a liquor that burned the throat and tongue like a devil's raki.

After returning from the worksite, washing quickly, and eating their evening meal, the men packed into the coffee-

house. Crowded so tightly there was little room to move, they
smoked and drank, argued and gambled. If a fight broke out,
the adversaries were thrown into the street to finish their
brawl. When it grew late, the shack fogged with the fumes of
tobacco and liquor, men stumbled back to their shacks. Those
who remained in the coffeehouse sat in a morose silence.
Sometimes then, one of these men played his flute, the lonely,
haunting sound reminding them of home.

Alone among the men in the camp, Stellios enjoyed the
challenge of the daily labor. As his strong, hard-muscled body
adapted to the long hours of work he grew stronger, doing
each task with such ease that within a few weeks he had become a driller. He pounded spikes with such swiftness and
strength, swinging the heavy hammer so accurately, that he
was regarded as superior even to men who had been drillers
for years. The Greeks were proud of Stellios and named him
"Hercules." They worked harder themselves to prove worthy
of his prowess.

All their best work, however, couldn't satisfy the foremen
led by the overseer Mishima, who berated them constantly,
cursing the slower, more awkward men, even poking them
with the butts of their clubs. These jabs were accompanied by
epithets like "sonofabitch!" "scum!" "Greek niggers!"

Heeding the counsel of Nikolaos, the Greek workers suffered in silence or angrily replied under their breath, waiting anxiously for payday.

But the man in the camp singled out for the most abuse
was the little Buzis. In spite of the help of stronger Greeks beside him, he couldn't sustain his share of the load. The
foremen would taunt him, and Mishima pursued his lapses
and stumbles and cursed him in English and Japanese. Even
the Italian and Slav workers came to regard his suffering with
pity.

"That bastard is on him constantly!" Nikolaos protested once to Stellios. "Genovese, who leads the Sicilians, asks why we don't do something. Speak to Buzis, Stellios, please, and convince him to let us ask for lighter work for him. If we don't, that yellow-skinned Turk will finish by killing him."

"He won't always have friends near to help him," Stellios said. "Even if he's a runt, he's Cretan, and he's got guts. This experience will make him tougher, so leave him alone."

By the end of each day's labor, Buzis could hardly walk and had to be lifted onto the flatcar by several men. He was in the infirmary for wrenchings and sprains at least once a week, and a cough wracked his slight frame. But he kept returning for each day's labor. Appreciating he had more courage than stronger men, the Greeks called him "Little Hercules." Buzis was overwhelmed with gratitude.

"Oh, fortunate Buzis! All his life to be called 'wretch!' 'cur!' and 'turd!' and now this honor! His spavined ass deserves only to be tossed into some ditch, but—God be praised —his good friends hold up his weak shanks and give him a noble and heroic title!"

For all of his physical infirmities, foremost among the Greeks Buzis developed a quick and supple tongue for the English language. He had only to hear a phrase spoken several times and was able to repeat it accurately. Soon he could speak better English than any of the Greek, Italian or Slav workers and acted as interpreter for the men.

In the evening, after Stellios wearied of the smoke and chatter of the coffeehouse, he returned to their shack to find Buzis studying a book of English he had bought in the company store. As much to pass the time as anything else, Stellios let Buzis tutor him in the English words and phrases. Struggling with the strange language, he grew frustrated and angry.

"Don't be discouraged, dear friend!" Buzis pleaded with

him one night when Stellios hurled the book aside in disgust.
"This is a new language and can't be learned at once."

"Then, how in hell have you learned so quick?" Stellios
asked resentfully. "To hear your chatter, you sound like you
were born here."

"Buzis has a petty facility with language." The little man
smiled wanly. "But this isn't important. More than anything
else, he'd like to be as strong and valorous as Stellios. If
Buzis were asked what on earth he'd most wish to do, he'd
answer to swing the sledgehammer and pound in the spikes."

About six weeks after their arrival in the Crow Mountain
camp and ten days before Christmas, the men heard they'd be
paid for the first time. After returning to the camp that evening, without bothering to wash or eat, they leaped off the
flatcars and raced to the camp office. They formed in long,
ragged lines, pushing and arguing with the Italian and Slav
workers.

Antonis was the first man to emerge from the paymaster's
shack. He stared at the waiting men with dismay.

"Eighteen dollars!" he said in shock. "And six of those dollars in scrip that can only be used in the company store!"

The men in line stared at him in disbelief. The babble and
laughter of other men farther back in the line ceased as word
was carried to them. A silence spread across the crowd.

"But the pay is twenty-five dollars a month!" Nikolaos said.
"And we've been working for six weeks now!"

"Eighteen dollars is all they gave me, too!" Thanasi, the
second man to emerge, swept his arm back at the office in disgust. "They said the balance was taken by charges and fees!"

An Italian who was the third man out rushed back to some
of his comrades, talking and gesturing angrily. A rumble of
agitation swept the line, growing in volume and anger as
other stunned, unhappy men emerged from the office.

"Eighteen dollars for six weeks of work!"

"Eighteen dollars for breaking my back!"

Genovese, the Sicilian, and Vlasevitch, the leader of the Slav workers, came to join Nikolaos. Both men were grim.

"The bastards are cheating us!" Mitsos cried. "Let's storm the stable of thieves!" The line surged forward.

"In God's name, wait!" Nikolaos called to the Greeks. "Let us first go inside and see what they're doing! Wait now and be patient!"

Motioning for Buzis to accompany them, Nikolaos, Stellios, Vlasevitch and Genovese entered the office. The paymaster, wearing the garb of a mourner, sat at a table with a large ledger open before him. The company interpreter sat beside him. Behind them stood Mishima and several other foremen, their fingers hooked on their belts near the holsters of their guns. When Mishima saw Stellios enter, he stepped closer to the table.

Stellios walked briskly to confront the paymaster.

The man fumbled at his ledger, looking up nervously at Stellios. He peered again at the ledger and then gingerly offered Stellios an envelope. Stellios ripped it open and counted the sum of cash and scrip that added to twenty dollars.

"Where's the rest of my money?" Stellios asked grimly.

The interpreter began to translate his query. Stellios cut him off brusquely and gestured to Buzis, who translated the question.

"He says the rest went for charges and fees."

"Ask the stinking toad what charges and fees?"

"Shall I translate stinking toad?" Buzis asked with his lips trembling.

"Just ask about the charges and fees," Nikolaos said quickly.

When Buzis asked the question, the paymaster pointed again to the ledger, speaking in a weak, shrill voice.

"He says the charges are for clothing they first gave you, Stellios," Buzis said, "and for items charged at the store. There is also a dollar a week fee paid to the labor boss, Leonidas Skliris . . ."

"A dollar a week!" Nikolaos said indignantly. "That snake at the dock in New York told us a dollar a month!"

Genovese and Vlasevitch caught some of the exchange and nodded in vigorous agreement with Nikolaos.

"He's a goddam robber!" Stellios said angrily. "Tell the bastard I said he's a goddam robber!"

His words didn't require translation. The paymaster blanched and Mishima snarled a warning at Stellios. The foremen grasped their pistols.

"Tell him!" Stellios said harshly. "Tell the leeching bastard I want the rest of my money!" He felt Nikolaos tugging urgently at his arm and shook him away.

"Stellios, listen!" Nikolaos pleaded. "They have guns! Let's take the money now and counsel with the others! We'll decide what to do later! If they shoot you now, that won't help anyone!"

Genovese and Vlasevitch added their own words of restraint to Stellios. Genovese stepped forward to receive his pay.

Stellios turned and started for the door. Mishima laughed hoarsely and when Stellios turned to look back at the smirking overseer, a current of hate passed between them.

Later that evening, the gloomy Greeks crowded into the coffeehouse.

"We're caught in a trap," Nikolaos said. "They have the ledger and the law. They claim those fees were agreed upon when we signed the labor contract with Skliris."

"I agreed to nothing like that!" Antonis cried.

"Nor did I!" Thanasi said.

"Greedy leeches!"

Nikolaos appealed for silence. "Were any of you able to read the contracts we signed in New York?"

"They weren't written in Greek, Nikolaos!" Antonis exclaimed in disgust. "How could we read them?"

"That's what I mean," Nikolaos said. "If we couldn't read the contracts, how can we know what fees and commissions we authorized to deduct from our pay?"

"We know what's right!" Thanasi snarled. "Let's rip the camp apart and hang the bastards by their greedy balls!"

"You're a valiant man, Thanasi," Nikolaos said patiently, "but common sense is needed here. These foremen have guns and they would shoot a few of us. Then more police and soldiers would come and toss the rest of us in jail. No, violence is useless. Common sense is needed."

"To hell with common sense!" Mitsos said, and motioned at Stellios, who sat drinking in silence. "Stellios and I are Cretans and know what men should do when they are cheated!"

"What would you do, Mitsos?" Nikolaos asked quietly. "If you were in charge here, what would you do?"

Mitsos tried vainly to muster an answer. He appealed to Stellios, who remained silent.

"I tell you what I think we should do," Nikolaos said. "We swallow this injustice for now, because we don't have any choice. But Genovese and Vlasevitch are meeting with their own people. We'll form a council with men from the three groups. The council will draft a letter of protest to explain we were told the deduction would be only a dollar a month . . ."

"Letters and talk! Talk and letters!" Antonis cried. "What good will they do?" He gestured at Stellios. "You haven't said a word yet, Stellios. What do you think we should do?"

"Stellios is the best worker in the camp and they respect him," Nikolaos said earnestly. "He'll head our council."

"I know nothing about councils," Stellios said impatiently. "The bastards have cheated me and I'll settle with them."

At that moment the coffeehouse door flew open and several men who hadn't attended the meeting burst in. They pushed their way through the crowd, and when one of them, a tall farmer named Kodrakis, reached Nikolaos, he waved his arms and hollered for silence.

"Four wagons of them!" Kodrakis cried. "Right here at the gate of the camp!"

"Talk sense, man!" Nikolaos said sharply. "Who's at the gate of the camp?"

"Whores!" Kodrakis shouted the word gleefully. "At least two dozen whores! Vasili and I have seen them and, we swear on our grandfathers, there isn't a gypsy among them! Some are fair-skinned, with hair like spun gold!"

In the bewildered silence that followed his words, a man asked, "What do they want here?"

"They're here for us!" Kodrakis shouted. "They sent us back here to invite you all over to the wagons! They've got liquor and women enough to handle us all and they take the goddam company scrip! That's why they're here, and we better get back there before the Dagoes and Bohunks steal the best ones!"

As they comprehended his words, men began to shout and stamp their booted feet on the wooden planks. A surge began toward the door. Nikolaos waved his arms in a futile appeal.

"Wait, you fools!" Nikolaos cried. "It's payday and they smell your money! The bosses have brought them to make you forget you've been cheated!"

But his words were helpless against the storm of lust. Men pushed and scrambled their way to the door, bellowing like a flock of wild goats in heat. In a few moments the coffeehouse was empty except for Stellios and Nikolaos and a few men who had left wives in Greece. Ashamed to join the stampede of single men, they stared unhappily at the floor.

For a moment Stellios hesitated, reluctant to chase the mob. What Nikolaos told them was probably true. The whores were there because it was payday. But he also remembered what Kodrakis had said about the whores being fair-skinned and golden-haired. In Rethymnon when he visited the market he had seen a few golden-haired women. He had often wondered if their bodies were as fair beneath their clothing.

He determined to go and see for himself. If the whores weren't as attractive as Kodrakis had described, he'd ignore them. He rose quickly from his chair and started for the door. As he passed Nikolaos, the older man gave him a gloomy and silent look of reproach.

Hours later, after the crescent of the moon had vanished from the night sky, Stellios returned from the wagons to the shack. His body ached and throbbed, a weariness making him feel light-headed. Although he had spent himself a number of times, his desire remained unappeased.

An old hag had finally cajoled him into leaving, pleading the girls needed to rest. If he could have mustered the vigor, he would have pounded a few more, astonished that such lovely creatures could be whores. They were golden-haired and creamy-skinned, wearing stockings of silk with lacy garters winding like black serpents around their smooth thighs. The liquor hadn't made him as drunk as the dizziness that came from smelling their powders and scents.

He clumsily lit the candle. Mitsos and Gravas, who had left the wagons and whores before he did, grumbled as the light fell across their faces. He ignored them, starting to pull off his clothes, bumping the cot on which Buzis slept. He hadn't seen the runt in the coffeehouse during the meeting or at the wagons during the revelry. He bent and shook him roughly awake.

"Why didn't you come to the whores, you little boob?" he laughed hoarsely. "They would have taken care of your third leg!"

Buzis didn't answer. Stellios leaned closer to him and saw his flushed, sweating face.

"What's the matter with you?"

"Nothing, Stellios," Buzis whispered.

"Are you sick?"

"No."

Stellios touched his forehead and jerked back his hand.

"You're hot as hell!" he said in disgust. "You've got a damned fever again!"

"Buzis is fine . . ." His voice was strained and weak. "He only needs sleep . . ."

"Don't start retching in here again like you did last time!" Stellios said. "And first thing in the morning, go and get some medicine. For a runt with a good-luck amulet you spend more time on your ass than any other man in the camp!"

He finished undressing and blew out the candle. As he climbed under his blanket, the fumes of liquor whirled in his head. He scratched his crotch and considered returning to the wagons, then tumbled into a heavy and sodden sleep.

The whistle blasts of the foremen cut into his head like knives. He opened his stone-lidded eyes and fought to keep from closing them again. He heaved his body from the bed, cursing as his feet struck the cold planks. Mitsos rose groaning from his bed and lit the candle. Gravas struggled up, erupting a series of noisy farts. They dressed, grunting and cursing, and when they were ready to leave, Gravas gestured at Buzis, who was still in bed.

"I'll wake the lazy squeak," Mitsos said.

"Leave him alone," Stellios said. "He's sick again. If he's still got fever, we'll get him some medicine."

He bent to look at Buzis. When he pulled the blanket away from the little man's face, the light of the candle glowed on his open and frozen eyes.

"Mother of Jesus!" Stellios said and quickly made his cross. He stared down at Buzis in shock.

"He's dead," Gravas said. "The little runt just died."

A foreman pushed open their door.

"Out!" he shouted. "All of you! Out!"

Gravas motioned at the body of Buzis. "We got a dead man in here, boss," he grinned. "I don't think he'll be able to work today."

Not understanding Gravas, the foreman started briskly to the bed. Stellios hissed a warning and the foreman stopped. He mumbled something and went back out the door.

"What shall we do, Stellios?" Mitsos asked in a low voice.

"Go and tell the men no Greek will work on the line today," Stellios said. His voice sounded strange and shaken in his ears. "And tell Nikolaos to come here."

Mitsos and Gravas left the shack. Stellios remained alone with the body of Buzis. He told himself that the little babbler had been a weak and foolish man who wouldn't be mourned.

He stepped closer to the bed, wanting to close the stark, staring eyes. But he was afraid to touch the body. Even the air in the shack had changed. The sweet scent of women had vanished, and a stench of death had taken its place. He hurried outside to wait for Nikolaos.

No man in the Crow Mountain camp worked on the railroad that day. When Genovese and Vlasevitch heard the news, they passed word to their men to observe the mourning. Some of the foremen argued with the men, Mishima threat-

ening them with beatings if they didn't climb up on the
flatcars. But the men were obstinate and when their tempers
grew menacing, the camp supervisor ordered Mishima to
leave them alone.

Stellios sent a crew of Greeks to dig a grave on a slope
above the camp. He gathered assorted boards and nails and
built a rough-cut box to serve as a coffin. Nikolaos and several other men prepared Buzis for the funeral. They stripped
and washed his body and dressed him in the best clothing
they could assemble. One man donated a clean shirt whose
sleeves were rolled up to fit the dead man's shorter arms. Another worker offered a coat and a third man gave a tie.

From a cluster of mountain shrubs they fashioned a crown
for his head and twined another stem around the marriage
finger of his right hand. They laid his body in the box, which
was suspended across two barrels in the coffeehouse. They
placed candles at his head and at his feet.

All through the morning and into the afternoon, the
workers in the camp filed past the body of Buzis, crossing
themselves and whispering their prayers. Afterward Stellios
nailed the lid on the box. He and Nikolaos and several other
pallbearers hoisted it to their shoulders. They carried it from
the coffeehouse, through the streets of the camp, and up the
slope.

Behind the pallbearers holding the box marched all the
workers in the camp, a solemn, silent procession of more than
a hundred men. The only sound was the scraping and
scuffling of their boots against the earth. Stellios noticed that
even the birds perched on the gaunt branches of trees were silent.

At the grave, they suspended the coffin across ropes held by
men on either side. The crowd of men pressed closer and
Stellios motioned for Nikolaos to speak.

"I'm not a priest, Stellios," Nikolaos said in a low, uneasy voice. "I'm not even a good, religious man. It isn't right for me to speak."

Stellios stared at the mountains in the distance, their snow-crested peaks outlined against the sky. He thought again how much they resembled the ranges of Crete.

"You're better than me," he said to Nikolaos.

Nikolaos stared down at the coffin.

"God forgive me for speaking," he said finally. "I only want to say that here is Eleftherios Buzis, from the village of Alones, on the island of Crete. We're burying him far from his home because this place is where he died. He wasn't the best worker, but he had courage and tried harder than anyone, and that's why he was called 'Little Hercules.' Please have mercy on his soul. Amen . . ."

The men holding the ropes lowered the coffin slowly into the grave, the ropes squealing and whistling beneath the wood. Nikolaos threw a sprig of oak into the grave, while other men tossed in fragments of leaves.

The coffin struck the bottom of the grave and the men pulled up the ropes. Stellios hoisted a shovel and dug into the mound of excavated earth. When the first load of dirt and stones he flung down clattered on the wooden lid of the coffin, the still and watchful birds scattered with a noisy beating of their wings.

When they had returned to the camp, Stellios remembered the pouch of earth Buzis had carried from Crete. He asked Nikolaos if he'd seen it.

"We washed his body and anointed him with oil," Nikolaos said, "and I didn't see any pouch."

Stellios went to their shack and lit the candle. He searched through the small bag containing the dead man's meager belongings. When he found nothing, he checked the bed where Buzis had slept, poking every part of the pallet. The pouch wasn't there.

He stood motionless for a few moments, wondering if Buzis had lost the pouch or whether it had been stolen. With a flaring of uneasiness, he carried the candle to his bed, holding the flame close to his pallet. He searched carefully and was relieved when he found nothing. As he started to replace the pallet, something caught his eye. He held the candle closer and saw the cord tied around one of the boards. He tore them apart and found the pouch of earth that Buzis had hidden in his bed.

Stellios sat on his bed for a while, clutching the pouch, confusion and frustration sweeping his flesh. When those emotions became shame and remorse, he vented his fury by tearing their shack apart. He broke the beds, ripped apart the pallets, hurled the litter and scraps into the street. A crowd of workers gathered outside but, thinking perhaps he had gone mad, they kept a safe distance from him. Even Nikolaos and Mitsos were afraid to speak to him.

His rage still unsatisfied after the destruction of the shack, he sprinted toward the center of the camp, the men hurrying to follow him. When he reached the dwelling where the foremen lived, a dense and silent throng had massed behind him.

Mustering every Greek profanity he knew and the vilest obscenities he had learned in English, Stellios cursed and damned Mishima, bellowing a challenge for him to come out and fight.

In a moment the Japanese work boss appeared on the porch. The other foremen came out behind him, several of them buckling on their holsters and guns. A rumble of warning came from the workers and they surged forward. Stellios motioned them back and continued to curse and taunt Mishima. The work boss flung his pistol to another man and leaped from the porch.

The men lunged at one another, their bodies ramming like bulls. At close quarters they jabbed and chopped, kicked and clawed, stabbing for groins and eyes.

Stellios took punishing blows to his body and head that sent waves of shock through his legs. But rage fed his strength and he returned blow for blow. For a brutal, merciless moment, neither man gave ground. Then Mishima shuddered, his body faltering, and then retreating. Stellios pressed him, battered his head and, in a final, savage assault, drove him to his knees. Mishima hung there stricken, spittle trickling from his lips.

Stellios brought his fist like a sledgehammer across Mishima's head. The blow stunned the work boss, and his arms flailed the air. Stellios struck him another thundering blow that catapulted Mishima backward. He sprawled on the ground, writhing in pain, blood bubbling from his shattered nose.

In the frozen silence that followed the short, fierce battle, Nikolaos and several other men leaped forward to grasp Stellios and dragged him quickly into the crowd. Other Greeks formed a protective guard around him and hurried him back along the street to the shacks. His blood still inflamed, Stellios tried to shake them away.

"You've got to leave, Stellios!" Nikolaos cried. "Do you understand? You can't stay here now! When they gather their senses, they'll shoot you or fling you into prison! We'll get one of the horses for you so you can try to make the mountains!"

Stellios wasn't afraid of death, but the thought of being imprisoned locked like a vise around his heart. He nodded at Nikolaos that he would leave.

Mitsos pushed through the men around him to clutch at his arm.

"Stellios, take me with you!"

"You better stay here, Mitsos!" Nikolaos warned him. "You haven't done anything! If they catch you with him, they'll punish you, too!"

"He's my brother!" Mitsos shouted. "Do you think I'm afraid to go with him?" He turned to Stellios. "Please, Stellios," he pleaded. "Don't leave me behind! We must stay together the way we've been together since we left Crete!"

Stellios nodded, and Nikolaos sent men running to the corral for the horses. In a few moments, they returned with the mounts saddled. Other men tied parcels of food and flasks of water to the pommels. Stellios and Mitsos swung up into the saddles.

"Ride to the west!" Nikolaos said urgently. "Even if they pursue you, it will soon be dark! God be with you both!"

They galloped through the camp and out the gate. From there, Stellios led Mitsos up the slope, pausing to dismount beside the grave of Buzis. He knelt and scooped a hole in the fresh surface of the grave. Then he took the small pouch of Cretan earth from his pocket and pressed it gently into the hole. Afterward he covered it with earth again.

When he had remounted, he and Mitsos reined their horses toward the mountains. Before crossing the ridge, Stellios looked back at the camp. The workers had massed outside the gate, and when they glimpsed Stellios and Mitsos, they started to wave and shout. In the first purple shadows of twilight, their hands became a field of wheat fluttering in the wind, while, over the distance that separated them, Stellios heard their voices calling a plaintive farewell.

CHAPTER SIX

Father Basil

After departing New York, the smoking black leviathan pulled their train through a hilly, forested terrain. On the ridges the foliage of the trees was burnished with the hues of late autumn.

From dawn until dark of that first day, the vistas remained unchanged except for clusters of houses. The train swept by these villages too swiftly for Father Basil to glimpse more than a few people and wagons in the streets. But the sight of at least one church steeple in each village reassured him that the natives of America were devout.

At night they were confined in narrow bunks. The jolting of the train made it impossible for him to sleep and he descended the ladder quietly in order not to wake Cristina and his children, in adjoining bunks. The car was silent and shadowed and, after whispering his prayers, he walked to an empty seat by the window.

The land they were passing was cloaked in blackness, but the sky shone with stars, a panoply so luminous it seemed a web snaring the crescent of the moon. He thought then of the skies above Rethymnon, the glowing stars and incandescent moon. These were the same celestial spheres, but now they seemed cold and inhospitable. They appear that way to me, he thought sadly, because, like a nostalgic child, I am pining for home.

Later in the morning, when Cristina, the girls and Andreas had risen, washed and dressed, they were joined by Krokas and Santilis. These were the representatives from the parish in Snowmass, Utah, who had met them in New York and were escorting them back home.

Santilis was a big, broad-shouldered man who towered over his smaller, slimmer companion. From the start of the journey the two men traded salvos of insults. This appearance of enmity didn't deceive Father Basil, who understood that the insults were a charade to entertain the children.

"What you've seen of this great country since leaving New York is only a fraction of the total," Santilis said to them on the second morning of their journey. "The state of Utah alone is 85,000 square miles and that is 35,000 miles larger than all the land acreage of Greece!"

"For an elephant like Mr. Santilis"—Krokas winked at the girls and Andreas—"size is obviously important."

Santilis waved his sally aside.

"Any talk of largeness mortifies a midget like Mr. Krokas."

"Largeness! Did he say largeness?" Krokas appealed to Andreas, who was listening intently to the exchange. "But you will observe, my boy, the good man isn't merely large, he has the proportions of a whale!"

Andreas giggled and Soula smiled.

"Elephant I might be . . . perhaps even a whale!" Santilis laughed robustly. "But if a sardine like Mr. Krokas had been born in our house in Crete, my mother, bless her sainted heart, would have thrown it back into the sea!"

Each evening, as the steward announced the call for dinner, Krokas and Santilis led them through several cars to the dining car. The other passengers stared up at what must have seemed to them an imposing procession. First the disparately sized men, then the small, slender mother, the lovely young girls, and the handsome Andreas. Finally, there was Father Basil, with his long, black cassock and tall, crowned ecclesiastical hat. Aware of the excitement they produced in each of the cars they passed, he affected a friendly yet dignified demeanor.

Seated in the dining car at tables covered with clean white cloths, they were served their dinner by courteous black men who treated even the children with deference.

"I feel so lazy and good-for-nothing," Cristina whispered to Father Basil at dinner on the second evening. "Why should these grown men, one old enough to be a grandfather, have to wait on the children and me? It isn't showing them respect. We should get up and bring the food to the table for ourselves."

"This is the way things are done in America," Father Basil replied in a low voice. "Trust Mr. Krokas and Mr. Santilis. They are here to show us what is proper."

"Mama, could I have some of that cake?" Andreas pointed to a frosted, yellow cake a steward served a passenger at a nearby table.

"You have eaten enough already."

"Let the boy have some cake, Papadia." Santilis motioned to the steward. "And let the girls eat all their hearts desire."

"No, thank you," Alexandra said firmly. "I would rather not get fat."

"Perhaps I'll have just a small piece," Soula said.

"You are both far too generous," Cristina said to Santilis and Krokas. "You'll spoil them."

"If you fear we are spoiling them on the journey, wait until we reach Utah," Santilis chuckled. "Our boys haven't seen a Greek family since leaving their homes in Crete. When they catch first sight of Alexandra, Soula and Andreas, they'll believe angels have descended on Carbon County."

"They'll discover soon enough Andreas isn't an angel," Soula said.

"I could be an angel someday!" Andreas glared at her. "Boys can be angels, but girls can't!"

"That's an old theological argument that remains unsettled," Father Basil sighed.

"Aren't there any Greek children in Snowmass?" Cristina asked.

"There aren't any married Greek men in Snowmass," Santilis said. "There isn't a single Greek girl in the town and less than half a dozen in Salt Lake City, almost a hundred miles away. Four of them are married, and the remaining one or two have each received fifty marriage proposals!"

"Fifty proposals!" Alexandra exclaimed. "How many young, unmarried Cretans are there in the town?"

"About five hundred who work in the mines and on the railroad," Santilis said.

Cristina looked nervously at her daughters and then shook her head. "How wretched they must be with no one to cook or care for them."

"They cook and care for one another," Krokas said. "That is different, of course, than the way it was back home, where their mothers and sisters treated them like princes. But, after a while, Papadia, men can get used to anything, even misery and loneliness."

"We must do what we can for them," Cristina said earnestly. "The girls will help me bake pastries and bread, which should remind them of home."

"They'll be grateful for that, I know." Santilis smiled. "But just having you there will make them feel less lonely. And, who knows, in a few more years Alexandra and Soula may choose splendid husbands."

"We'll have an army of men to choose from," Alexandra said smugly.

"Talking of marriage is premature!" Cristina said sternly. "The girls are far too young! They'll have plenty of time to find husbands later on . . . much later on!"

"They'll be all right," Andreas frowned. "When I grow up and it's time to be married, I'll be having trouble." He whistled. "Five hundred men!"

"Don't start grieving yet, my son," Father Basil smiled. "By the time you're ready to marry, Utah may be swarming with fine young Greek girls."

"Amen!" Santilis and Krokas echoed fervently.

On the day they were scheduled to arrive in Salt Lake City they were packed and ready several hours before reaching the city. The girls were restless, and Andreas ran up and down the aisle, ignoring his mother's warnings to sit still.

"Will there be anyone at the station to meet us, Mr. Santilis?" Andreas asked.

"I hardly think so, my boy," Santilis shrugged. "As I've told you, Snowmass is almost a hundred miles from Salt Lake City, and few of our men have any transport besides some horses and mules. One or two might make the trip and be at the station when we arrive, but I can't even be sure of that."

The final hours of the journey dragged by, the train traveling through a panorama of magnificent mountain ranges.

"But these mountains look like Crete!" Father Basil said excitedly. "That tall peak there might almost be Psiloriti!"

"The first Cretans who came to Utah saw that resemblance," Krokas said. "That brought other Cretans and has helped keep them here too. A man opens his eyes in the morning and, for a few moments, believes he is in Crete."

"Salt Lake City! Salt Lake City!" The conductor's loud and clear voice rang through the car. The girls and Andreas rose, slipping into their coats, moving to say goodbye to a few of the passengers they had met on the journey. Krokas called a porter to assemble their luggage. Father Basil peered out the window, saw the light of the midday sun reflecting from the façade of ornate stone buildings. In the streets he saw the figures of men and horses, all of them rushing about. He fumbled to clasp Cristina's hand, squeezing her fingers to pass on a reassurance he didn't feel.

The rattling, swaying train gradually slowed. As they passed beneath the roof of the station, the interior of the car darkened and they came, finally, to a stop. The locomotive's bell kept ringing loudly and the steam hissed up from the wheels to obscure the windows.

"All Cretan families off now!" Santilis called gaily. "Soula, Andreas! Don't get left behind on the train!"

Santilis and Krokas led the younger children up the aisle. Father Basil followed with Cristina and Alexandra behind him. As the train's bell fell silent, he became aware of a din and clamor outside, a rumbling suggesting the sound of a stormy sea. When he reached the platform, the racket mounted in volume. Santilis held the children aside and eagerly motioned him ahead.

"You step off first, Father!"

Father Basil moved to the doorway. Holding the bar, he looked out across the station area and caught his breath in amazement. Hundreds of shouting, cheering young men, many waving small Greek flags, were jammed across the tracks and around the station. When they saw him, the shouting became a roar, and a fusillade of gunshots cracked in the air.

Still dazed, he stepped from the platform to the stool. He stumbled and would have fallen but for the hands of half a dozen men who caught him and lowered him safely to the ground. He felt his hands clutched and kissed. Those men who could not reach his fingers snatched at his cassock, raising the hem fervently to their lips. He was jostled and pressed back and feared suddenly he might be knocked down and trampled.

As quickly as the roaring had begun, the thunder of voices ceased. A few gunshots, trailing smells of powder, still sounded from the perimeters of the throng, and then those guns, too, were silent. With every man staring again at the train, Father Basil looked up to see Soula in the doorway of the platform. Her dark, long hair crowning her lovely face, her bright, flowered dress visible under her open coat, she made an enchanting, dreamlike vision.

Santilis leaped down past her and then reached up to swing her off the train, raising her carefully to a perch in the curve of his arm and shoulder so she'd be visible to every man in the station. As Andreas followed her to the doorway, a big Cretan stepped forward and gently swung the boy off the train and onto his shoulder. Finally, Cristina and Alexandra appeared, staring in bewilderment at the huge assembly.

A long, heartfelt sigh swept through the crowd. Father Basil saw men crossing themselves, murmuring prayers, wiping tears from their eyes. He was shaken to his soul and, by the tears that glistened on Cristina's cheeks, he knew she had been intensely touched as well. For the men stared at the children and at her as if they were witnessing a miracle, an endearing fragment of their native land transported into the crowded station.

In that matchless moment, Father Basil felt the fears and tribulations of their long journey redeemed. And he confirmed once again the glory and wisdom of the Lord, who had brought them safely to a place where they were sorely needed and loved.

The weeks that followed their arrival in Utah were a frigid and winter-assaulted time. Snow fell from an overcast sky, mantling the mountains, trees and houses. The cold winds, so unlike the temperate climate he had known in Crete, chilled him to the marrow of his bones. When he stepped outside, he wore his collar pulled up and a long, woolen scarf wrapped about his throat to prevent icicles forming in his beard.

Yet, in that icebound span of days and nights, he often remembered the tumultuous welcome, the outpouring of affection that embraced them in the station, and he felt warmed. When he and Cristina spoke, as they often did, of the wild procession of mules, carts, horses and a few rattling automobiles, horns blowing and banners flying, that carried them from Salt Lake City to Snowmass, they knew they'd treasure the experience as long as they lived.

When they arrived in Snowmass, segments of their caravan strung out for miles behind them, they were taken to the Greek section of the town and greeted by a crowd as noisy and enthusiastic as the one that had met them in Salt Lake City. Men rushed from the coffeehouses, from the shanties, boxcars and rooming houses. Some were dressed in suit, shirt and tie, while others came directly from their shifts in the mine. The faces of these men were coated so thickly with coal dust that only white circles were visible about their eyes.

Amidst another deafening barrage of gunshots, the singing, cheering crowd swept them along to the domed, stone Church of the Holy Trinity. While the crowd surrounded the church, the bell in the belltower pealing madly, Father Basil was led ceremoniously inside by a group of men who pleaded with him to conduct a mass. Making certain that Cristina and his family were secured in the cantor's loft he agreed, and the doors were opened to the crowd. Men swarmed and pushed into the church, packing the nave from the doors to the steps below the sanctuary. Hundreds of men must still have remained outside, for Father Basil could hear volleys of gunshots.

Made nervous by the continuing explosion of the guns, Father Basil removed his Bible and chalice from his bag and draped his cassock across his shoulders. Walking into the sanctuary, he inhaled the oppressive odors of mustiness and dampness. Behind the altar table, he saw the crustings of mold and the droppings of animals that had nested in the deserted church, which was unused except for the service once a month by the circuit-riding priest. He understood that the neglected, mournful atmosphere couldn't be helped. A church that wasn't used regularly was like a table laden with food that no one ate.

He emerged from the sanctuary, holding his Bible aloft. Word was carried to the men surrounding the church, and the shooting ceased. The interior of the church grew still as well. He glimpsed Cristina and his beloved son and daughters watching him intently. He was imbued with gratefulness, because he was once more in a church.

Afterward, he chanted his prayers and sang that first mass with such fervor and power that many of the men before him were, once again, moved to tears.

The house given to them as a parsonage was walking distance from the church. The sturdy, stone dwelling contained a large, central room built around a potbellied stove. They lived around the warmth of that stove and the fireplace, fed by the wood the parishioners brought, cut and stacked in piles outside the door. There were also a narrow kitchen area, and several bedrooms on the second floor.

Although the men had made an effort to clean the house for them before they arrived, the premises at first appeared as cold and desolate as the church. But Cristina and the girls began a vigorous, thorough cleaning. When they finished, they decorated the walls with fringed laces they had brought across the ocean from Rethymnon. The surroundings began to resemble a home.

Meanwhile, a crew of volunteers led by Santilis cleaned and scrubbed the church from the ceiling to the floor. Despite the protests of the men that they "would do the dirty work," Father Basil rolled up the sleeves and hem of his cassock and joined them at their labor.

"This is my church now as well as yours," he told them. "No harm will befall a new priest if he spends time washing and scrubbing. Those are good exercises for a wavering spirit and an indulgent waistline."

By the end of a week of robust labor, most of the mustiness had been dispelled. The candleholders sparkled and the scrubbed stone glowed. In the process of scouring every crevice, they had dispossessed at least two score squirrels, pigeons, mice and assorted lizards, all of which must have believed the church was destined to remain their domain forever.

But nothing in the world of animals and men is forever, the priest thought as he surveyed the brightened church. If I do not prove a worthy spiritual father and help my parish to thrive, the Lord will banish me as we drove out the animals and insects.

Once the house and church had been reclaimed, Father Basil began to familiarize himself with Snowmass. He discovered there were two sections of the town, as rigidly divided as the border between two countries. One section comprised the neat houses and well-provisioned stores of the native-born Americans: the Mormons, Danes and Norwegians who had settled the town many years before and now worked as merchants or foremen and supervisors in the Snowmass mine.

Father Basil had been bewildered when Santilis first drove him through Old Snowmass and pointed out the signs in grocery and restaurant windows that read: NO NIGGERS OR GREEKS ALLOWED.

"Because of their dark complexions, they think our boys have African blood, and they don't allow Negroes into their stores," Santilis said. "Besides, they don't understand our language, our customs or our religion. Then, they resent our boys' looking at some of their pretty girls. And they resent it because many of those girls look back at our handsome young men!"

"So our boys can't shop in their stores?" Father Basil asked.

"They have learned not to, Father," Santilis said. "If any of our boys wander over the tracks, a deputy sheriff keeps them moving. If they offer resistance, they are clapped into jail and we have to bail them out. So, resenting the slurs and resenting being harassed, they stay on our side of town."

The Greek section of Snowmass, dominated by the unsightly cables and wheels of the mine tower, was a sprawling settlement of rooming houses, shanties and railroad boxcars used as living facilities by the miners. There were about a dozen shabby lunchrooms where men could purchase meat skewered and sizzled over charcoal and bread soaked in olive oil. There were shops selling cheeses, dried octopus and spiced sausage.

But the most common businesses in the Greek section of Snowmass were the two-score coffeehouses, all of them thriving. Many of them were labeled "Private Club" and restricted to the men from a particular region of Crete, such as the Sfakians or Lasithians. All day and all night men would cluster around the bare tables in these places, drinking, playing cards, and arguing about mine conditions, or politics in Greece.

The young Cretans, who totaled the largest number of

miners, were in their early to middle twenties, clean-shaven except for black mustaches bristling under their black, curly hair. Some still wore the patched faded breeches and boots they had worn at home, but most had acquired the nondescript woolen trousers and drab gray shirts bought in the company store. They were as Father Basil remembered young men in Crete: handsome, energetic, proud and high-spirited.

They were dutiful in their church attendance. Every Sunday morning, even on the coldest days, the nave was jammed, with an overflow crowd of men swathed in jackets and scarves standing outside. In addition, during the week and on Sunday afternoons, a steady procession of men came to the priest for communion and confession. From these confessions, repeated to him by several hundred young men, he first learned about the extent of drinking and gambling in the coffeehouses, the quarrels and sometimes the despair at losing a paycheck they had planned to send home to Crete. Then, through the faltering, anguished confessions of sinners, he learned also about the cribs of prostitutes at the outskirts of the town. He was shocked to discover how many young Cretans visited the women in these cribs.

While he omitted mention of the prostitutes, he confided in Cristina about the drinking and gambling.

"The entire parish is caught in this web of vices," he told her late one night as they lay in bed. "I know this is because they haven't had a regular priest for so long, but it is distressing and worrisome to me."

"They are good young men," Cristina said. "Courteous and respectful. When I pass with the girls, they take off their caps and stand and watch us in silence. As for the drinking and gambling, Father, now that you're here to tend to their spiritual needs, they'll change, I'm sure."

They fell silent. He felt weariness seeping through his

bones and curled deeper into the warm bed. He wondered whether Cristina would be as confident about the men changing if he also told her about their visits to the prostitutes.

Spurred by the confessions, each Saturday evening for several weeks Father Basil zealously prepared an eloquent sermon against dissolute and hedonistic lives, reminding them of the trust and devotion of their families in Crete. The men listened earnestly, nodded zealously in agreement, and, after church, thanked him warmly for his admonitions. By Sunday afternoon the coffeehouses were packed again, and drinking and gambling resumed as if the Sunday sermon were a trivial interlude. And in their next confessions, Father Basil learned that many of them continued their visits to the cribs.

On an afternoon when he sat with Santilis in his grocery, Father Basil confided his despair.

"I think they truly want to be devout Christians, Father," Santilis tried to console him. "But they've fallen into morally corrupt habits."

"But if in spite of my counsel," Father Basil said, "they continue drinking and gambling and . . . and visiting those poor, wretched women in the cribs, why, then, why do they come to church?"

"Faith and prayers, Father!" Santilis said. "They want to come to church on Sunday and have you remind them what their lives should be like. They need you to hear their confessions, to intercede for them with God, to have you ask Him to have patience with them!"

"But I am a priest and not simply a petitioner!" Father Basil said. "They must free themselves from this debauchery or they make a mockery of church, priest and God!"

"Don't lose patience with them, Father," Santilis said

earnestly. "As long as they have you, there's always a chance for them."

When Father Basil had been in Snowmass almost two months, he met the circuit-riding priest for the first time. He was sorting candles in the narthex of the church late one afternoon when he heard a horse's hoofs on the cobblestones. He emerged from the church as the rider dismounted. Bundled in a fleece coat and fur cap, a big man with a scruffy beard, swarthy complexion and defiant black eyes, there wasn't anything to suggest he was a priest until he spoke.

"I'm Father Grivas," he said in a hoarse, strong voice.

"God be thanked for bringing you here safely!" Father Basil said. "I'm Father Basil, from Rethymnon, in Crete. I've heard how hard you labor all over the mountains, bringing the blessings of God to fifty hamlets. I've been most anxious to meet you. Here, let me tether your horse and please come inside."

As they entered the church, Father Grivas tugged off his coat and untied his cassock, which he had raised and knotted about his waist, letting it fall across his grimy boots. A pungent smell of sweat and wine rose from his body. As he walked beside Father Basil through the church, he released a low, hoarse whistle.

"You've sure cleaned the place up, Father." He grinned. "Polished like a monk's knees and smelling like a nunnery."

"Scrubbing and washing are easily accomplished," Father Basil said stiffly, nettled by the cleric's mocking tone. "How long will you be staying, Father?"

"I'll spend the night here and leave again at first light," Father Grivas said. "I've an early-morning service in Provo."

"Then, tonight you must come and share supper with my Papadia and our children."

"I'm not used to family suppers." Father Grivas frowned.

"That's because I've never married and have no Papadia but my horse. She never nags me about my manners, so I've never learned the graces. I better eat in town and sleep where I fall."

"You must come home with me, please!" Father Basil spoke with added fervor because of the unchristian antipathy he felt toward the gruff priest. "Papadia Cristina will be distressed if you don't, because she has been looking forward to meeting you as well."

"I won't keep arguing with you, Father." Father Grivas shrugged. "If you insist, I'll come and enjoy a warm meal in the bosom of a Christian family."

When they arrived home, Cristina greeted the priest warmly and told them supper would be ready shortly. While they waited, Father Grivas warmed himself at the stove and stared at the girls and Andreas with admiration.

"You've a handsome family, Father," he said. He spit into his palm to discourage the devil. "In another couple of years, you'll have to hold off the young men with a gun."

Andreas stared at the priest with fascination.

"Andreas, you're being rude!" Father Basil said sternly. "Go and do your homework now until supper is ready."

"Leave the boy alone, Father, I don't mind." Father Grivas winked at Andreas. "He can't help it, because he's never seen a bear in a cassock before."

In a few moments they sat down to supper. The unkempt priest ate heartily, complimenting Cristina on the food and regaling the girls and Andreas with stories of adventures in the mountains, tales of storms, thieves and bears.

"I woke up as my horse pounded her hoofs and shrieked," Father Grivas said. "Opened my eyes to look into the eyes of the biggest, ugliest, devil-driven bear I'd ever seen. I tell you, I saw my funeral in his bloodshot eyes!"

"What did you do?" Soula asked tensely.

"What did I do, young lady? I let out a roar like the devil had bitten me and leaped straight up into the air, at least five feet high! I landed running, that bear hot at my heels! God gave my boots wings or I'd never have made that tree!"

He paused, gesturing a warning at Andreas.

"Are you taking another serving of the chicken, boy?" he cried. "But there won't be a bone left for me! Hands off that wing now or I'll challenge you to wrestle in the courtyard, the loser taking only the bird's ass."

Father Basil made an effort to smile, wishing the raucous meal were over. Afterward, as they sat sipping tiny cups of Turkish coffee, Cristina suggested Father Grivas spend the night with them.

"Father Basil and I would be pleased to have you under our roof," Cristina said. "Andreas loves to sleep here before the fireplace and will gladly let you have his bed."

"Thank you kindly, Papadia," Father Grivas said, "but my crusted carcass would stink up the boy's bed for a month. I'll just unroll my bedsack on the floor of the church. I'm used to worse than that."

Even as Father Basil joined his wife in urging the priest to remain for the night, he was grateful when Father Grivas left the house to walk to the church.

The following morning, Father Basil slipped quietly from the bed in which Cristina still slept and dressed quickly. He emerged into the darkness and cold, hurrying the short distance to the church. When he arrived, the first glimmerings of dawn rimming the mountains, he found Father Grivas saddling his horse for departure.

"I hope your night here wasn't too uncomfortable, Father," Father Basil said. "Cristina and I were distressed that you didn't stay with us."

"I was fine, Father," the burly priest said brusquely. He tightened the cinch straps and fastened his bedroll on the saddle. Father Basil watched him, feeling a prickle of remorse.

"Shall we pray together before you leave, Father Grivas?" he asked. "I'm sure you know about the dreadful problems that face us here. I'll require all the good, Christian prayers I can muster."

Father Grivas stared at him for a moment. "All right, Father," he said finally. "A prayer has never hurt anyone. Let's pray."

They walked through the damp, shadowed church to stand before the altar table. They crossed themselves and Father Basil bent his head to pray. He heard Father Grivas praying swiftly, while his own prayer took longer. When he finished, he looked up to see the shaggy priest watching him. Once again he sensed a mockery in the priest's demeanor. He felt another flare of resentment and tried to think Christian thoughts about his brother in Christ as they returned to his saddled horse.

"How soon will you be returning to Snowmass, Father?"

Father Grivas patted his horse's neck, soothing him as he prepared to mount. "Maybe in a month or so . . . maybe longer," he said. "Now that you're here, my visits aren't important."

"I'll always be grateful to have you share supper and a prayer," Father Basil said earnestly. "As I am grateful for all you've tried to do for this parish in the past. You must have been as saddened and disheartened as I am at the vice and debauchery so rampant here. But I pledge to you I'll remain dedicated in my mission to return these young men to a moral environment and a Christian existence . . ."

His voice trailed away. The mockery he had sensed on the circuit-riding priest's face erupted into a glare of scorn.

"That's enough, for God's sake!" the priest snapped. "You are prattling a stableful of shit!"

Father Basil stared at the man in shock. He started to answer sharply, until he remembered this man was a rough, uneducated cleric whose parish was the wind and a score of rude hamlets.

"Have a good journey, Father," he said in what he felt to be a dignified tone. "We'll offer you our hospitality whenever you return to Snowmass."

"Don't practice your Christian forbearance on me!" Father Grivas snapped. "You know you'll be damned happy never to see my hairy, ugly head again. I won't miss your sanctimonious pap, either, although I'll miss being near your Papadia and children, to remind me what human beings are like!" He paused for breath, his big hand wiping away the spittle that ran from his mouth into his beard. "You may not want my advice, but I'll give it to you anyway. If you truly want to help these men, bring your righteous ass down off the holy mountain and try to understand something about their lives!"

"But I do understand!" Father Basil said indignantly. "There is a dreadful immorality rampant in this parish . . . you must admit that's true! It isn't the men's fault, I know, because they want to be good Christians and to live good Christian lives—"

"Shit!" Father Grivas cried balefully. "Holy and unholy shit! You're blind as a monk who's never left the cloisters! I'll tell you what they want! They want to believe that God cares about them, that he'll salvage them from their terror and despair!"

Taken back by the ferocity of his voice, Father Basil stared at the priest in confusion.

"It isn't bad enough that proud young men cross an ocean to find themselves treated like lepers!" Father Grivas cried. "Scorned and mocked by snots who only came a few years earlier! No, that wound to pride and spirit isn't enough, for, each day and each night, they have to burrow like moles into the ground. In those subterranean pits they run danger of cave-ins, gas explosions, injuries to leave them at the mercy of those company butchers who amputate arms and legs with the compassion they'd show a goat! So the young men drink and gamble and whore to forget their misery and to forget their terror!"

"I appreciate your effort to help me . . ." Father Basil felt his voice trembling.

"I don't give a shit about helping you!" Father Grivas snarled. "I'm just trying to penetrate your dense, pious fog to tell you what kind of parish you have here! How long have you been in Snowmass now? Six weeks? Two months? Long enough by far to have made a trip into the pits! Have you gone down?"

Father Basil shook his head slowly.

"How can you console and reassure them if you don't know what their lives underground are like? Go down and see for yourself those catacombs and the brutality of their labor! I once saw mules brought up to daylight after spending a year down in the mines! When the sun touched them, they went mad with joy, shrieking and kicking their heels in the air! Do you think men suffer less than animals?"

He slipped one boot into the stirrup and swung his body into the saddle. The dawn glinted across his angry, bitter face.

"I've been down with a rescue crew of miners digging out men caught in a cave-in," he said. "We dug for five days and five nights until we uncovered them, mouths jammed full of dust and their eyeballs bulging from their heads like the eyeballs of men who've been hanged. If you had looked into those mutilated faces, my good Father, you'd understand how senseless is all your prattle about a Christian existence. This is the devil's parish, and if you want to help your poor, cursed parishioners, then you have to enter the devil's damned playground!"

He spurred his horse away and started riding up the path, his broad body rocking in the saddle. A short distance from the church a gaunt hound woke to run baying and barking at his horse's heels. The priest hurled down a strident curse, and then man, horse and dog were lost in the mist of dawn.

Several days after the circuit-riding priest had departed from Snowmass, Father Basil asked Santilis and Krokas to obtain permission for him to go down into the mine.

"What are you asking, Father?" Santilis said in shock. "We have been praying and waiting for you for years! If we arrange for you to go down into the pit and if anything were to happen to you down there, a hundred men would have the flesh hot from our bones!"

"He's right," Krokas shuddered. "Be merciful, Father, and let us forget you asked such a thing."

But with his pride humbled and his assurance shaken, Father Basil pressed them to do as he wished. The words of Father Grivas had been brutal, but they had also had the disturbing ring of truth. He determined to find out for himself what those catacombs were like.

For several days he prayed for strength, because the prospect of descending into the mine terrified him. When the mine supervisor delayed giving him permission, he felt a keen relief. But he continued to press for consent and, finally, approval was granted.

The night before his trip underground, he couldn't sleep. He rose from his bed a half-dozen times, staring out the windows into the darkness, slipping into the adjoining rooms to look at his sleeping daughters and son. His restlessness kept Cristina from sleeping, and she fretted with him. He knew she wanted to ask him to change his mind, but she didn't speak. Finally, he closed his eyes wearily as the breezes of dawn shook the sash of the window. He couldn't have been asleep more than a few moments when Cristina shook him gently awake. He dressed quickly to greet Santilis and a tall young miner.

"You know Leonidas Varvarakis, Father," Santilis said. "He's one of the best men in the Snowmass mine, sure-footed as a mountain goat and with the eyes of a cat. He'll be your guide and look after you."

"As I would protect my own father," Leonidas said gravely and bent to kiss the priest's hand.

"Have some bread and cheese before you go, Basil," Cristina said anxiously.

"We'll be glad to wait, Father," Santilis said. "Don't go to work on an empty stomach."

"I don't want anything now," Father Basil said. He couldn't tell them the reason he wasn't able to eat was because of the nausea churning in his belly. As he forced a smile to reassure Cristina, he thought of feigning illness, but shame kept him silent.

Clearing the settlement of shanties at the edge of the mine property, they followed the same path the miners walked each day and night. Their shoes crunched on the roadway of slate and shattered coal, while the dawn cast a gloomy haze around the tall, cross-beamed tower of the mine. Father Basil had never noticed how forbidding and grim it was before that moment, like an unsightly totem raised to some pagan idol.

Passing beneath the tower, they entered an alcove where they changed clothing. Father Basil removed his cassock and slipped on a stiff, coarse jacket. Santilis helped him into a pair of boots, and then Leonidas handed him a cap, a headpiece hard-crusted as a turtle's shell, with a small gas-flame lamp at the brim. When he placed the cap on his head, he felt the weight squeeze his temples.

"You look like a ten-year veteran of the pits, Father!" Santilis made an effort to speak lightly. "If you really like it down below, we'll get you on a regular shift!"

The priest nodded and tried to smile. When he and Santilis clasped hands, his clammy palms must have betrayed his fear, because Santilis pressed his fingers in reassurance.

They stepped into the elevator, a three-walled cage secured by overhead pulleys and strands of oily, black cables.

"We should be able to get you a quick look around before the shifts change, Father," Leonidas said. He pressed the brake release and, for a moment, nothing happened. Then a bell rang loudly and the cables squealed and slid free. Father Basil held tightly to Leonidas' arm as the cage began to descend.

The square of light above them grew smaller and then faded completely. Darkness enveloped them except for the tiny hissing flames on their caps. The priest felt his stomach, heart and lungs constricting as if these organs were being squeezed. When the cage jarred to a stop, he stared into a gloom blacker than any night he'd ever known.

"Careful now, Father." Leonidas spoke quietly as he led the priest from the cage. "Stay close to me and watch for overhangs of rock."

With only the frail, wavering beams of flame to guide them, they moved slowly along a narrow corridor. The air was cold and damp, a pervasive chill seeping beneath his clothing to enter his bones. Fear made him breathe more quickly, and he tasted the grainy film of coal dust on his tongue.

The ground became slippery and he stumbled and would have fallen except for Leonidas' support. They splashed through several inches of stagnant water fed by trickles dripping from the rock above their heads. He saw gruesome patches of fungus growing between the timbers holding up the roof. A metallic smell burned his nostrils and his throat.

The corridor widened and they entered a large chamber where he saw the shrouded figures of men working and heard the dull echoes of their picks striking the walls of rock. They seemed inhuman apparitions, dark except for the whites of their eyes and their gleaming teeth and the flames bobbing at their heads. Several men lay between ledges of rock, striking up with short-handled picks, while another man on his belly, wedged into a narrow crevice, had only his booted feet visible.

They moved on, the dust growing thicker, the fumes stronger. He saw a canary in a small wire cage and asked Leonidas why the tiny creature was penned beneath the earth.

"To test for gas, Father," Leonidas said. "If the bird dies, the men are warned and quickly leave the tunnel."

In another chamber he saw men working with mules that were dragging carts filled with coal. The creatures, with great white circles about their eyes, looked wretched and mournful, and he remembered the circuit-riding priest's story of the liberated mules that shrieked for joy when they were returned to the sun.

Leonidas tugged him aside as one of the carts rolled past them. He caught a swift glimpse of a dwarfish figure perched on the mound of coal: a boy no more than nine or ten, with a pinched, scrawny face and haunted eyes.

"He's only a child!" he exclaimed to Leonidas.

"He's a breaker boy." Leonidas shrugged. "If he doesn't get hurt or die in an accident, he'll grow up fast. By the time he's twelve, he'll be an old hand."

From that chamber they walked along another corridor and then turned several times. One corridor seemed to resemble another, and he had an irrational feeling they had lost their way. His disorder grew and he resisted a compulsion to cry out.

"Seen enough, Father?"

He could not uncake the dust from his tongue to answer and nodded mutely. Shuffling his way back through the narrow, winding tunnels, he fought his terror. He prayed under his breath, his voice hissing eerily in his ears.

They entered the cage and he walked quickly to the rear, bracing himself against the wooden planks. Leonidas stood beside him, and other men joined them. He saw their silent, exhausted faces as they filled the cage. The bell sounded again.

The cage began to ascend, the cables squealing, the floor shaking. He stared up, hardly daring to breathe for a long, burdened passage of time until he saw the first tiny frame of light. When they reached the surface and he saw Santilis waiting for them, the earth behind him suffused with light, his heart burst with joy.

In that resurrected moment, for the first time in all his years as a priest, he truly understood the reborn, restored Lazarus on the day when the Lord delivered him from the dead.

CHAPTER SEVEN

Manolis

During his first months in America, living in the gloomy city of Chicago, Manolis often longed for the tranquil island and life he had left behind. He was repelled by the numerous wagons, carts and clattering autocars that rushed through the streets. He was dispirited as well by the severe weather. On Crete, even the winter solstice produced only mildly cool nights, so he wasn't prepared for the stinging wind and raw cold that penetrated layers of clothing to numb his flesh.

He found it hard to believe that only a few months had passed since he and Starkas had boarded a freight train in New York and headed west. On the journey, Starkas had taught him to climb the narrow metal ladders to the roofs of cars and how to balance on the rocking catwalks of trains, where a clumsy step might mean injury or death.

Sometimes they jumped off a train before it pulled into the freight yards, to avoid brakemen and special railroad guards (Starkas called them "bulls"). That early descent saved them in Pittsburgh, where the bulls ambushed the train, flailing with their billy clubs at a score of hoboes.

From Pittsburgh they had ridden West again across a hilly terrain that leveled off into prairies and the most fertile farmland Manolis had ever seen. He had to restrain himself from leaping off the train to walk in the fields.

When they reached the outskirts of Chicago, they left the train at dawn and ate with a dozen hoboes squatting around a fire. They shared a stew that, Starkas informed Manolis with a grin, was made with ingredients that included a hobo's old shoe.

Later that morning, they found Manolis a ride on a produce wagon going into the city and cajoled the driver, a taciturn Armenian, to drop him on Halsted Street. Then, after a felicitous embrace and a heartfelt prayer that their paths cross again, he and Starkas had parted. Watching his friend plodding back toward the tracks, where he'd board another train and continue his journey west to Colorado, Manolis felt an ache of foreboding. For the first time in the strange, unfamiliar land, he was alone.

When he first saw Halsted Street he was cheered by Greek names on the signs of stores and the familiar aromas of olive oil and cheeses coming from several groceries.

He spent the first day wandering from coffeehouse to restaurant to grocery asking about his uncle Agrios. A number of Greeks knew his uncle or had heard of him, but none of them had seen him since summer. By twilight, hungry and weary from walking and dragging his bag, he had found a grizzled old cook named Javaras who had been a close friend to his uncle. The cook couldn't provide him any more information than the other men, but he told Manolis he was certain his uncle would return to the street. He gave him food to eat and offered him work in the kitchen as a dishwasher.

After Manolis had eaten two heaping plates of rice and lamb, Javaras, chewing the sodden stump of a cigar, instructed him in the art of the old iron tub.

"Like many of the deluded young men who come here now

to find gold under their feet," Javaras said, "you might think dishwashing is a menial, unworthy task. But the kitchen of a restaurant, like the heart in a human body, is where the activity begins. It doesn't matter how palatable the food one serves, if the dishes and glasses don't sparkle, the meal is diminished. Remember that and remember that I began as a dishwasher ten years ago. Look at me now. While I do not own this restaurant, I am undisputed chef in this kitchen and I have earned the respect of patrons who come here to eat, many of whom are not even Greek. That, my boy, is the American way!"

When Manolis had practiced washing a few plates and scouring a pot to the cook's satisfaction, Javaras asked if he had any place to stay. Manolis shook his head. Javaras chewed thoughtfully on his cigar.

"For the wage you will receive here, you won't be able to afford a room," he said. "And you can't sleep here in the restaurant, because the rats from the cellar forage at night for food. You can't stay with me, because my hotel room barely fits my wizened shell and wouldn't hold half your big, Cretan frame but there's a bakery about two blocks from here called the Corinthian, owned by a churlish, abrasive man named Kastris." The cook scowled, exposing his tobacco-stained teeth. "That man wouldn't offer a chair to his old mother or give Jesus Christ a glass of water. But we buy a dozen trays of bread and pastries from him each week and he's obligated to me. Go tell him Javaras asks him to allow you to sleep in his kitchen at night. Tell him you'll watch the oven fire. He'll do me the favor, because he'll fear I'll find another baker."

Later that evening, when Manolis walked to the bakery, he found the dark-cheeked Kastris as sullen and unfriendly as Javaras had described him. But when Manolis told the baker who had sent him, Kastris reluctantly granted him a pallet in

the bakery kitchen. In return Manolis pledged to keep the fire
in the large clay oven from going out during the night.

Through the last days of November and into the beginning
of December, waiting anxiously for his uncle Agrios to return, Manolis labored from dawn to dark in the restaurant
kitchen. At night he returned to the bakery to tend the oven.
Between these tasks he had only a few hours to relax and
sleep.

While he found Javaras a stern taskmaster, he admired the
old cook's ability in the kitchen. Under his fingers and eye,
ordinary food took on an appealing luster. Despite his age,
his energy seemed boundless. He was at work when Manolis
began his day, and after he'd finished the last dishes and
scoured the final pots, Javaras was still at the restaurant.
Sometimes, after they had closed and Manolis was still washing dishes, Javaras helped him at the tub.

"Some cooks would expire before putting their hands to
dishwashing," he told Manolis wryly, "but a man's dignity
cannot be washed away by a few suds. If you ever become a
famous man, remember the lessons you learn in this kitchen
now."

Kastris, the baker, was a different man from Javaras. He
spent only a minimal time in the bakery each day, generally
early in the morning, when he baked the day's bread and
pastries. Then he'd leave the shop to be managed by his wife,
a slender, weary-faced girl named Vasso. She was five or six
years older than Manolis and, in the beginning, he found her
as sullen and unfriendly as her husband. After a while he
came to understand that she was peevish and melancholy because she was unhappy. She and Kastris quarreled frequently
—loud, bitter arguments about his gambling and his chasing
of other women. They made no effort to conceal these arguments from Manolis.

When he first started sleeping at the bakery, Vasso usually locked the shop and walked to her apartment soon after Manolis arrived. After the first two weeks, she began to stay at the bakery later each evening. She began speaking to him about the city that existed beyond the boundaries of Halsted Street.

Little by little, through those cold, gray weeks of the winter, he started to know her better and began looking forward to their time together each night. She seemed to like him more, for she started carrying him food from her own table.

"You don't have to go to this trouble for me, Mrs. Vasso," he told her one evening after she had offered him a plate of lamb and beans. "You know I eat at the restaurant."

"That cold jumble of scraps isn't enough for a child," she said scornfully. "You work hard, long hours and you need warm, filling food."

"Well then, I thank you," he said, touched by her concern. "You're a very kind lady, Mrs. Vasso."

"I'm not so kind," she said quietly. "But I'm not inhuman either—" She paused. "Manolis, do something for me in return."

"Anything I can do!"

"Don't call me Mrs. Vasso, please," she said. "You make me feel like your grandmother. There is, after all, only a slight difference in our ages."

"If that's what you wish," he said. "As long as you and Mr. Kastris don't feel I'm being disrespectful . . ."

She dismissed his concern by a wave of her hand. In the silence that followed, something in the way her sad, dark eyes looked at him caused a curious unrest in his body.

After she had left the bakery to go home, he settled himself on his pallet beside the warm oven. The white shift Vasso wore in the bakery during the day hung on a hook, and, in the light of the glowing coals below the oven, the folds of cloth shimmered as if she were still standing there.

Although Vasso didn't resemble his Sofia, who was lovelier and not as somber, he found that the baker's wife merged into thoughts about his beloved. He had written several letters to Sofia and hadn't yet received an answer. Her father might have intercepted and destroyed them, but he also knew letters took months to cross the ocean. He might not have any answer from Sofia or his parents and sisters until spring. He hoped to hear sooner in answer to the letters he'd written the kind priest and his younger daughter, Soula, in Utah. He thought of them as his family in America.

In those restless hours when he couldn't sleep, the walls of the bakery reflecting the glowing coals, he wondered impatiently when his uncle Agrios would return. He thought bitterly of Stellios and Mitsos Trombakis hiding somewhere in the vastness of America, gloating because they had escaped retribution for the murder of Aleko. He swore again his oath that they wouldn't escape.

When weariness pushed him nearer to sleep, his thoughts of blood and vengeance grew dimmer. He recalled pensively the life and girl he had left behind. Fashioning a vision of Sofia's flawless face, he carried his beloved into the lonely, solitary night.

Sometimes between lunch and dinner at the restaurant when Manolis had a respite from the dishes, he questioned the old cook about his uncle Agrios.

"I wasn't any more than a child when he left and barely remember him," he said to Javaras one day. "What does he look like now?"

"Your uncle Agrios is like an Achilles!" Javaras said fervently. "When you first see him, he looks destined for challenges and feats! He is big, taller even than you, dark, with a warrior's bristling mustache! And he is strong! Once he gripped my hand and I felt clutched in the paw of a lion!"

"What work does my uncle do, Barba Javaras?"

"To tell you the truth, Manolis, I don't really know," Javaras said. "He always has money in his pocket and is generous in buying drinks for his friends."

"Where does he live?"

"I don't know that, either." Javaras chewed on his lumpy cigar. "He'll just show up here at the restaurant and we'll smoke and talk together. Then he'll leave, saying he has somewhere to go or someone else to see."

A waitress called in an order for a bowl of soup. Javaras rose and walked to the steam table. He stirred the soup with a ladle.

"I think I know your uncle as well as anyone on this street knows him, Manolis," he said. "Yet, I suppose even I don't really know him. He is like one of those wanderers in the old legends, men who sometimes build and sometimes destroy. No, Manolis, I don't know where your uncle is or what he's doing or how soon he will be back. But he'll return or we'll have some message from him." He took the cigar from his mouth and waved the stump reassuringly at Manolis. "Meanwhile, my boy, all you can do is wait."

The winter grew colder. When Manolis left the restaurant, he'd run the blocks to the bakery, huddling beside the oven until his body had thawed. He was grateful for that warm, hospitable shelter, and he was grateful for Vasso Kastris.

That winter, the baker's wife became his friend. She continued to bring him food from home and showed him other kindnesses. She gave him a discarded, fleece-lined jacket of her husband's, which, though frayed and worn, was much warmer than the coat he'd bought in a used-clothing store. Then, during the evening, after closing and locking the bak-

ery door against any intrusion by customers, she helped
Manolis with his reading and writing of English. Those hours
in the bakery, the aromas of pastries and bread weaving a fragrant mist about their heads, became the best part of his day.

Sometimes when Vasso remained at the bakery late at
night, he'd walk her to the building where she and Kastris
lived. He'd stand in the street below her dark apartment until
he saw the light in her window. He'd linger in the street for a
while, reluctant to return to the bakery, which would be
lonely without her.

He wasn't certain when his friendship for Vasso altered and
became desire. He was deprived of the companionship of any
other friends, his body urgent and restless. When they bantered and laughed, with her somberness erased, he saw that
Vasso was a pretty girl with sensitive eyes and fine cocoa-
brown hair that his fingers tingled to stroke.

He was often bewildered by her swift changes of mood. At
one moment she seemed as young and flighty as his sister
Eleni, chattering about some gossip on the street. He felt no
discrepancy in their ages then. At other times she exercised
some mystery to tease and bewilder him. Once, after they'd
eaten and drunk some red wine, a trickle of the juice of the
grape spilled across her lips. Her tongue slipped lazily between her lips to retrieve the drops. He stared at her in fascination.

"What are you looking at, you cuckoo?" she laughed.
"Haven't you ever seen a woman's tongue before?"

Enjoying his discomfiture, she continued to lick her lips, so
intimate and erotic a movement that he was swept by a wave
of longing.

The bakery was always warm and, when Vasso baked, she
removed her stockings and changed from her dress to a white
cotton shift. A small stain of sweat appeared beneath her

arms, and the contours of her breasts and thighs were evident as she walked or stretched. When she bent to inspect the bread in the oven, he held his breath as the shift hiked up her glistening, bare legs. He thought of caressing her smooth calves and of kissing the slim, shaded hollows behind her knees. With his cheeks feeling flushed, he looked away quickly, fearing she'd turn around and understand the reason for his agitation.

Vasso had been kind as a sister to him, and he made an earnest effort to conceal his wanton feelings. Even if she teased him from time to time, that didn't excuse the boldness of his fantasies. In the last moments before he slept at night, his thoughts were no longer of his beloved Sofia, but of the baker's wife, indecent visions that saw her naked on his pallet, her slender, supple legs hot and pressing against his naked body.

Several days before Christmas, Manolis was wakened by Vasso and her husband quarreling. He understood, at once, that the conflict was angrier than any he had heard between them. Shrilly and tearfully Vasso unburdened herself of complaints and accusations. Their voices spiraled into shrieks and, suddenly, the sound of a blow exploded across the bakery. Vasso cried out in pain and Kastris shouted a curse and a warning. A moment later, the front door slammed closed.

Manolis dressed slowly. He found Vasso at the table kneading the dough for the day's bread. She worked quickly and silently, her fingers flailing the dough, tearing it apart and then beating it to form the loaves. She did not look up at him, but an ugly, red bruise discolored her cheek. He wanted to say something to reassure her, but he had to leave for his day's work at the restaurant.

He thought about her throughout the morning, remorseful that he hadn't offered her a single word of comfort. He asked

Javaras to let him run back to the bakery for a few moments before the lunch rush began.

"Are your pants torn?" Javaras asked sharply. "Did you forget to wear clean underwear? Why do you need to go to the bakery in the middle of the day?"

Manolis explained about the fight between Kastris and his wife and told Javaras he wanted to see how Vasso was faring. The old cook told him bluntly he couldn't leave.

"Stay clear of their shit, boy," he said grimly. "What that woman has in store for her may be much worse than a bruise. Kastris has squeezed his brains into his balls and is cuckolding a Sicilian. They have more-violent tempers than Turks. Everyone on the street knows, and when the Sicilian finds out, he'll roast the baker in his own oven. You keep your eyes and ears dumb as a statue."

When Manolis returned to the bakery that evening, Vasso had heated noodles for his supper. While he sat and ate, she moved about quietly. Some of the redness on her cheek had faded, but the bruise remained. After he had finished, she carried his dishes to the small sink in the corner.

"Let me do them, Vasso."

"You do them all day," she said. "I'll do them now."

After washing the few dishes, she dried her hands. She drew her chair close to the oven and sat down, folding her fingers in her lap.

"I'll walk you home, Vasso, whenever you want to leave," he said.

"The kitchen is warm and the night is cold," she said. "I will stay here in the bakery tonight."

In the silence that followed her words, he heard the beating of his heart.

"Come and sit here, Manolis," she said softly. "I know you enjoy being near the oven. Bring your chair here."

He carried his chair nearer to the oven, being careful not to place it too close to her. When he looked at her, he found her watching him.

"Won't Mr. Kastris be angry with you if you don't go home?"

"He won't be back here or at home until after Christmas now," she said. "The fight this morning gave him an excuse to spend the holidays with his Sicilian bitch."

She spoke the words bitterly and stared down at her hands. In that moment, she appeared so forlorn that he impulsively reached across the span that separated them and touched her hand in reassurance. She looked at him gratefully and clasped his hand between her fingers.

"You have a strong hand, Manolis," she said. "A man's hand . . . but, always remember, a strong hand must still be gentle with a woman."

The flutter of her fingers against his palm swept him with unrest.

"Our life wasn't always like this morning," she said. "You have only known us fighting, but once, in the beginning, I loved and respected him. I looked forward to the night we'd spend in bed together. That was how it was once."

He listened to her intently, understanding that talking might ease her burden.

"But all that happiness is gone now," she said. "I've become a bitter, unhappy woman, needing to love because life without love is hopeless."

He sensed the shadow of the things she was saying. He thought uneasily of Sofia and of Vasso's husband, who had married her in church, their vows sanctified by a priest and by God.

"You, too, must need love," she said quietly. "You're a healthy, handsome young man. There should be more for you in life than washing dishes and tending an oven."

She watched him, and he was conscious of her breasts rising with her shaken breath.

"Someday you'll return home and marry that girl in your village," Vasso said. "Perhaps bring her back here to build a new life together. But now it's winter and you're thousands of miles away from your village. For a little while now you need to feel warm and close to someone who cares for you."

Her fingers pressed his hand and he felt her trembling.

"I care for you, Manolis." She spoke in a low, wavering voice. "Being with you in the bakery, night after night, having you speak so gently to me, I've come to care for you. God help me, I know that's not worth the love you have back home, but it is something." She paused, her eyes pleading with him. "I've seen you watching me, too, Manolis, and I think there's a part of you that cares a little for me, too."

He divined that she wished him to reveal his feelings about her, encouraging him to speak the truth. He couldn't unscramble his thoughts and words or unbind those years in the village, when no one could speak of desire and love.

As if she understood the reason for his silence, she moved from her chair and slipped slowly to her knees beside him. Without awkwardness or hesitation, she laid her head lightly against his knee.

She's like a child, he thought with a rush of tenderness, an unhappy child, and his tension and fear of her vanished. He clumsily stroked her hair, feeling the fine brown strands curling beneath his palm. He was careful not to press too hard, for he remembered her saying a man's hand must be gentle.

She expelled her breath in a sigh that he felt through the cloth of his trousers, warm against his leg. When she raised her head to look at him, her face appeared more flushed and beautiful than she'd ever been before.

Holding his hand, she carried it slowly to her breast. He

felt the bud of her nipple and the soft, pliant flesh around it. Suddenly he understood the meaning of what was going to happen between them. Vasso had fed his hunger with food, clothed him against the cold with a coat, and now she needed him to console her loneliness.

He kissed her then and felt her tongue between his lips, remembering how she had licked up the trickle of wine. When they broke apart for breath, she unbuttoned the row of buttons at the bodice of her shift. A strip of elastic and a faded, pink ribbon cupped her breasts. She looked at him and, not certain whether she wanted him to go on, he fumbled to untie the ribbon.

In a time when he and his sister were still young, he had glimpsed Eleni's tiny tits when she bathed, but he had never looked at a woman's full-blooming breasts before. For the first time, he saw the pale blue veins beneath her flesh, the rose-hued corona about her nipples, the dusky cleft between her mounds. He was stunned by her loveliness.

He drew her down to the pallet on which he had dreamed they'd sleep together, her naked breasts and naked legs assuring him she wasn't a dream. He was content just to look at her, feasting his eyes on her body. Without warning, his fluid burst from him while he gasped in mortified passion. Afterward, consoling his shame, she drew him tightly against her body, whispering endearments. They caressed one another and he felt his desire strengthening again. When he pressed beneath the patch of downy amber hair, entering a moist sheath more pleasurable than anything he could have imagined, he felt as if he had entered her blood.

Fearing not to be gentle, he remained immobile, until she began twisting her body beneath him. She thrashed more wildly, causing him to probe and thrust, and, finally, as he felt his fluid erupting again she cried out a long, shaken wail.

He rested his head happily against her breast, his cheek ris-

ing and falling with the tumult of her breath. She whispered,
"Manolis," then repeated it softly several times: "Manolis
. . . Manolis . . ." He had never heard his name spoken so
tenderly before.

During that night he rose to add a few coals to the fire
burning in the oven and then hurried back beneath the
covers. Because the pallet was narrow, Vasso and he had to
hold tightly to each other to keep from slipping off onto the
floor. The touch of their naked bodies rekindled desire and
they caressed and made love again. Finally, weariness forcing
him reluctantly to sleep, he hadn't closed his eyes more than a
few minutes before he felt Vasso shaking him gently, telling
him it was time to go to work.

"No!" he said. "This day is special now, like a feast day or
a names day! I'm not going to work!"

Through heavy-lidded eyes he watched her slender, naked
body spring from the pallet. She slipped quickly into her shift
and came to stand laughing down at him while he gazed up at
her with adoration.

"You're laughing!" he said. "You think I'm fooling? I'm
not fooling! I'll dress and go to the restaurant only long
enough to tell Barba Javaras I can't work today!"

Vasso knelt on the pallet beside him, stroking his cheeks
and lips with her fingers. He kissed the hollow of her palm.

"Yes, my dearest," she said. "And will you tell him the
reason you can't work is that you want to stay in bed with
me? Greedy young bull that you are, you want more of the
honey you're tasting for the first time?" She swooped down to
give him a quick, light kiss. "Don't be impatient, my dearest.
Go and do your work. I have work here, as well, the baking
to do for customers who'll want their bread and cakes for the
holiday. Tonight, when you return, I'll be waiting for you.
Oh, my dearest! I'll be waiting for you!"

"What if he comes back?"

"He won't come back. Not until after Christmas. I know him."

Still disgruntled at having to get up and leave, he rose and dressed. Before leaving, he hugged Vasso and kissed her fervently.

"I love you, Vasso! I love you!"

She stared at him quietly without responding to his words.

"I mean it! I love you!"

"I love you, too, my dearest," she said softly.

He remembered and savored her words as he walked from the bakery to the restaurant. Men and women hurried past him along the cold, gray street, heads down, necks drawn grimly into their collars. The previous morning, he'd been as wretched and cold as they were, but now the tumult in his blood kept him warm.

All morning he washed dishes with such vigor that Javaras marveled at his zest.

"Between yesterday and today you seem reborn, my boy," he said. "Have you heard the world is ending and only dishwashers will be saved?"

"I had some good dreams last night, Barba," Manolis said. "Dreams that bear favorable omens for my future."

"Dreams, is it?" Javaras sniffed. "I know young men, and you bounce today with the strut of a rooster who has frolicked the night with a frisky hen. Well, you've been here a while and I suppose it's about time. What hen have you found? One of the Polish factory girls? A waitress in the Italian's restaurant?" He shook his head uneasily. "I hope it isn't one of those tarts over on Blue Island. Whoever it is, take the advice of an old rake whose atrophied sacs forced him into retirement. Pace yourself! Men and women are like plants and pots. The plant needs sun and water, time and patience to bloom. The pot needs only to be filled. A man can go mad trying to keep up."

"Thank you, Barba Javaras," Manolis said cheerfully. "If I ever do any planting in pots, I'll consider your sound advice."

The lunch hour began, and for a while there was the usual bedlam in the kitchen. Manolis was grateful to be busy, anxious for the hours to pass swiftly so he could return to Vasso. When the activity quieted after lunch, he went to stand in the doorway to the alley, relishing the cold air on his flushed cheeks. He imagined Vasso moving lightly about the bakery, perhaps humming as she worked, feeling the same joy he felt. With a shiver of excitement he recalled their lovemaking.

The old cook's voice calling from the kitchen intruded on his ardent reveries. He walked back inside. Javaras stood by the tub, chewing in agitation on his sodden cigar.

"Karabatos, from the Apollo, just brought in the dreadful news," Javaras said. "You better find another place to spend your nights."

"I don't understand, Barba . . ."

"There isn't anything to understand," Javaras said grimly. "It's all clear. Last night the Sicilian caught Kastris, the baker, in his wife's bed and cut his throat. They say he bled like a pig before they found him, and the Sicilian and his wife have fled."

Manolis felt the words like blows. He fumbled at the cord of his apron. "I have to leave now, Barba! I have to go and see Vasso . . ."

"Stay away from there, I tell you! That isn't any of your business! Don't mix in their dung hole!"

Manolis started quickly for the door. Javaras called his name. When he looked back, he saw the shock spring to the old cook's face.

"Holy Mother of Christ!" Javaras cried hoarsely. "I understand now! You and that baker's skinny wife! You damned young fool!"

When Manolis reached the bakery, the front door was locked, the shade drawn across the glass. He walked through the alley and opened the back door with his key. The kitchen was empty and silent, the shapeless lumps of dough strewn on the table. He walked to the front of the bakery, the counter shrouded in shadows. He returned to the kitchen and lay down on his pallet, cradling his head in his arms. He closed his eyes and heard his heart pounding. He counted the beats and, after a while, fell wearily asleep.

The opening of the alley door wakened him. He rose quickly from the pallet as Vasso entered the kitchen. He'd considered the things he'd say to her, the words of consolation he might offer. But before he could utter a word, she rushed like a wind into his arms.

"Listen to me, my dearest!" she whispered. "We'll be separated for the next few days. It's better that way. There will be the wake and the funeral. His sisters and my brother will come to Chicago tomorrow. You stay here in the bakery! Don't come to the wake! Don't come to the funeral! Stay here and wait for me!" A frenzy entered her voice. "Promise, Manolis! Promise you'll wait for me here! When it's all over and everyone is gone, I'll come back to you! We'll be together again!"

"I promise, Vasso," he said. He paused. "Will you have to leave right now?"

"Tonight I'll stay with you," she said. "In the morning I'll leave and be gone for a few days. But tonight you'll hold me in your arms again."

After a while they undressed in the shadowed kitchen and lay together on the pallet. He took Vasso into his arms, feeling the spasms that swept her body. He was tense, uncertain

whether she expected him to make love to her. The baker was
more menacing in death than he'd been in life.

For the first moments, neither of them spoke. He heard the
beating of her heart. There were noises from the street: the
voices of people passing the bakery and the clatter of a
wagon. Vasso began to speak, her voice an unsteady whisper.

"I was kneading the dough for the bread when the police
brought the news," she said. "They drove me to a building
and took me into the basement, into a cold, damp death
room. They showed me a slab with a sheet-covered body. One
of the policemen lowered the sheet and asked me if it was my
husband. I told them yes, it was Kastris, it was him . . ."

She shivered, drawing closer, her thigh pressed against his
thigh, her cold feet groping for his ankles.

"We called the undertaker to come and take his body," she
said. "And then I went to our apartment and brought back
his clothes, his good suit, a clean shirt, socks. At first I chose a
new pair of shoes he'd just bought and then I discarded them
because they pinched him and he wouldn't wear them. I knew
he'd feel nothing but I couldn't put those shoes on him."

Another fit of trembling seized her body.

"I have been thinking all day of the two of us making love
last night," she said. "I wondered, when Kastris was killed,
whether he screamed at the moment I cried out in passion
with you. I thought of that."

She reached up to his face, caressing his temples, his cheeks
and his hair.

"Do you understand, my dearest?" she said earnestly. "Do
you understand that it was a miracle? On the same night Kastris was killed in that whore's bed, God blessed me with you!
On the same night Kastris died, God brought us together!
Yes, that was a miracle!"

Her voice grew wearier until he couldn't make out her
words. He continued to hold her tightly and she grew quieter,

her breathing less labored. He tried not to move until he was certain she had fallen asleep.

But he couldn't sleep. In the silent kitchen of the bakery, holding the wife of the slain baker in his arms, he didn't believe their union was a miracle.

Froso and Aleko, Kastris and the Sicilian's wife, Vasso and himself, all their lives were linked by passion and murder. That brought them together and then nurtured the furies that tore them apart. Those twin furies, he now understood, existed in the cold, winter city of Chicago as they existed in the sun-swept village in Crete, the way they existed in every country, among all men and women who had lived and would live on the earth.

In that moment of grim and sorrowful awareness, he felt he'd finally left youth and innocence behind him forever.

CHAPTER EIGHT

Stellios

When he fled from the Crow Mountain camp with his brother, Mitsos, after his savage battle with the work boss, Stellios couldn't reason beyond his rage. As they rode their horses through the darkness, his blood cooled. He understood Mishima would never forgive the beating and humiliation he had suffered before the workers and foremen. Goaded by a fury for vengeance, he'd pursue Stellios wherever he tried to escape.

In Crete, Stellios knew the land and mountains, the caves and hidden valleys. He and Mitsos would have been able to elude any pursuers. But America was strange to him. In any village where they sought shelter, their inability to speak the language would brand them as foreigners. They'd be identified as runaways and sent back to the camp or to jail. Their only hope would be to find a sanctuary away from houses and farms.

That first night, after leaving the camp, they rode through the darkness without pausing until daybreak. When the dawn rimmed the peaks of the mountains before them, Stellios felt a surge of hope. The mountains might provide them a place to hide.

By late afternoon they were both weary and their horses were exhausted. Pushing the mounts a little farther, they rode a short distance into the forest on the mountain slope. Within a clearing formed by the trunks of some lightning-shattered trees, they dismounted and fed and watered their horses.

"These trees are spruces and firs, like our trees back home," Mitsos said gratefully. "I feel better here."

In spite of the protection of the forest, Stellios felt an oppressive foreboding. Somewhere in the landscape behind them, he sensed their pursuers.

"We'll rest for the night," Stellios said. "At daybreak we'll climb the mountain as high as we can go. There should be caves there where we can hide."

"Will we be safe there, Stellios?" Mitsos asked nervously.

"If you're worried about being safe," Stellios said gruffly, "you should have stayed back in the camp. I told you not to come with me."

"I had to come with you!" Mitsos cried. "Since we were children, Stellios, you've looked after me and I've looked after you! How could I have stayed behind now?"

They took beef and bread from their bags and ate in silence. By the time they finished, darkness had settled around the trees and the forest prepared for night. Cicadas droned from the hidden thickets, the birds grew quiet, an owl hooted from a nearby tree. They unrolled their blankets and draped them around their shoulders, sitting close together for warmth.

Stellios lit a cigarette and smoked it slowly. When he had snuffed out the butt, he closed his eyes and dozed. He didn't know how long he'd slept when an alien sound startled him awake. At the same instant, Mitsos wakened. Both of them listened tensely until they heard the sound again, the fearful baying of hounds carrying in a warring chorus across the night.

They scrambled to their feet and ran. As they stumbled forward, their feet and arms tangling in the brush, Stellios looked back and saw the bobbing lanterns of men entering the forest. The howls of the animals grew louder and the forest erupted into a clamor.

He was shocked at how swiftly the hounds closed on them. Mitsos screamed as the first dog leaped at him, and then Stellios was attacked. He caught a dog by the throat and hurled it away. Other animals pounced on him, their teeth ripping his clothing, tearing at his flesh. While he tried to beat them away, men leaped on him.

He rocked one man back with his fist, his booted foot leveled another. They closed in a tighter circle around him and he pounded furiously at bodies he couldn't see. He was driven to his knees while they battered at him with fists and the butts of guns. When a terrible blow struck his temple, the night was shattered and his senses fled.

Later, he opened his eyes, his head pounding and blood trickling down his throat. Fearing he'd strangle, he coughed, trying to spit the blood from his lungs. He called weakly for Mitsos, but there wasn't any answer. When he struggled to rise, he felt his wrists and ankles bound. He slipped into a stupor once more.

He was roused by the loud voices of men arguing. He couldn't understand their words, but he suddenly recognized a harsh, angry voice that dominated and beat down the others. He wondered strickenly how Mishima could have recovered so swiftly from the beating and led the pursuit. His hate must have driven the hunters and the hounds.

As the first gray daylight became visible through the crowns of the spruces and firs, several men came and pulled him to his feet. One bent and cut the rope that bound his ankles and they pushed him onto the saddle of a horse. For a confused moment, he thought they meant to return him to the railroad camp. Then he saw the twin nooses dangling from the tree above his head. His spirit plummeted into terror.

The men whose heated voices he had heard earlier must have been arguing about sparing their lives. A few might have sought a lesser punishment, but the will and fury of Mishima must have prevailed. In a land where men could be hanged for stealing horses, their identities and the reason they had died would be hidden in the forest forever.

With the awareness that he was going to die, his courage fled cravenly. He babbled to the men in Greek, pleading for mercy for Mitsos and himself. Then, as a revelation burst upon him, he fell silent. He understood suddenly they weren't being hanged because he had beaten up the work boss. That ruffianism didn't warrant death. He and Mitsos had to die in a retribution decreed by God for their murder of Aleko, in Crete.

Even in his despair he marveled at the patience and artfulness of God's plan. He had allowed them the journey from Crete to America, the labor in the camp, the fight and their flight. The hunters and the hounds were part of that relentless design. Finally, Mishima and the hangmen were the instruments of God's will.

The men brought Mitsos and pushed him onto the saddle of a horse. He must have seen the nooses, and let loose a wail of anguish. "Jesus, Stellios! They're going to hang us!"

"Yes, brother," Stellios said quietly.

"Stellios, in God's name! Ask them for mercy!"

In God's name Stellios knew that pleas were useless. "Stay calm, brother," he pleaded with Mitsos. "All we can do now is show them that Cretans can die with courage."

"I don't want to die! Holy Jesus, I don't want to die!" His brother's voice trailed away into a shaken prayer.

Stellios whispered his own last prayers. In those final moments of his life he was grateful that he wasn't afraid to die. He had always believed that death was a debt a man owed from the instant he was born. If he hadn't broken God's law, his debt might not have come due so soon.

The noose was slipped over his head, the cold, hard strands tightened about his throat. Mitsos struggled as the men placed the noose around his throat. Stellios called reassuringly to him again.

The men around them waited in silence for them to finish their prayers. One man whispered to another and a third man coughed hoarsely. Above them dawn lightened the sky. The massifs of the mountains became visible beyond the trees. From one of the crags, an eagle suddenly took flight, soaring slowly and majestically across the sky.

"Mitsos, look!" Stellios cried. "A sign God forgives us . . . !"

As Mitsos raised his head, a man struck the rump of his horse. The animal leaped forward and Mitsos flew off its back, his last cry strangled.

An instant later, Stellios was hurled from his horse. His body whirled and spun, sky, forest and mountains converging upon him. His tongue clawed for air.

The men watching him expected him to die, but he didn't die. With every tormented second of survival, his longing to live gained force. He mustered his will, bracing the strong muscles in his back and shoulders, trying not to thrash or kick so the noose would not tighten and sever the frail channel of his breath. Pain worse than any he had ever known seared his eyes.

As his strength and spirit faltered, the men mounted their horses. An eternity passed until they rode off, their horses noisily trampling the brush. A roaring began in his ears and Stellios resigned himself to death.

Below him he glimpsed movement. A man darted from

behind a tree and swiftly shinnied up the trunk of the tree from which he and Mitsos dangled. He saw a bearded face and an arm stretched toward him. His rope was cut and he fell to the ground, gasping great drafts of air into his burning lungs. The man cut his brother's rope and Mitsos tumbled to the ground.

The man leaped down and crouched beside Stellios, carefully cutting away the noose and freeing his hands. Stellios moaned as he touched the raw collar of blood the rope had burned around his throat.

There wasn't any sound or movement from Mitsos. The man went to kneel beside his brother, looked back at Stellios, and slowly shook his head. Stellios cried out a grieving, bewildered cry, because Mitsos had died while he had been spared.

They buried his brother in the shadows of the spruce and fir trees that had reminded Mitsos of Crete. They covered his grave with a mound of earth and stones. Stellios was grateful that his brother's final resting place was a tranquil site that would remain undisturbed except for small forest creatures and birds.

Afterward the woodsman, whose name was Anders, took Stellios to his cabin, secluded in the woods. He washed his wounds and gave him a blanket to lie on before the fire. For a day and a night Stellios didn't move, fearful to break the dream that he had survived. In the days that followed, the bruises on his body mended and he slowly regained his strength. His throat healed, but the noose left a ridged, mottled scar he'd carry forever. Each time he saw the raw blemish reflected in a glass, he was amazed again that he had lived.

At the beginning of his second week in the cabin, Stellios joined the woodsman in the forest. Each morning, they left the cabin to spend the day cutting down trees. They sawed the trunks into logs and, with the woodsman's mules, dragged and hoisted them onto the wagon. Once a week, Anders drove the wagon down the mountain to a railroad section house and water tank set in the sagebrush. From there the logs were loaded onto a freight car to be shipped to copper and coal mines farther west.

The lean, strong man, whose blue eyes glinted like the sea of Crete, had been living in the forest for five years. Until Stellios joined him, his only companions had been a trio of huskies who trailed him closely. At night, when Anders settled on his blanket before the fire where both men slept, the animals would nestle beside him. He'd whisper to them in a cajoling, affectionate voice and, as if they understood his words, they growled and whined at him in response.

In the beginning the two men communicated mostly by gestures and signs and the few words Stellios had learned from Buzis. Anders began teaching Stellios additional English words and phrases, pointing to objects in the cabin and in the woods. Stellios repeated the words over and over again. They practiced during the day and in the evenings before the fire. Throughout that autumn, while the earth and forest faded into the neutral hues that foreshadowed winter, Stellios improved the rudiments of the language. Yet, even after he had gained the facility to speak to Anders in English, their dialogue remained spare exchanges about the woods, the weather and the dogs.

The days and nights grew colder. They went to work in the mornings bundled in woolen jackets and fur caps. The strokes of their axes echoed like thunder in the chilled, crisp air. At the end of the day they sat and ate in the warm, nested cabin. After they climbed under their blankets, Stellios stared at the fire, while Anders whispered and laughed with his dogs.

As weary as he was each night during that autumn, Stellios

resisted sleep. Falling into that merciless darkness brought him apparitions that whirled angrily through his dreams. He recognized them as the accusing trinity of men for whose deaths he felt responsible. When he saw the murdered Aleko, the little saint, Buzis, and his ill-starred brother, Mitsos, he pleaded with them to forgive him and leave him in peace.

When the first heavy snows of winter covered the trees in the forest and confined them to the cabin for days at a time, he had endless, tranquil hours to meditate upon his life. Sitting before the fire through the day and evening, he was able for the first time to examine the years he had lived without the distortions of passion. He saw clearly that he hadn't truly cared about anyone but himself, his motives always self-seeking and base. He had indulged selfishness and envy, avarice and cruelty. Finally, he had murdered one man and had caused the deaths of two others as surely as if he had murdered them, too. He couldn't understand why God had chosen to spare him.

But even as he anguished about his past, he came to understand that he had it in his power to fashion his future. He needed to banish pettiness and evil from his heart, extending his hand in compassion and comradeship to other men, even as Anders had given him his own hand. The possibility of redemption suddenly warmed his spirit.

Seeking to prove to God his faith and his conversion, he renounced any vengeance against Mishima and the men who had hanged Mitsos. That renunciation wasn't easy for him. There were nights he burned with the dark joy of planning that vengeance. In the end, his longing to redeem his life prevailed, and he vowed he would never kill another human being again.

He began to feel in some mysterious, bewildering way that God had a purpose in saving him. That intimation grew stronger and he prayed for a sign to help him understand that divine intention.

Spring came to the forest. The snow melted on the lower slopes and swelled the streams that rushed water down the creeks. The sun grew warmer, and Stellios felt his spirit lighten with the promise men had felt in spring since the beginning of time.

Then, on a morning near the end of March, in the radiant blue sky above the forest, Stellios saw the eagle again. His heart leaped as he remembered the great bird appearing to him on the day he'd been saved. The bird soared and wheeled above the mountains and the trees, and he followed its buoyant flight until it had disappeared into the sun.

That evening, he told Anders he had to leave. The woodsman seemed to have anticipated his departure, and the following morning Stellios mounted the wagon beside him for the drive down the mountain to the railroad spur. They made a final stop in the woods where Mitsos was buried. Mimosa and daisies had begun to blossom from his grave, which was taking on the coloration of the woods. In the span of a few more seasons, the grave would no longer be distinguishable from the forest. Trees, leaves, roots and flowers would merge with bones and dust to become part of a timeless landscape once more. Soothed by that thought, Stellios knelt beside his brother's grave and whispered a last prayer.

At the section house beside the water tank, Stellios and Anders shook hands. As they had rarely needed to speak to one another while they lived together, words weren't needed for their parting. The woodsman prodded the mules and drove the wagon away from the spur. The huskies riding in back barked at Stellios in farewell.

He waited at the spur through the day and at twilight boarded a westbound train that stopped at the tank for water.

He climbed into a freight car that was occupied by some railroad section hands. They seemed ordinary immigrant laborers, but after nodding a wary greeting to them, Stellios sat alone in the shadows at the opposite end of the car. Remembering the merciless hunters who had tracked them like furies from the Crow Mountain camp, for the first time in his life he was afraid of other men. He was still a fugitive, and if he was recaptured, death by hanging might still be his fate.

He left the train early the following morning when it stopped in a small town set among the sagebrush and boulders. Grateful that he could speak English, he made several inquiries for work and was told a labor agent was hiring all the men he could find for work in the Sharp's Creek coal mines, about fifty miles away. Using the name of Petros Ladas to conceal his identity, he signed papers of employment with the labor agent, noticing that, once again, he was obligated to pay the padrone, Leonidas Skliris, a percentage of his wages. But, anxious to work and trying to avoid drawing attention to himself, he didn't complain.

Within an hour, he joined a dozen other men who were being transported by wagon to Sharp's Creek. An armed deputy carrying a Winchester rifle rode on the wagon seat beside the driver. An Italian sitting beside Stellios in the wagon told him that the reason for the guard was that a strike had been in progress in the Sharp's Creek mine for almost two months.

"That's why they hired us so easy," the man told Stellios gloomily. "We're being brought in as strikebreakers. I've heard if the striking miners catch a strikebreaker, sometimes they break his arms or legs."

"We'll be all right now," a bearded man near them said. "Most of the miners who went out on strike have been jailed or kicked out of Sharp's Creek. The strike has been broken."

The wagon reached Sharp's Creek in early afternoon. The streets of the dingy coal town bristled with armed deputies and police. As their wagon rolled past a series of taverns and coffeehouses, a few men standing in the doorways hurled curses at them.

"What is that curse they're calling us?" a man in the wagon asked.

"Sonofabitch?" the bearded man asked. "Bastards?"

"I know those curses. I learned them from a sailor on the ship that brought me to America. But what is that other profanity?"

"Scabs," the bearded man said.

"What does that mean?"

"It means we're taking the jobs of miners who are on strike," the bearded man answered. "To them that's a crime worse than horse stealing or murder."

"If they want their jobs, why did they leave them in the first place?" the Italian who had first spoken to Stellios asked. "But let them curse me if they want as long as I can work and eat."

They were fed that night and quartered in a dormitory. In the morning they were given clothing, boots and caps and crowded into a creaking cage that descended into the bowels of the earth. When they emerged into the tunnels, Stellios saw men at work resembling dark phantoms. A despair about them came—he felt it himself—because it was unnatural for human beings to be confined beneath the stony, enormous weight of earth, denied sun and sky, unable to distinguish between night and day. Men were confined in the underworld after they were dead, but his first impression of the mines was as an entombment for the living.

Those early reactions were strengthened during the first weeks of his labor, when Stellios understood some of the fears that had driven the miners to strike. The labor underground wasn't only exhausting and despairing, but dangerous. Sometimes the small charges of powder that miners tamped behind the faces of rock failed to go off until the miner checked to see what had gone wrong. In the first week Stellios worked, a young miner in an adjoining tunnel brushed an unexploded blasting cap with his pick and it exploded, severing all five fingers of his right hand. The man's screams echoed through the tunnels for a long time as the cage carried him to the surface.

As dangerous as the explosives were the odorless and colorless gases that seeped through the tunnels, gases that could suffocate a man within a few moments or cut off his supply of oxygen and permanently damage his capacity to move and speak. The metallic, black dust that entered a man's eyes, nose and throat made him breathe as though stones were rising and falling in his lungs.

They worked like animals, and outside the mines they lived like animals, occupying shanties that were no more than planks of wood nailed together, and dilapidated rooming houses. These dismal dwellings were divided into ethnic groups so that Greeks, Italians and Slavs lived separately in rooms with cots lined up in rows. The same divisions prevailed in the taverns and coffeehouses, which were otherwise identical in being dens of stale, smoky air where the men thronged between shifts to drink and play cards and backgammon, shouting and spitting on the dice for luck.

The bearded man in the wagon had been right about the strike being broken. Within a few weeks of their arrival in Sharp's Creek, the last of the militant strikers had been driven from the town. A few of the striking miners who pledged good conduct in the future were allowed to return to work. These miners resented Stellios and the other strike-breakers. Stellios felt their hostility and contempt in the locker rooms and bathhouses. While they sometimes mocked and taunted other newcomers for their clumsiness, they accorded Stellios a grudging respect. Part of this came as the result of a day when he lifted the end of a coal cart by himself so that a man whose foot was trapped could be pulled free. They thought such strength inhuman. There was also the strangeness they perceived in him because he always wore a scarf around his throat, even when he bathed. Only in the darkness of the dormitory room where he slept did Stellios ever loosen or remove the scarf. When he touched the rough, ridged scar that circled his throat, the memory of that fearful day burned his fingers.

Gradually the resentment of the strikers against the new-comers dissipated in their common misery. Following the breaking of the strike, the miners were paid less than they had received before they walked out. Part of the pay was also in scrip, good only for purchases in the company store, where all the items were overpriced. And then, every payday, the agents for the padrone, Leonidas Skliris, came to deduct his percentage. Even to these poor devils who risked injury or death every time they went to work, Stellios thought grimly, the "Czar of the Greeks" stretched out his greedy hand.

Men grumbled about the conditions and the reduced pay, but no man dared complain openly. The mine was riddled with company spies, who reported any malcontent. The next payday, the grumbler would be fired. So men worked wearily and hopelessly, resigned that nothing could be done to help them.

On a night about eight months after Stellios began work at Sharp's Creek, a young Greek miner named Cristos, who slept on the cot beside him, motioned him aside as they were getting undressed for bed.

"There is a Greek, big as a colossus, who has come to Sharp's Creek to talk to the miners, Petros," he whispered. "I heard him last night and his words set me on fire. There were only five of us there and he asked each of us to bring another man with him tonight. Will you come with me to hear him?"

Stellios believed the man had to be one of the union organizers the foremen were constantly warning them about: men, they said, who were "bomb throwers" and "bolsheviks." He hesitated, because he hadn't any wish to join with dissidents or to foment trouble. But he was curious to hear the man, and he agreed to go.

After the dormitory grew quiet except for the snores and mutterings of sleeping men, he and Cristos dressed quietly. They walked from the dormitory to the outskirts of the town and into a grove of trees, where they joined about a dozen men. They waited in a nervous silence, men clearing their throats and coughing. Then the huge, burly organizer appeared and motioned to them to gather in a tighter circle. He started talking to them in a low, yet vibrant voice.

"You're brave men for coming here tonight," he told them. "Miners suffer enough and don't need anyone bringing them more trouble. I can't promise to keep trouble away from you. I can only help you prepare for it by asking you to join a union of miners that will include every mine in the West."

That was the way he began. In the following half hour he recounted a litany of mine disasters in which miners were killed and crippled. He talked of the agony of men who had legs and arms amputated and of older miners who coughed black blood until they died. He spoke scornfully of mine owners who wouldn't correct the safety defects that caused these deaths and cripplings because of their greed for profits.

"They won't improve these conditions in any single mine," he said. "That is how the strike here at Sharp's Creek was broken. Miners grew angry and simply walked out. There wasn't any plan or organization so that strikers knew what to expect and what to do. As long as the owners have the money and the police, they have the power to dictate to us. But if we

unite the miners in all the mines, then we, too, gain power.
The aim of our union isn't revolution or anarchy, as the
owners would have you believe, but to demand safer working
conditions in the pits, clean clothing, decent food, a good
bed. We want better wages for our labor, less of those wages
paid in the damn' company scrip, and we want the damned
padrones off our backs."

He spoke of the history of the miners' union, of men called
Wobblies, of Big Bill Haywood, who had a dream of a day
when no child would labor, when every aged working man
and woman would be free of poverty. He spoke of men like
himself traveling across America, seeking to organize not
only miners but those who worked as timberbeasts, hobo har-
vesters, itinerant laborers, and the immigrants exploited as
strikebreakers.

Stellios was caught and stirred by the big man's words and
passion. He had never heard anyone speak with compassion
for other human beings before.

Somewhere in the darkness beyond the grove, several dogs
began to bark. As that sound shattered the stillness of the
night, Stellios felt his skin crawl with fear. The darkness was
suddenly altered, a whisper of wind carrying the scent and
tremor of danger. Every man in the grove tensed, and the
speaker fell silent. Then they heard the jangle and clatter of
armed men.

The miners scattered in panic, each man desperate to save
himself. Impelled by terror to flee with the others, Stellios
looked back once at the speaker and saw the big man hesitating as if uncertain which way to escape. Stellios ran back to
him, grabbed him by the arm, and rushed him into the darkness.

They took refuge in the Zenith coffeehouse. Ganaras
brought them a bottle of mastika and they drank, taking each
other's measure.

"You haven't yet given me your name, friend," the giant said with a smile, "so I'll know who to thank for saving me."

"Petros."

"Well, Petros, my name is Starkas and I thank you warmly. You saved me from a beating or worse." He shook his head grimly. "The last battering I took from the Coal and Iron Police left boot marks in my back for months. When I stretch out to sleep at night, my bones poke me like nails."

"But you go on talking," Stellios said.

"Someone must talk," Starkas said. "Someone must speak for those men who cannot speak for themselves."

"Even if the things you say are true," Stellios said, "you're only one man. How can one man change anything?"

"I'm not alone," Starkas said. "Other men like me have been caught and beaten many times and tossed into jail and beaten again. They get their teeth knocked out and they piss blood from their damaged kidneys. But they go out and talk again."

Suddenly Cristos appeared from the crowd of tables and came to stand crestfallen before them. "I'm ashamed enough to die." He spoke to Starkas in a low, contrite voice. "I thought of helping you myself, but my guts turned to pudding. Forgive me for being a coward." He turned morosely to leave.

"Come back here, man!" Starkas called after him. "When he's scared, a man's primal instinct is to flee. I've been so scared myself at times I've run and left comrades behind. So sit down and console yourself with a drink."

His face flushed with gratitude, Cristos started to join them. He hesitated, to make sure Stellios didn't object. When Stellios nodded, Cristos quickly took a seat.

There was a commotion at the door as a group of noisy men entered. Starkas stared tensely toward them. "Have the bastards found us?" he asked.

"They wouldn't dare set foot in this place," Cristos said

proudly. "They'd have to fight a hundred men, who'd rip their teeth from their mouths."

Starkas nodded approvingly. "That's all I was trying to say tonight," he said quietly. "A hundred men joined make the weakest among them stronger and the frightened more courageous. That is what a union does. Men banded together for the good of all."

After that first meeting, Stellios joined Starkas each night at locations where the organizer spoke to miners. The gatherings were small in the beginning and then, as word about him spread among the miners, larger groups assembled. Captivated by his vision of a better life for them, men overcame their fear of beatings by the police or dismissal from their jobs and came to hear him.

As he listened to Starkas, night after night, Stellios formed an altered vision of America. He began to see it as a vast land of exploited men seeking a liberation from their bondage, as the Cretans sought freedom from the Turks. From the young immigrants with whom he traveled on the ship, innocents as Mitsos and he had been, to the young men from a dozen countries, he felt his own struggle submerged into their dream of a fair life.

He was grateful to Starkas for that insight. At the same time, he felt his bonds of friendship to the big man growing stronger. Remembering what the organizer had told him of the beatings and tribulations he had endured in jail, Stellios gathered several strong young Greek miners he trusted to join him in guarding Starkas.

As their gatherings grew larger, their chances for betrayal increased. Once, when the Coal and Iron Police attacked their meeting, the young miners managed to get Starkas away just in time to avoid his capture. After that encounter, they didn't meet for a few days and their first assembly was poorly attended. Little by little the numbers grew again, due, in large part, to Stellios' urging miners to attend. He began taking added precautions. When a meeting had to be canceled because they suspected they had been betrayed by a company spy, Stellios led Starkas to an alternate site. Meanwhile, the miners who had been alerted to the change also assembled. As the room filled with them, an astonished Starkas grabbed Stellios in a bearlike embrace.

"You're a canny devil!" he said. "Crafty and bold! You're a born organizer!"

"I could never say the things you say so well," Stellios said.

"You wouldn't have to say nearly as much," Starkas said. "The men respect you enough so that one word from you would carry the weight of ten from me."

There was a night when Starkas spoke to the largest gathering of miners he had yet addressed. He made a plea for them to sign up with the union, to contribute a few coins to show their membership was in earnest. The miners stared uneasily at one another, afraid their names written on a list would subject them to punishment. As eloquently as he spoke, Starkas couldn't overcome their fear. He turned away, finally, shaking his head grimly as if conceding the struggle was lost. Something in his despair made Stellios rise to speak.

"When I was a boy in Crete," he said quietly to the men, "there was a cave on the mountain above our village we all believed was inhabited by a monster. On nights when the wild winds blew down from the peaks, we swore we heard the creature roaring. For a long time, none of us dared enter that cave until, one night, one boy went in alone. We waited for his destruction, but he came out unharmed. Then all of us rushed in and the cave became our sanctuary, a secure place where we could meet to counsel and talk."

His words rang strangely in his ears. The men watched

and listened. He was conscious of Starkas watching him as well.

"The union Starkas speaks of is like that cave of my childhood," Stellios said. "Once the first man enters, others will follow. So now I will be the first to join and sign."

"And if we follow you, Petros," a miner called out, "can we be certain the owners and police won't find out who we are and punish us?"

"We can't be certain they won't find out," Stellios said. "Nor can we be certain that tomorrow the timbers in the mine won't collapse and bury us. Nor can we be certain how long we will live or when we will die. But uncertainty shouldn't weaken our courage."

He walked to the small table on which Starkas had laid out the papers and slowly signed his name. He took from his pocket the coins required to pay his first dues. He heard men rising behind him, coming to join the line, bending to sign their names. For a moment, he saw Starkas watching him, approval on his face and, most rewarding of all, the warmth of friendship and affection.

In the days that followed, more miners joined the union. Realizing that there was safety in numbers, that the owners couldn't fire them all, those who had signed zealously encouraged those still unsigned. The union membership went from 40 to 50 and, finally, to 68 percent of the workers in the Sharp's Creek mine. That night, there was a celebration in the Zenith, the men as jubilant as if they had achieved a major victory. Starkas and Stellios drank with them, responding with smiles to the toasts of men who cheered them.

"They have a right to a small celebration," Starkas said, "but they must understand that all we have accomplished so far is that we've organized a single mine. Every mine is another battlefield, and every battle needs to be won before we can win the war." He sighed. "Even today I had word from a courier that there's been a tunnel cave-in at the Commonwealth mine, in Big Table, Utah. Eleven young miners are trapped who may never come out of the pit alive." He cursed in a low, bitter voice. "I visited that mine six months ago. We knew the timbering was unsafe, that it needed further shoring. The owners scoffed at us. Now, this is the result."

His voice trailed away and he looked earnestly at Stellios.

"I'm leaving early in the morning for Big Table," he said. "There's something I want to ask you before I go. I know nothing about your past, but I know you're a born leader. Because of that gift, you have a choice to make. You can remain a miner, blasting and chipping away at seams of coal. Or you can join us, traveling from mining town to mining town, using your gift to bring miners an awareness of their stake in joining the union. For, make no mistake, Petros, a war is coming. And in that war our union is an army."

He sipped his mastika and shrugged.

"You'll be beaten up, have your bones broken, your spirit assaulted," Starkas went on. "You'll spend wretched days and nights in filthy jails at the mercy of deputies with fear and hate in their hearts. You'll move like a hunted wolf, eyes and ears alert for a hundred dangers. The only home you'll know will be a score of dirty pallets in the back rooms and shanties of dingy mining towns. Even men you try to help will scorn and curse you for bringing them trouble. And, God help you, there's the chance it may cost you your life, martyred like Joe Hill, who died before a Utah firing squad crying his last words, 'Don't mourn for me. Organize!'" Starkas paused and stared grimly at Stellios. "Do these things I am telling you make you afraid?"

"Yes, they make me afraid," Stellios said. "Once, I wasn't afraid, but I've learned what men can do to other men."

"A man who isn't afraid is a fool," Starkas said. "Now, in spite of that fear, will you join us?"

Stellios remembered the moment when his body dangled at the end of the rope. He recalled the vision of the eagle, a sign that his life belonged to God. If he chose now to help others, he might in some way atone for the men he had destroyed. "I'll join you," he said.

The eyes of Starkas shone with pleasure. "From that first night when you shepherded me to safety," he said, and his voice trembled, "I've felt our destinies linked to forces beyond us, forces over which we haven't any control."

He finished his mastika and rose to go.

"Do you want me to leave with you in the morning?" Stellios asked.

"You better remain here for a little while," Starkas said. "Make sure the men who've signed don't backslide. I'll get word to you as soon as I can where we'll meet. Be ready to move fast and travel light."

"As light as the clothes I'm wearing," Stellios said.

"That's just light enough for a good organizer," Starkas laughed. He started from the table and turned back. "Answer one question for me, my friend," he said. "That story you told the night you inspired the men to sign for the union. Were you the boy who first entered that cave?"

"That was another boy," Stellios said. "He was the bravest in our village, always the leader in everything we did."

"Is he still as brave?"

"He would have been braver," Stellios said. "Boys followed him as men would have followed him later. In his presence we felt we were able to accomplish great deeds."

"Where is this man?" Starkas asked. "The union could use him."

"He's dead now," Stellios said, and as he spoke the words a tremor shook his heart.

AMERICA
1911

❖❖❖❖❖❖❖❖❖❖❖❖❖❖❖❖❖❖❖❖❖❖❖❖❖❖❖❖❖❖❖❖❖❖❖❖❖

CHAPTER NINE

Papadia Cristina

There was a night in early April when Cristina dreamed she was lost in a dark, tangled forest. She heard her father's and mother's voices calling her and she pleaded for them to find her. Their voices grew fainter and, terrified she'd be lost forever, she snapped awake. Her heart pounded and she shifted her body closer to the warmth of her husband's body.

A tracing of moonlight seeped through their window and illuminated the base of the bed. She imagined the glow lightening the rooms in which her son and daughters slept.

As she often did when she woke and couldn't sleep again, she sorted her grievances. In addition to her anxiety about the young miners who labored in the dangerous tunnels while she and her family slept, she shared her children's struggle to make a place for themselves in the town. During their first year in Snowmass, while the other children taunted them by calling them "dirty Greeks" and "garbage from Europe," Andreas had fought constantly. He returned from school each day with bruises on his face and his knuckles raw.

"We are the strangers here," she pleaded with him many times. "Even if the other boys provoke you, keep your dignity and try to turn the other cheek. Remember, your father is a priest and you must set an example."

Because they were girls and less belligerent than Andreas, her daughters had overcome some of the animosity and developed a few friendships. Only fools and bigots wouldn't have sought their companionship. Alexandra, who was a month from sixteen, and Soula, who was fifteen, had grown into slender, young beauties with long, black hair. When they bathed, Cristina saw their small breasts grown fuller, the floss thickening between their legs. Some of these physical changes could be hidden when they dressed in loose frocks, their hair bound in seemly plaits. But their beauty was becoming harder and harder to conceal.

While the men on the street still doffed their caps in respect to the girls as they had in the beginning, there was an altered tension in the way they stared. Cristina suspected they were affected by the changes in the girls, the blossoming of their young womanhood. The young men would have had to be statues instead of flesh-and-blood mortals not to have felt some desire. She doubted that any sober man would dare lay hands on one of them, but a lonely man or a drunken one might speak indecently to them. God forbid, some poor devil might even try to harm them.

Yet, neither she nor the children carried the burdens of Father Basil. All during the winter, when he returned home late at night, particles of ice frozen in his beard, she saw his weariness and despair. In the absence of any other leader, he had become spokesman for the miners with the superintendents representing the eastern owners. These men listened to Basil's pleas for the men's safety and an improvement in their living conditions and then did nothing. Because he wasn't able to help his flock, his frustration and resignation made him seem years older.

She tried to console him, but he seemed distant and strange.

She recalled with nostalgia the tenderness and affection between them on those afternoons in Rethymnon when he came home from the church to rest. They had made love lazily in their bedroom, splashed with sunlight while laughing like newlyweds.

Now Basil left the house early in the morning and didn't return until long after the children were home. On those rare occasions when they made love, the act was flurried and unsatisfying because of the children in adjoining rooms. They might also be interrupted by miners who came to the house to see him. So the spontaneous joy of their lovemaking was gone.

Perhaps she contributed to that joylessness by her fear that she might become pregnant again. As fulfilling as her other conceptions had been, she couldn't endure the thought of bearing a baby in the dismal mining town, an infant who, with its mother's milk, would suck in her feelings of hostility and sadness.

Did Basil have any intimation of her unhappiness? Sometimes as the two of them sat before the fire in the evening, she looked up from her knitting to find him watching her. She sensed an accusation in his eyes, and she felt remorseful without being sure of the ways she might have failed him.

More than anything else, she missed the company of women, whose voices were gentle and not hoarse and gruff like men's voices. She longed for women, who smelled of baking and who wouldn't mind chattering about the small things that only concerned women. Sometimes she felt that if she had just one other woman, with whom she could share her hopes and fears, she'd pull her embittered life together.

The mine whistle tore away the night. Keeping her eyes closed might conceal the faint daylight, but she couldn't close her ears to that infernal sound. She rose from the bed trying not to disturb Basil so he might sleep a little longer.

After adding more wood to the fire and putting water on to boil, she woke Andreas and the girls. They dressed quickly and hurried downstairs to warm themselves before the fire. As Cristina set eggs in the boiling water, Basil descended to the kitchen, slipping into his cassock. They gathered at the table and bowed their heads while he said grace.

"Mama, don't worry, because I'll be coming home later today," Alexandra said. "We're making a history chart and the teacher has asked a few of us to stay and help."

"I'll be late too," Andreas said. "We're going to play ball."

"Does this mean you're getting along better with your classmates?" Basil asked.

"I have a couple of friends," Andreas shrugged. "The other whiteheads leave us alone."

"They've given up trying to crack Andreas' hard skull." Soula smiled.

"Even one good friend is enough, my son," Basil said. He spoke to the girls. "How about your friendships?"

"Things are better now," Alexandra said. "Only the worst haters still bother to taunt us. The more enlightened girls even seem to enjoy talking to us."

"Why don't you invite a couple of them to have dinner with us on Sunday?" Cristina asked.

"They're not that enlightened, Mama," Alexandra said. "I think a few still believe Cretans eat raw meat and drink blood."

"We do drink the blood of Christ in our communion; don't you know that?" Andreas scoffed at Alexandra.

"We know that," Soula said. "But you better not tell the whiteheads. They won't understand."

They finished their breakfast and rose and kissed their parents goodbye. Cristina followed them to the door, making certain they wore scarves. Soula lingered behind the others.

"I wrote a letter to Manolis last night, Mama," she said in a low voice. "Will you mail it for me?"

Cristina nodded and Soula hugged her tightly.

"Don't worry so much about us," she said to her mother. "We're sturdy and we'll be all right."

Cristina nodded gratefully. She often found this child evidencing compassion, an uncommon emotion in one so young. Sooner than she anticipated, Soula might provide her the female companionship she sought.

She returned to the table. With the children gone, the house seemed strangely silent, the only sound coming from the logs crackling in the fire.

"Would you like more tea?" she asked.

Basil nodded and she brought him hot water. These last few moments before he left the house for his church were the only time during the day she spent alone with him. There were always so many things she wanted to say, but they weren't the words she finally spoke.

"I had letters in the mail yesterday from Kyra Doulakis and Kyra Stathos, in Nipos," she said. "Both women complain they haven't heard from their sons in a year."

"I'll speak to the boys," Basil said.

Sometimes the parents of the young Cretans wrote to Basil, but often the mothers wrote to her, pouring out their anxieties in letters written for them by village scribes. The letters pleaded for Cristina to be mother to their sons, to make sure the boys rested enough, attended church regularly, ate well and, most important, kept away from foreign women, who might snare them into marriage.

As if Basil understood what she had been thinking, he sighed.

"They cannot understand what life here is like," he said. "This isn't the village and our concerns aren't those of the village. It isn't enough to keep the boys coming to church, we must struggle to help them avoid injury and death." He finished his tea and pushed aside his cup. "I stopped by the hospital on my way home last night," he said. "The boys in the ward carried on about your visits and your baking. You do more for them than anything Barba Sotiris or the doctor can accomplish."

"I baked *koulourakia* I'll take to the hospital today."

He rose to leave. She wanted to urge him not to hurry into the gray, chilled dawn but to linger in the warm kitchen. She felt constrained and didn't speak. That is the way we live now, she thought ruefully, not like loving husband and wife but as if we were strangers, afraid to say what we wish to say.

He bent to kiss her cheek and she turned her face so he'd have to kiss her mouth. He brushed her lips uneasily with his lips and straightened up stiffly. There was remorse in his eyes, as if he wished her to know there wasn't any rejection of her in his turning away. The day had begun and the pressure of his duties occupied his emotions. There wasn't time now to consider Cristina or himself.

He drew his coat from a hook near the door and draped it across his shoulders for the short walk to the church.

"I think the worst of the winter is behind us now," he said, as if wishing to offer her some final reassurance. Then he left the house. She listened to his steps on the gravel walk until she couldn't hear them anymore.

She washed the dishes, as she washed everything in the kitchen, several times a day. Nothing remained unsoiled in the house for long, because of the coal dust, the grainy film coating the windows and powdering the bedclothes and the clothing. Even the food she cooked tasted of the pervasive dust.

Packing the koulourakia in a napkin-covered basket, she left the house, following the path that ran by the church. Basil had been right about the weather changing. She could smell the first warming traces of spring.

Outside the church she saw the line of waiting miners. Another group waited inside the narthex. All day long they would pour out to Basil their confessions, remorses, and longings, the laments that came from wretchedness and a homesickness that had no cure.

Beside the church was a small graveyard unlike the ancient cemeteries in Crete, which were packed with stone and marble monuments. She could count the eleven graves in this cemetery, each with a simple wooden cross bearing the name of a young miner killed in a mine accident. These bodies had been recovered, but for each one of them there was another body unreclaimed from the earth. She paused by the graveyard to cross herself and murmur a prayer for those mothers in Crete who would never see these sons again.

She stopped in the railroad freight office to mail Soula's letter to Manolis, in Chicago. Although she and Basil had written the young man from time to time in the past two years, Soula wrote him regularly and eagerly awaited his answers. Cristina thought it strange that her daughter, only thirteen when they were together with Manolis on the ship, had forged such a durable bond to the young man. That was additional confirmation that the girl was emotionally older than her years.

Leaving the railroad office, Cristina followed the crushed slate path along the tracks to the river and toward the Snowmass mine. Although a pall of soot and smoke was visi-

ble everywhere in the town, in the midst of the works the sky
was almost night-dark. Not a bush, blade of grass, or sprout
of vegetation could survive in the withering landscape.

Hurrying along with her head down, trying to avoid breathing in the smoke and dust that singed her throat, Cristina entered the long shed that held the infirmary and hospital. At
the far end of the building she saw the infirmary jammed with
miners in pit clothing and boots being treated for beat knees,
cut fingers and coughs.

Pausing at the threshold of the ward, Cristina felt again
how unnatural a setting the gloomy room was for young men.
They belonged in a sun-filled landscape of orchards and
mountains. Instead, their unhappy fate had confined them
here.

There were ten beds in the ward, two rows of five along
each side of the room. Seven of the beds were occupied.
Nikos, Stavros and Elias were recovering from severe burns
incurred in a tunnel fire. Their bodies would bear the scars
for as long as they lived. Another miner, Fanos, had inhaled
pit gas, his gray face and listless eyes showing little improvement. Alexis had been admitted with pneumonia and hadn't
been expected to live. His healing was due to the curatives of
Barba Sotiris, the old folk healer who had achieved miracles
with many of the boys.

Cristina saw the wiry little man at the end of the ward beside Lenos. When that eighteen-year-old youth had his legs
shattered in a tunnel collapse, the company doctor wanted to
amputate them. But Barba Sotiris, working feverishly for a
day and a night, had set the youth's legs and wrapped them in
a sheep's-wool poultice he'd mixed from spices and herbs. Two
months had passed since then and—another blessed miracle
—the young man's legs seemed to be mending.

Mustering her spirit, Cristina entered the ward. In the bed
nearest to the door, Nikos was the first to see her. He waved

one bandaged hand excitedly in the air. "Papadia is here, boys!"

The men called blessings and greetings to her with such fervor that tears rose to her eyes. She moved slowly from bed to bed, greeting and visiting each patient.

"How are you feeling today, Stavros?"

"Better now that you're here, Papadia!"

"Are you taking your medicine?"

"That's poison, Papadia! I think the nurse with the sour face is trying to kill me!"

"She is trying to help you! I want you to take your medicine!"

"Papadia!" Nikos called from another bed. "I have a letter from my sister I want you to read!"

Tugged from bed to bed by their entreaties, she adjusted their covers, tried to cheer and console them. When she passed out the koulourakia, some men savored them slowly while others clasped them in their hands like amulets to remind them of home.

"They are just as delicious as the baklava you brought last week, Papadia!" Elias said.

"Papadia bakes as good as my blessed mother bakes," Nikos said.

"Nobody in the world bakes as good as one's own mother," Cristina said.

Passing down the ward, she came finally to Lenos. She felt a special affection for this handsome youth not only because he was the youngest patient in the ward but also because he came from a village near their town of Rethymnon.

She gently kissed him, inhaling the sweat of weakness from his pores. Then she greeted the folk healer, who knelt and massaged the youth's feet, which protruded from his casts.

"How are you today, Barba Sotiris?"

"Miserable like all my days in this place," Barba Sotiris

growled, "among these young hellions eager to get well only so they can indulge in some new deviltry."

"Then, why do you work so hard to make us well?" Lenos smiled.

"I cannot help myself, because I was born with a gift to heal." The old man feigned somberness. "At my birth, my mother's blessed womb ejected me and then, miraculously, closed without a trace to show she'd given birth."

"I know of only one other born in that fashion," Cristina said gravely. "He was born in Bethlehem and also grew up to be a great healer. Are you suggesting, Barba Sotiris, that you're related to him?"

Barba Sotiris chuckled and then leveled a stern finger at Lenos. "Careful, boy! Are you snickering at the way the Papadia skewered me? I'll snap off your toes and fling them to the cats!" He winked at Cristina. "Papadia, how does our young Diomedes look to you today?"

"Healthier and stronger!"

"My legs are getting stronger, Papadia!" The young man's black eyes shone. "In the night I hear them cracking like nuts and know the bones are mending! If Barba Sotiris would take off the casts, I'd race up the mountain!"

"Have patience, boy!" Barba Sotiris cried. "Believe me, Papadia, there's impertinence in this ward, but patience . . . that's in short supply!" He rose from his knees with a groan. "Enough massaging now," he sighed, "or my own poor back will need a cast."

He moved to another patient. Cristina pulled up a chair close to Lenos and sat down. After a moment he shyly reached out to grasp her hand. She felt his fingers trembling against her palm.

"When I'm well again, Papadia," he said. "I pledge I'll mend my life, as well." He shook his head remorsefully. "I've done things that would make you and my mother ashamed of me. I think that's why God broke my legs, to punish me, and warn me I must change my ways."

"God is merciful and wouldn't do such a thing!"

They sat in silence for a moment. The voices of men drifted to them from the other beds. Barba Sotiris, comforting one of the patients, snapped his fingers and stumbled a few steps in an awkward parody of a dance.

"Will you believe me, Papadia?" Lenos' face was suddenly flushed. "I was the best dancer in our village. The girls always watched me and that made me dance even faster."

"You'll dance again, Lenos," Cristina said. "You'll dance here in this new country and in your village again someday when you visit there as a rich and respected man."

"I don't pray to dance again, Papadia." He clasped her hand tightly. "And I don't care if I'm always poor and never own anything but tattered breeches and a shabby coat. I only pray God lets me walk on His earth again."

For as long as Basil and Cristina had been in Snowmass, their custom on Sundays after church was to open their house to the young miners. All afternoon, men filled the rooms, which grew crowded, noisy, and warm with bodies.

By twilight on that first Sunday in May, a larger group of men lingered into the evening celebrating Alexandra's sixteenth birthday. Cristina distributed figs, cakes soaked with honey, and glasses of cider and coffee.

Alexandra was dressed in a shimmering white frock with a lace collar. She looked regal and tall, her loveliness buoyed by the numerous compliments she received from the men who lavished little presents of candy and charms upon her. A few of the men, emboldened by the celebration, began to tease her in the gentle, sportive manner they might have teased younger sisters back home.

"Now that you have become a grown lady of sixteen years,

Alexandra," Leonidas said, "you should begin thinking
seriously of marriage. Can you tell us, please, which province
of Crete you'll someday choose your husband from?"

"How can you ask such a question?" Dinos scoffed. "The
province of Sfakia has the bravest, strongest Cretans. Alexandra, being fair and beautiful, deserves only the best and
therefore she will, of course, choose a man from Sfakia!"

"Rethymnon produces leaders and learned scholars," Vasili
said. "She should choose a man from Rethymnon."

"Perhaps I won't choose a Cretan at all," Alexandra said.

The men burst into exclamations of shock and dismay.

"I won't choose a man because he comes from a particular
province!" she said sternly. "That would be a foolish marriage! The man I choose must have qualities more important
than the place he was born."

"What are those qualities, Alexandra?" Vasili asked.

"Manliness, gentleness and pride," she said.

"Those sound just like me!" Nikos said loudly. The other
men hooted and jeered at him, gesturing boastfully at themselves.

"You're all making fun of me now," Alexandra said, and
Cristina noticed a flaring of temper in her daughter's eyes.
"But I will only marry a man with a great heart and a shining
spirit. You'll respect him as the first and best among you.
We'll have a grand wedding and you'll all celebrate with us
on that day."

The girl spoke with such conviction that the men ceased
laughing. A few nodded in approval.

"We all hope that prophecy will come true, Alexandra,"
Leonidas said quietly. "And we'll be honored to share your
joy on that happy day. But now!" he clapped his hands
briskly. "The sun has gone down and the rooms are chilled.
To properly celebrate your birthday, Panos has brought his
lyra and Kostas his clarinet. We'll dance now to warm up!"

The men clapped their hands and shouted as they leaped to push back the furniture and clear a circle in the center of the room. As Panos and Kostas raised their instruments, the dancers assembled quickly, tugging Andreas with them into the line. A tempest of Cretan mountain music wailed through the house.

The dancers whirled and leaped, kicked and dipped, circling faster and faster. The floor rocked under their boots and the walls trembled so that Cristina feared for her plates. She watched Andreas, who, sustained by swift Cretans on either side, matched their furious pace. Basil smiled at her, both of them savoring the boy's delight. The only shadow over the moment came when she thought of Lenos in the hospital ward and his pride in the way he had once danced.

When the boisterous dance finished, Leonidas motioned to the girls. "Andreas danced like a Cretan *palikari,*" he said. "Now it's time for you young ladies to show you are Cretan heroines. Is that all right, Father?"

Basil nodded and the girls joined the dancers. Alexandra headed the line, Soula behind her, and Leonidas following. He solemnly furled his handkerchief to link Soula's slender fingers with his own big hand.

When the music began again, the lyra and clarinet were quieter, the dance more restrained. Alexandra led the circle swiftly and gracefully, her black hair whirling about her shoulders. Soula followed her with nimbleness and ease. The men jammed along the walls and crowded into the doorway watched the girls with adoration.

There was a flurry of activity at the door. Beyond the dancers, Cristina saw Santilis enter the house with a man she had never seen before. They greeted a few men and then made their way slowly through the crowd toward Basil, who stood a short distance away from her. When they reached him, Santilis introduced the stranger, who bent and kissed

Basil's hand. Santilis saw Cristina and waved at her, and then he and the man turned to watch the dancers.

The stranger was taller than any of the men in the room. His thick, dark hair and coal-black beard curled about his lean-fleshed face, which was burned copper-brown from the wind and sun. Clad in a high-necked shirt and jacket, his broad and powerful body appeared hewn from rock.

She felt something disturbing about him and couldn't understand why. Perhaps it was in the way he stood, his body suggesting agility even in repose. While his gaze followed Alexandra at the head of the line, there wasn't any disrespect or brashness in his face. But neither was he staring at her with the shyness or veneration exhibited by the other men. Cristina had the resentful feeling that he had entered the crowded room and, somehow, claimed it as his own domain.

As the dancers whirled by him again, for an instant she saw Alexandra's eyes catch the stranger's level gaze. Cristina felt a shock as though their glance had made a physical contact. The dancers swept on, but she retained an unexplainable foreboding.

When the dancing ended, a while later, she didn't get a chance to meet the stranger, because a phalanx of men surrounded him and pulled him to a corner. She caught a sharper glimpse of him as they passed and saw the damage to his face she hadn't been close enough to see before. His nose had been broken and healed crookedly, with a slight ridge creasing the bridge. The discoloration and webbing of a scar wrinkled his temple. Yet, she had the feeling that these visible wounds, as well as any others that were concealed by his clothing, added to the man's imposing presence.

Before she and her daughters went upstairs to prepare for bed, while wishing Santilis goodnight Cristina heard Alexandra ask him about the stranger. Santilis told her that throughout the mining towns of Utah and Colorado, he was the Cretan organizer known as "Giant Petros." When miners were in conflict with owners, when grievances festered and violence seemed imminent, he appeared to join the struggle. His legend had grown, Santilis told Alexandra, until the miners swore he wasn't mortal, but the embodiment of some ancient Cretan spirit.

The meeting of the men carried long into the night. Lying awake in bed in the darkness of her room, Cristina smelled the trailings of smoke from their cigarettes and pipes, and heard the surge and echo of their voices.

She remembered Santilis referring to the stranger as a spirit. He wasn't a spirit, Cristina thought unhappily, but a man of palpable flesh and blood with an aura of primitive energy and violence that might impress an innocent young girl. Now he sat downstairs with the young miners while they recited their complaints about poorly timbered tunnels, working ankle-deep in ice-encrusted water, breathing the dreadful black dust. They told him of the abuses of foremen, who treated them as if they were beasts of burden. When they spoke of the hated labor czar, Leonidas Skliris, their voices grew louder and trembled with rage.

"He's a greedy bastard! They say he lives in a fine hotel with a suite of twenty rooms!"

"What does an honest man need with twenty rooms?"

"If we were in Crete, a bullet would finish the vulture! Maybe that's the way to handle him here!"

Cristina heard Basil's voice, urging moderation and an avoidance of violence.

"There's another way to war on the bastard." She recognized the resonant voice of Leonidas.

"Don't start preaching the union again! A union is for foreigners!"

"Don't you understand we are the foreigners?"

"A union will only take more of our money from us!"

"A union will make the owners listen to us, will join us to other workers who might join our strike!"

The wrangling and contentious voices went on. She couldn't understand why the stranger remained silent. He didn't appear to be a man without an opinion in these matters. Then she imagined him listening, weighing what was being said, waiting until their indecision turned them to him and they asked him what they should do.

Trying to stay awake until she heard him speak, she grew weary. Drifting slowly into sleep, carrying their voices like furies into her dreams, the last thing she remembered was the way the stranger and her daughter had looked at one another.

The week following Alexandra's birthday brought a sequence of warming days. Cristina discarded the old woolen sweater she'd worn to work in the garden. She cleared the last tangle of weeds from the newly sprouted buds. The first petals became visible under the nurturing sun.

She continued to visit the hospital ward each day. Several of the young patients had been discharged and others had taken their places. Lenos had the casts on his legs removed, but the bones hadn't mended properly. With each of her visits, she watched his condition worsen. On a morning in the second week of May, she drew the folk healer, Barba Sotiris, into the corridor outside the ward.

"God knows how much I wish the tidings for the boy were good, Papadia," he said grimly. "For a while I thought we might save his legs. Now, every day, you see how the legs grow worse. I am afraid of . . ."

"Gangrene?" She whispered the dreaded word.

"I think they will have to amputate soon," the old man said sadly.

Cristina made her cross and mumbled a prayer as she entered the ward. She distributed koulourakia and visited with the patients briefly. As soon as she could, she went to Lenos.

The youth lay with his eyes closed, a stubble of beard shadowing his cheeks. One of his bare feet lay outside the blanket, and she stole a glance at his discolored toes. Doubting that he was sleeping, she bent over him and touched his cheek gently. When he looked at her, she saw the terror beneath the moist surface of his eyes.

"You look better today, Lenos!" she lied earnestly. "That's a good sign!"

He didn't answer and, after a moment, she drew several koulourakia from her basket.

"These are freshly baked," she said. "They are—forgive my immodesty—delicious. Would you like one now?"

"Not now, thank you, Papadia," he said. "But put them here, by my pillow, where I can see them."

He continued to stare at her, and she restrained an impulse to cry.

"Papadia, I saw the doctor's face when he examined my legs this morning . . ."

"They'll only do what's best for you, Lenos . . ."

He shook his head, rejecting her words. "Papadia," he said in a low, shaken voice. "Come closer, please."

She bent closer, a tremor pinching her flesh. He clutched her hand.

"Please listen to me, Papadia," he pleaded. "You are a woman like my mother with a mother's loving heart. Make them understand they mustn't cut off my legs! They might as well cut out my heart!"

"Lenos, please . . ." she tried desperately to find words to sustain his spirit.

"Please talk to them, Papadia!" He squeezed her hand until her fingers ached. "If they do such an inhuman thing to me that will be my end. I'll be sent back to my village, a half of a man, a cripple and a beggar! Explain that to them, Papadia! Ask them to show God's mercy and not cut off my legs!"

She sat with him for more than an hour, listening to his pleas, murmuring the same futile words of reassurance. When he finally closed his eyes, she wasn't sure whether it was from weariness or to allow her a chance to leave. She kissed his temple gently, whispering she'd return in the morning. His eyelids fluttered, but he didn't speak.

She walked the length of the ward to the door. The other young men were gloomy and tense, making her anxious to escape.

"Pray for Lenos, Papadia," Stavros said quietly, "and pray for the rest of us as well."

"I will pray for you all," she said.

That evening, Basil didn't come home for dinner. Cristina waited an hour for him, and then she fed Andreas and the girls. After dinner they worked on their school books before the fire and then went up to bed.

Cristina opened the door and looked along the deserted path that ran from the church to the house. A trace of moon glistened across the bell tower. She saw and heard nothing but the wind and, in the distance, from the shanties and rooming houses where the miners lived, the sad strains of a flute. She pulled a shawl around her shoulders and sat before the fire.

She dozed, and was wakened by Basil's steps on the gravel walk. She rose quickly as he opened the door and entered the house. When he walked slowly into the firelight, she saw the tears gleaming like crystals on his cheeks and in his beard.

"The boy Lenos," he said softly. "Tonight they amputated his legs."

She heard a cry wrenched from her soul.

"There wasn't any way to save his legs," Basil said. "Barba

Sotiris told us if they didn't operate, the boy would surely die."

He walked to the fireplace and stood with his head bent, staring into the flames. She waited in silence for him to go on.

"I prayed for him and tried to reassure him," he said wearily. "But the greatest strength for him in his ordeal came from the man Petros. He spoke to the boy gently, yet without pity, and told him a Cretan's heart and spirit would not be lost because he lost his legs." He shook his head slowly. "He remained with the boy all through the operation. I don't know how he endured it. Even waiting outside, the smell of blood almost made me ill."

How strange, Cristina thought, that a man who emanated such an aura of violence could be so gentle. That disparity in his character perplexed and frightened her even more. From the first time she had seen him on the night of Alexandra's party, she'd felt he would change their lives in ways she couldn't foresee.

After a few moments, Basil left the fireplace and picked up the lamp. He started upstairs and Cristina followed him. While he undressed, she removed her dress, stockings and shoes and slipped into her gown. She crawled into bed beside her husband, shivering as she touched his chilled arms and legs.

She held him until she felt warmth returning to his body. From time to time he whispered words she couldn't understand but which she felt were prayers for the stricken boy. She thought of Lenos and how much he'd need her love and devotion in the weeks ahead.

Suddenly, unprompted by any thought or caress, there was a quickening in her blood, a heat rising through her legs. She tried to move away from Basil, fearful he'd think her excitement at such a time licentious and shameful. Then, because he'd sensed her desire or because of his own need, he gently touched her breast. She released her breath with a sigh.

For the first time in months, they made love that night. Afterward they lay together quietly, their hearts linked by a single beat. Basil fell asleep but she remained awake, listening to the sounds of the night. There was a gusting of wind that rattled the frame of the window and the haunting cry of an owl. Even as she grieved for the boy whose legs had been amputated, she couldn't subdue the glow of fulfillment that suffused her body.

"I love you, Father Basil," she whispered to him as he slept.

In that revelatory moment she understood there were hundreds of young men who needed and relied on Basil's strength and faith. She felt herself the means of renewing that strength and faith by taking his pain and weariness into her body. That was the force of womanhood, which Alexandra and Soula would share someday, a power women held since the beginning of time to render bearable the raw, harsh world men wrought for one another.

Grateful for the consolation of love in the sorrowful night, she whispered a prayer for Lenos, for his mother, father, sisters and brother in Crete. She prayed for her daughters and her son, for the young miners so far from home, for the stranger named Petros, who had helped the youth in his time of anguish.

She shifted closer to Basil, her legs touching his legs, her toes grazing his ankle. She closed her eyes and, almost at once, felt herself slipping into a deep and reposeful sleep.

CHAPTER TEN

Manolis

In the spring of 1911, Manolis had been living in Chicago with Vasso for nearly two years. He felt the time to have been longer, because he had lost the cycle of the seasons he had known in Crete. Without planting and harvesting, there wasn't any way for him to mark the passage of a year.

Early each morning he rose and walked the blocks from their apartment to the bakery. He shook the coals beneath the oven in the kitchen and added chunks of wood. As Vasso's husband had done before him, he kneaded the dough to form the loaves of bread. Shortly before he drew the first trays of bread from the oven, Vasso joined him. She'd change from her dress into a white shift and then she'd unlock the front door of the bakery to admit the first customers.

At lunch they'd lock the door for a half hour and snack in the kitchen on bread, sausage and cheese. Afterward Vasso would leave to do some shopping. That was the quietest part of the day for Manolis and, between waiting on an infrequent customer, he'd read the papers and write letters.

Every few months, in answer to one of his letters, his sister Eleni would write to tell him they were well. At the bottom of the page would be labored scrawls from his parents. His

mother's postscript sent love and prayers, but his father's note
asked for word on his mission. Manolis imagined the villagers
questioning his father on the progress of the retribution.
Those notes from his father left Manolis restless and de-
pressed.

He also wrote letters to the family of the priest in Utah.
Sometimes Father Basil or Papadia Cristina answered him
with friendly, solicitous letters. The most faithful corre-
spondent in the family was their younger daughter, Soula. She
wrote Manolis almost every week, warmhearted letters de-
scribing her life in Utah and always asking him how soon he
might come to visit them. He was gratified and sustained by
her affection and looked forward eagerly to her letters.

When Vasso returned to the bakery, in the late afternoon,
he'd leave to visit the old chef, Javaras, in the restaurant
kitchen. Each day, Manolis asked him if there was word from
his uncle Agrios. Each day, the chef's answer was the same.
Finding it harder and harder to explain his impatience and
frustration about his uncle's silence, one day near the end of
his first year in the city Manolis had confided his mission to
the old man.

"Butchers! Assassins!" Javaras cried wrathfully. "You were
right to pursue them to America! Murderers must not go un-
punished! Now I understand why you are frantic for word
from your uncle! I wager he must be hot on those devils' trail!
I know the man and he will not rest until they have been
punished!"

"I hope he doesn't take vengeance without me," Manolis
said. "I pray he has me join him when he finds them!"

"Your uncle Agrios will do what he must do. Trust him!"

But in the months of silence that followed, Manolis grew
more discouraged. He feared his uncle had forgotten him.

"Why hasn't he sent me some word, Barba?" he lamented

to the chef one afternoon. "Just a note telling me where he is
and when he might send for me. That's all I ask."

"Your uncle Agrios is like the wind, my boy," the old chef
said gravely. "Do you carp at the wind when it blows or
doesn't blow? One day he will appear like an avenging angel!
Until then you must be patient!"

After closing the bakery each evening, Vasso and Manolis
returned to the apartment. She shunned any public place
where she'd be recognized as the wife of the murdered Kastris
and they ate dinner at home. Afterward she'd take a bath in
water scented with rose crystals. While he undressed and
washed, she'd light the small incense burner in the bedroom
as well as several candles, which cast a flickering glow across
the bed. She'd wait for him on the bed wearing only a silken
chemise. Slowly, alluringly, she'd unloop the sash and open
the chemise to reveal her naked, glistening body. He'd join
her on the bed and they'd make love.

He couldn't recall how many nights they'd made love since
their initial, fumbling unions. In the beginning Vasso had patiently guided him in ways to please her. After a while he became adept at providing her pleasure. He came to understand
the shadings of a woman's moods, how close her joy could be
to tears.

Vasso loved him, he felt sure, but she also suffered guilt because they were living together in a relationship not sanc-
tioned by the church. Soon after her husband's death, she had
spoken to Manolis of marriage.

"We must wait a proper interval of time," she said, "so that
people will not gossip that I haven't shown respect for the
dead. Kastris was a cruel man and the devil's fool. God forgive him, he deserves nothing. But I don't wish people to
think badly of you and me. Therefore, my darling, we'll have

to wait a year and then we must do what is decent and right. We are bound by our love now, but marriage in a church will sanctify that bond."

Spurred by a sense of obligation and by his affection for Vasso, Manolis agreed they would be married after the mourning period. But when he first told Javaras of their plans, the old man was vehement in his disapproval.

"How many times I've cursed the day I first sent you to their hellish pit!" Javaras said bitterly. "If you have chosen to be her lover now that her husband is gone, that's your affair! But it's madness to think of marriage! Have you forgotten why you came to America? Your uncle Agrios might summon you at any time! He might show up on the day of your wedding! What would you say to him then? 'Forgive me, Uncle Agrios, but our family honor will have to wait because I am getting married!' Shame on you, Manolis, for even considering such a thing!"

"You are right, Barba," Manolis said contritely. "I am grateful that you've reminded me of my first responsibility. I'll explain to Vasso there are personal reasons why we can't marry, at least for a while. I'm sure she'll understand."

"I'm not so sure," Javaras muttered. "Women balk at reason. Give one of them a logical thought and they'll smother it between their tits."

Manolis didn't speak to Vasso that night or in the nights that followed. She was so happy in anticipation of their marriage that he didn't wish to disappoint her. The longer he delayed telling her, the more difficult the explanation became for him. Finally, just before the year of mourning had ended, she asked him to set a date for their nuptials.

"I think October would be a good time," she said. "Let's plan the wedding for the first or second Sunday in October."

"I had a cousin in Crete who married in October," Manolis

said. "The marriage was an unhappy one. October isn't a good month."

"Well, then, we can marry in November. The first Sunday in November will be a good day."

"It's too cold here in November," Manolis said. "We'll be bundled up in heavy coats and it may snow. That isn't a good month."

She looked tensely at him and he grew uneasy under her stare.

"I don't think you're telling me the truth," she said fretfully. "Your unhappy cousin and the cold are not the reason for delay. I think the real reason you're hesitating is because of that girl back in the village you told me about. Do you think I've forgotten her? What was her name? Sofia? Admit it, Manolis, she is the reason, isn't she?"

During the first months he'd been in Chicago, he had enclosed short messages for Sofia in the letters to his sister. She had never answered and he had about given up hope that he'd ever hear from her. But when Vasso brought up her name, he grasped at that reason for the delay.

"There was an understanding about us with her parents," he said. "I don't want to reject her and shame her before the village."

"You'll hurt and shame her more later by letting her dream of a marriage that can never take place," Vasso said. "You are thousands of miles away from Crete. You won't return home for years and she'll never be able to come here. It is cruel to have her pining her youth away for you. Please, Manolis, for her happiness and our happiness, you must write her at once."

Grasping the chance to buy more time, he agreed. The following day he lied to Vasso and told her he'd written Sofia.

"I don't think we should even set a date for our wedding

before I have word from her parents releasing me," Manolis said. "That is the decent thing to do."

The excuse served him a while longer. As the weeks passed into months and there wasn't any word from the village, Vasso grew moody and unhappy. On a night they were lying in bed together, she began to cry. When he made an effort to console her, she pushed him away.

"You don't love me!"

"I do love you, Vasso!"

"You don't! I know you don't!"

"Vasso, don't be a foolish girl! I swear I love you!"

"Then, why do you make me suffer?"

"I don't mean to make you suffer."

"You are cruel! You do make me suffer! I've been kind and generous to you from the beginning and you repay me with ingratitude and cruelty!"

"Vasso, don't say that I'm ungrateful! I know how much you've done for me!"

"Then, if you have any feeling at all for me, Manolis," she said, "tell me the truth! Perhaps you don't want to marry me because you don't respect me? You are like a man who has been sipping the cream for free and sees no reason why it should be paid for! Even Kastris would not shame me as you are doing!"

Shocked by her accusations and stung even more because he knew they contained some truth, he confessed to her the true reason for his hesitation and delays. She was overwhelmed with relief that it was vengeance and not love for another woman that obsessed him.

"Dearest Manolis!" she cried. "What a noble and heroic thing for you to cross the world to avenge your beloved brother! That makes me respect and love you even more than I do already!" She embraced him tightly, kissing his temples and cheeks with ardor. "I swear I will help you take ven-

geance! Now those evil brothers have become my mortal enemies as welll"

Grateful for her understanding and excited by her em-
braces and caresses, he began kissing her and they made pas-
sionate love. Afterward she traced her fingers gently across
his sweated chest.

"Oh, my darling," she whispered. "You are a wonderful
lover and a wonderful man. How fortunate a woman I am to
be able to love you."

"I love you, too, Vasso," he said fervently. In that felicitous
afterglow, he wanted to remain with her forever.

She spoke, finally, in a soft, reassuring voice. "You must
understand, my darling, that the vengeance you seek won't be
easy to accomplish. This is an immense country and you'll
have to find two men when you don't even know what state
they have settled in. They will have changed their names, I'm
sure, and will have taken other precautions to hide their identities."

"They won't escape!" Manolis said. "Uncle Agrios is on
their track now and he'll let me know when it is time to join
him! Those bastards won't escape!"

"Of course you'll find them, darling," Vasso said soothingly. "But the search may take many more years. You
have waited for word from your uncle for two years now and
you must be prepared to wait longer. As your wife, I will join
and aid your vow for vengeance. There isn't any need for us
to delay our marriage any longer."

The following day, Manolis and Vasso locked the bakery in
midmorning and walked to the small neighborhood Greek
church. The swarthy Messenian priest, Father Gregorious,
approved a date for their marriage about a month away.
Knowing the lurid background that had made Vasso a widow,
the priest somberly advised they have a small, unpretentious

wedding. Vasso agreed that only a first cousin of hers from Detroit and a few neighborhood friends would be invited.

Later that day in the restaurant kitchen, Manolis told Javaras of their decision. The old man crossed himself and muttered a few gloomy words.

"I haven't lost my senses, Barba!" Manolis said earnestly. "I think you're being unfair to Vasso. She loves me and accepts the Trombakis brothers as her enemies. She swears after we're married to help me in any way she can. What more do you expect her to do?"

"Perhaps I am unfair," Javaras said. "Perhaps I've grown so hoary and cynical that I no longer trust anyone. But I've always been suspicious of women. She appears to accept your mission now, but she may be wagering she can make you forget your quest for vengeance. When a man is fed and loved, it takes an earthquake to rattle him loose."

"We aren't talking about an earthquake, Barba, but about a wedding," Manolis said. "That is my news today, and I want to ask you to be my best man."

"Your koumbaros!" Javaras said in shock. "Knowing how I feel about this marriage, you still want me as your koumbaros?"

"You're the most treasured friend I have here," Manolis said quietly. "You are closest to my uncle Agrios. There isn't anyone else I'd rather have beside me when I marry Vasso. Please do this for me."

"All right, my boy," the old man said in a low, doleful voice. "God forgive me, I'll hold your wedding crowns."

The following day, Manolis received a letter from Soula. He read it several times in the bakery and carried it home to their apartment that night. Although he usually kept his correspondence in a box in one of the drawers, when he left for work the next morning the letter remained on top of his dresser. An hour later, when Vasso came to the bakery, she stormed up to him and angrily waved Soula's letter in his face.

"So you weren't content with dreaming about a little virgin in Crete!" she said bitterly. "You also have a nymph over here!"

"Vasso!" He stared at her in dismay. "That letter is from the daughter of the priest who befriended me on the voyage from Crete. She's only a child."

"A child, is she?" Vasso tore the letter from the envelope and read from a page, shrilly mimicking the words. " 'I think of you before I go to sleep and light a candle for you each time I go to church.' How touching! How spiritual! What other endearments has she written you?"

"I told you she's only a child! She isn't any more than fifteen!"

"Fifteen is a child? You're the child if you think a girl at fifteen isn't a woman! She is a woman who is in love with you! That's obvious in her letter! She loves you, and your male vanity has probably encouraged her!"

He stared at her face, made ugly and swollen by jealousy and rage. He resisted a compulsion to strike her. She must have seen the storm in his face, for she rushed to hug him in a tight, remorseful embrace.

"Forgive me, my darling!" she cried. "Only my great love for you makes me act the bitch! I have been through so much misery and pain and I feel so insecure! We aren't even married yet and I feel everyone plotting against us! That dreadful old cook you have asked to be our koumbaros hates me! Now there is this virgin in Utah! You might be thinking of a bride unsoiled by marriage and murder! That thought drives me crazy!"

"You're making up your own devils, Vasso!" Manolis said

angrily. "Javaras and Soula are my friends and don't deserve the things you're saying about them!"

"Manolis, my darling, please try to understand," Vasso pleaded. "Forgive my outburst and I will promise to be better . . ."

He reluctantly allowed her to pacify him, venting his aggravation by roughly kneading the dough. They worked in a tense silence, Vasso stealing nervous glances at him. When he thought of what she said about Soula loving him, he was surprised at the glow of pleasure he felt seep through his body.

In the dismal, winter city, spring appeared like a listless messenger dropping meager buds on the branches of stunted trees. In the vacant lot on Blue Island Avenue where the men of the neighborhood dug trenches to barbecue the Easter lambs, drab patches of grass turned a pale green.

Baking extra quantities of bread and pastries for the holidays, Manolis walked to work while it was still dark. Vasso joined him later and they worked until late at night, when they returned to the apartment and climbed wearily into bed. Manolis slept fitfully, while Vasso tossed restlessly beside him. They didn't speak and, in the morning, he rose to begin another weary and monotonous day.

On the Orthodox Sunday of the "Palms," he and Vasso went to church. She had always insisted they enter church separately, a deception Manolis knew fooled no one, since he was aware of the hostile stares leveled at them by the parishioners. Now, emboldened by their forthcoming marriage only a few weeks away, Vasso held his arm tightly as they walked into the nave.

After the service, carrying the small palm crosses, they emerged from church into a balmy spring day. A few patrons from the bakery murmured congratulations and slipped quickly away. Other men and women turned their backs on

them. The rebuffs made Vasso nervous and Manolis angry.
When Vasso turned down the street leading to the bakery, he
pulled her back.

"To hell with the bakery today!" Manolis said. "We have
been working like dogs for weeks. We deserve a day of rest."

Vasso stared at him for a moment and then looked at the
sky. She inhaled deeply. "All right, my darling," she said.
"The day is so lovely, let the baking wait. We'll take a trolley
east to the lake we haven't seen since last October."

They walked to Harrison Street and boarded a trolley that
carried them through the downtown area of the city. At the
lakefront they descended from the car into a throng of men,
women and children. They strolled toward the water, the
scents of spring curling around them. In the distance he saw a
steamer, its silhouette low and gray against the horizon. A
few gulls soared gracefully above the water. The ship and
birds made him think of journeys, and he felt a longing to return to Crete.

"What are you thinking of, my darling?"

"Nothing."

She stared at him uneasily. "I'm glad you made me come
here today!" she said. "We'll do this often after we're married.
In the summer we'll pack our lunch and picnic here in the
park. Would you like that, Manolis?"

"Who wouldn't like it?"

"Then, I promise we'll do it! You'll see I can think of other
things besides work. We must allow ourselves time to enjoy
life!"

A group of children ran by them, shrieking and leaping as
they tossed a ball back and forth.

"Look there, Manolis," Vasso said. "Aren't they beautiful
children?"

"Yes, they are beautiful."

"That golden-haired child resembles a little angel," Vasso

said pensively. She looked at Manolis and he saw tears glistening in her eyes. "I never wanted children with Kastris, because I knew he would be a brutal, uncaring father. But I want to bear your children. Perhaps we could have a little girl like that angel. Would you like us to have a child, Manolis?"

He stared at the child. She was lovely, but he had difficulty casting himself in the role of parent. Vasso waited anxiously for his response and he didn't wish to hurt her, so he smiled and nodded. He was troubled by the joy that illuminated her face.

The following morning, he rose at his usual time and dressed and walked to the bakery. He had just slipped on his apron and was shaking the coals beneath the oven when he heard a rapid knocking at the kitchen door. He opened it and was surprised to see Javaras. The chef wore a battered felt hat and an oversized wool coat. His cheeks were pale and he seemed distraught. He peered nervously past Manolis into the kitchen.

"You're alone?" he asked anxiously.

Manolis nodded and motioned him into the kitchen. Javaras walked quickly to the oven and extended his hands to warm them. He spoke with his back turned to Manolis.

"Late last night, just before closing," he said in a shaken whisper, "a man came to the restaurant asking for me. Gorgios sent him to the kitchen. He brought word from your uncle Agrios . . ."

Manolis felt his heart leap as if trying to escape from his body. He hurried to Javaras and pulled him around. "Where is he? Is he coming here? When will I see him?"

"He's in a city called Denver of Colorado," Javaras said. "He wants you to meet him there right away. You must leave today!"

"Today!" Manolis stared at the chef in shock. "Barba, how can I leave today?"

"I am only a messenger," Javaras said nervously. "You do whatever you want to do. Don't blame me!"

"I'm not blaming you," Manolis said, his voice trembling. "But my wedding is only two weeks away. What will I tell Vasso?"

"I am only a messenger!" Javaras cried. "You do what your conscience tells you is right! Stay and get married if that's what you want!"

"But Uncle Agrios needs me!"

"Then, go to him! A train leaves for Denver at two o'clock today! Be on that train!"

"Will he meet me there?"

"In Denver go to a restaurant in Greek Town called Acropolis. The owner, Skountzos, once worked for me here. Wait there and you'll hear from Uncle Agrios!" As if fearful suddenly that Vasso would catch him in the bakery, he hastened to the door.

"Barba, please, don't go! I need to talk to you!"

Javaras paused at the door. He stared back at Manolis, grimacing as if he were in pain. "Don't blame me, Manolis! I'm only a messenger! You do what you want to do!"

He opened the door and stumbled into the alley. Manolis heard his flurried steps echoing in the stillness of dawn.

He had only a few moments to collect his rattled senses. He knew that to abandon Vasso so close to their wedding was a cruel, heartless act. Yet he couldn't ignore the message from Uncle Agrios he had been waiting two years to hear. What if his uncle had tracked the Trombakis brothers to Denver and was waiting for Manolis before confronting them? Even if he left at once, he might already be too late! The thought swept him with panic! To have waited so long and then be cheated of sharing in the vengeance would torment him for as long as he lived!

The kitchen door opened and Vasso entered. He watched her remove her coat and hang it on a hook. She started to unbutton the bodice of her dress to change into her white shift and saw Manolis staring at her. For a moment, neither of them spoke. Then her hand fumbled to her breast. He saw the agitation of her breathing as if she sensed some calamity.

"Holy Mother Mary," she whispered. "Blessed Mother of Jesus . . ."

"Vasso, listen to me!"

"Holy Mother Mary." She made her cross with trembling fingers. "Blessed Mother of Jesus, protect me now . . ."

"Listen, Vasso, please! My uncle Agrios has found the Trombakis brothers in a city called Denver! He has sent word for me to join him at once! Vasso, I have to leave today!"

He braced himself for her rage, for her tears and pleas. She remained transfixed except for her fingers trembling at her breast.

"I had the dream again last night," she said in a voice so low he could barely hear her. "The same dream I have had for months. I was a bride beside the grave of Kastris."

She paused and, in the silence, the coals cracked and hissed beneath the oven. She drew a labored breath.

"I have seen that dream so many times," she said mournfully. "A bride in a graveyard with a tombstone for an altar and the wind for a priest. When I first saw that dream, I knew we would never marry."

"We will marry, Vasso!" he said earnestly. "I will come back to you! When my brother has been avenged, I will come back!"

She walked slowly to a chair and sat down. "I loved you and wanted you," she said softly, "and when Kastris was murdered, I was glad. That was a sin against God and I am being punished for it now." She clasped her fingers tightly in her lap and stared down at them. "I wore widow's black as if I mourned him, but in my heart I hated him and was glad he was dead. Now God is punishing my sin by taking you away."

"You haven't sinned, Vasso! This hasn't anything to do with you! Uncle Agrios needs me and I can't stay here and betray my honor and my family's honor!"

"Each time I saw that dream I knew we would never marry," she said wearily. "My soul is black with sin and God's wrath is on me."

"Vasso, I'll come back! I swear to you I'll come back as soon as I can and then we'll be married!"

She raised her head to look at him, and he saw her tormented eyes.

"Yes, you'll come back," she said, her voice like a lament. "You'll come back when Kastris comes back."

He left the bakery and returned to the apartment to pack a bag with clothing. From there he went to the bank where he had been depositing money regularly and withdrew most of it, leaving only a small balance. He stopped by the restaurant to say goodbye to Javaras, but the dishwasher told him the old chef hadn't felt well and had gone to his room.

Outside the restaurant, Manolis hailed a taxicab for the station, telling the driver to pass the bakery. The front door was locked and the shade on the glass was drawn. He thought of Vasso grieving inside and felt a surge of remorse.

At the station he purchased his ticket for Denver and sat in the cavernous waiting room. When the loudspeaker announced his train, he hurried to the gate. He handed the conductor his ticket and then looked back toward the station. He thought he saw Vasso standing in the shadow of one of the pillars. He stifled an impulse to rush back to her and waved. He couldn't be sure if the woman waved back.

The conductor called a final boarding. He hurried along the platform and boarded the car. Perhaps, he thought as he took his seat, he hadn't really seen Vasso but another woman who had resembled her.

He spent his time on the train staring out the window, watching the changing landscape. There were farms with huge barns and small towns clustered about the railroad crossings. Then the terrain of level fields changed and he glimpsed a land of mountain ranges that reminded him of the massifs of Crete. The following morning, the train arrived in Denver. Asking directions of a station attendant, he was sent to a shantytown of coffeehouses and cafes.

After locating the Acropolis, he entered a narrow, unpainted lunchroom with a few tables and a dozen stools running the length of a ramshackle counter. The owner, Skountzos, was a somber-faced man with a soiled apron looped about his waist. When Manolis explained that Javaras had sent him, the owner's face lit up. Manolis asked about his uncle Agrios.

"Maybe he comes in here," Skountzos said, "but I don't recognize that name. What does he look like?"

"He is a big man, taller than I am," Manolis said. "You would remember him if you saw him."

"I don't remember anyone like that."

"Do you have any message or letter for me?"

Skountzos shook his head.

"Then, I haven't missed him," Manolis said with relief. "He'll be meeting me here, so I'll have to wait."

"Sit there, close to the door," Skountzos said. "I'll bring you a bowl of soup and a sandwich."

Manolis thanked him and seated himself at the table, where

he could watch the men who entered the cafe. He scrutinized each of them, looking vainly for the fierce-eyed giant he would recognize at once as uncle Agrios.

He waited all afternoon and into the evening. When it grew dark, Skountzos brought him a plate of greens and a salad but refused the money Manolis offered to pay him.

"I owe my life, whatever it's worth, to Javaras," the owner said. "I was drinking myself to death, not an uncommon fate for men who labor in kitchens, and he helped me detour my rush to hell. If you're his friend, you're my friend too. In here, my friends don't pay."

Late that night, the cafe emptied of its last customers, Skountzos came from the kitchen, tugging off his apron.

"I'm closing the dump now, Manolis," he said wearily. "After eighteen hours here I need a few hours sleep."

"Let me wait here, Mr. Skountzos," Manolis said. "My uncle may come during the night."

"You're a good boy with strong family feelings." Skountzos nodded approvingly. "If you're that eager to see your uncle, then wait. I hope he comes soon."

After he had left, Manolis sat in the shadowed cafe, his coat draped about his shoulders against the chill. Men emerged from the coffeehouses along the street, their laughing, drunken voices splitting the darkness. Afterward the street grew quiet. Manolis rested his head in his arms and slept fitfully. He was awake when the first glimmers of dawn lightened the roofs of buildings across the street. Back in Chicago, Vasso would be rising to begin her day. He thought of her working alone in the bakery and felt another pang of remorse.

A short while later, Skountzos opened the lunchroom and brought Manolis a mug of steaming, black coffee.

"Maybe your uncle got delayed," Skountzos said.

"He should be here today," Manolis said.

He waited again all day, staring at each man who entered

the cafe, listening to their surly, cheerful, brooding or jok-
ing voices and to the bitings and suckings they made while
eating.

That night, Skountzos made him a pallet of potato sacks
with a wadded sack for a pillow. After the owner closed the
lunchroom, Manolis lay down on the pallet. Weariness made
him lightheaded and he fought sleep, afraid he'd plunge into
so deep a slumber that he wouldn't hear his uncle hammering
on the door. Finally he slept, and in what seemed only moments later, woke to someone shaking his shoulder.

"Uncle!"

"It's only me, Manolis," Skountzos said regretfully. "I'm
opening the door now and you better get off the floor so the
herd won't trample you." As Manolis rose from the pallet,
Skountzos clapped him reassuringly on the shoulder. "He has
to come soon now," he said. "Meanwhile, would you mind,
my boy, waiting in the kitchen? Some of the customers are
complaining that the way you stare at them makes them think
you're crazy." He grinned and shrugged. "That's the way
things are in this country," he said. "If you show loyalty and
love for your family, they think you're crazy."

Manolis waited that day in the kitchen, sitting beside the
stove or staring through the serving aperture. The day passed
as the others had passed. Late that night, Skountzos sat down
beside him.

"You haven't asked for my advice, Manolis," he said
quietly, "but I'll offer some anyway. You can't keep sitting
here or you will go crazy. You need a real bed and, forgive
me, a bath and a shave. There's a cheap hotel about a block
from here. Get a room there so you can rest properly. We'll
leave a note tacked on the door if your uncle comes during
the hours we're not here. You can return in the morning and,
since you'll be spending so much time here, you can work for

me a few hours a day. I can't afford much but I'll give you something to help pay your rent."

He knew that what the owner was saying made sense. Earlier in the evening he had seen his reflection in the toilet mirror and had been shocked at the gaunt, disheveled countenance that stared back at him.

They closed the lunchroom and walked to the hotel, a dilapidated, two-story frame building with a honeycomb of sleeping rooms. In his cubicle, which contained only a cot and a small table with a candle, Manolis tugged off his shoes and sprawled across the pallet. Beyond the thin wall that separated him from an adjoining room, a man snored in loud, drunken sleep. But, that night, for the first time since leaving Chicago, Manolis slept as if he were in the grasp of death.

Easter Sunday and the week in which he was to have been married to Vasso passed. The beginning of May brought a sequence of warming days. Each morning as he walked from the hotel to the Acropolis, above the roofs of Greek Town he saw the slopes of the mountains gleaming with foliage. The wind carried an aroma of flowers that made him homesick for Crete.

He worked with Skountzos in the lunchroom each day until noon. He spent his afternoons idling in a nearby coffeehouse with about a dozen young Greeks who had been injured or fired from the railroad section gangs. Linked by futility and boredom, they drank and played cards all day and most of the night. Within a few days after joining them, Manolis was drinking and gambling with them.

At night in his room, sitting on the edge of the cot, he wrote his first letters under the light of the candle. He wrote to Javaras telling him of his impatience and asking him to relay any word from his uncle to him as soon as he heard. He wrote to his father, telling him that Uncle Agrios would be joining him soon so they could continue the pursuit. He wrote to Soula in Utah. Without revealing the reason he had come to Denver, he found himself telling her of his loneliness and homesickness for Crete. Finally, he started several letters to Vasso that he never finished or mailed, because he was ashamed to tell her that he hadn't yet heard from his uncle.

The first answer he received, about a month after he had written her, was from Soula. When Skountzos handed him the letter in the lunchroom, he recognized her handwriting with a quiver of pleasure. He took the letter from the owner with assumed indifference and slipped it casually into the pocket of his jacket. All morning he resisted an impulse to open it. As soon as lunch was over, he left the Acropolis. Finding a deserted alley beside a coffeehouse, he took the letter from his pocket and opened it.

> My dear Manolis:
> How surprised I was to hear that you are in Colorado! Papa says there are mountains there like those we have in Utah. Do you realize how close you are to us? We are getting along better in school. Sometimes the whiteheads still call us names but they are afraid of Andreas who fights with them. I become angry too but Mama says we mustn't pay attention to them.
> Summer will be starting here soon. I remember it from last year as a beautiful time. How wonderful it would be if you could come here to share this summer with us. I understand why you feel homesick for Crete. But homesickness is easier to bear if there is someone to share it. That is why you should write me as often as you can. I keep all your letters in a box and, sometimes at night, I

reread them. They are wonderful letters although sometimes you write to me as if I were still a little girl. If you saw me now you'd see I'm not so little anymore. Papa and Mama send their love. Andreas and Alexandra would also send you love if I told them I was writing you but I keep that private. That means you and I share a secret.

I send you prayers that you stay safe and well. I never forget to light a candle for you in church on Sunday.

Your dear friend,
Soula

P.S. I think something special is happening to Alexandra. There is a man here who has come to help the miners and I think she loves him. She hasn't told me that, but she suddenly seems older and not concerned about school or the other things she used to feel were important. I think he loves her, too, not in anything he has said that I've heard but in the way he looks at her.

He finished the letter and read it several more times. Then he folded it carefully back into the envelope and tucked it safely into his pocket.

By the middle of summer there still wasn't any word from his uncle Agrios. He couldn't understand the reason for the silence and he rocked between feelings of frustration and of self-pity. He began drinking more intemperately and remained in the coffeehouse most of the night, stumbling back to his hotel at dawn to fall into a sodden sleep. Unable to rise for work, he apologized to Skountzos and pledged he'd be more diligent. But he couldn't forsake drinking and gambling, because they were his only means to relieve his anxiety and impatience.

He thought of returning to Chicago and Vasso. He considered picking up the search for the Trombakis brothers alone. The possibility that Uncle Agrios might arrive in Denver looking for him an hour or a day after he departed, terrified and immobilized him. So he waited, day after day, continuing to drink and gamble and growing more despondent. At the beginning of his stay in Greek Town he had felt himself different from the men who idled in the coffeehouse, because he had a purpose in waiting and a mission. As the dismal summer wore on, he felt he wasn't any different from the rest of them.

In late August he had a letter from Father Basil with the news that Alexandra was going to be married. An engagement had been announced and the wedding would take place in late September.

> This man she will take as her husband, is remarkable in many ways. He has strength and courage and has quickly become a leader for the men in the mines. He has organized them into the union and brought their grievances into focus. Every night there are stormy meetings and talk of a strike. The owners have hired more coal and iron police and I am fearful of violence. You know how angry our Cretans can be once they have made up their minds and have the right man to lead them.

> But the other side of this man is one of compassion and gentleness. Alexandra loves him, I am sure, and glows with a joy that is awesome to see. Petros has told me he loves her, too, and I believe him and believe he will care for her with all his heart. At the same time, I am uneasy, because I

don't think he is a man destined for a peaceful house and a serene old age.

But I am consoled when I consider that all is in God's hands. He is not concerned with our fears or plans but with his own design, which we mortals can never understand. Meanwhile, Manolis, Papadia Cristina joins me in sending you our blessings and our fervent hope you can visit us soon. All of us, especially Soula, would be overjoyed to see you again. How wonderful if you could come for Alexandra's wedding!

Father Basil

Within a week after receiving the letter from Father Basil, there was another letter for him, a roughly scrawled one from Javaras, which he read in the kitchen of the lunchroom.

I know you will be angry with me, Manolis, and curse me for being a liar and a wretch. God forgive me, for I am both these things. Let me tell you now that Vasso has just married a man who came from Greece in the spring and who worked for her all summer in the bakery. They were married in the church last Sunday.

Meanwhile, God help me, I am now free to tell you that there was never any message from your uncle Agrios. I invented the message to prevent you being married. I felt responsible for first sending you into that hellhole and for allowing you to fall into that woman's clutches. You never had a chance with her, because she was older, more experienced, and tainted by blood and murder. I could not sit by and watch your life destroyed.

So, Manolis, there is the grim truth of how your friend betrayed you. You will probably hate me and

curse me, which I deserve, and if you come back to
Chicago, you might want to beat me, which I deserve. But I did what I thought was best for you
so try not to hate me too much. Your disgraced
friend,

Javaras

Manolis finished the letter and reread it with his fingers
trembling and a heat searing his body. He was shocked because he didn't feel any anger or resentment at Javaras. He
felt liberated, as if the letter had discharged him from prison,
released him from his aimless and dissolute days and nights.
He would write Javaras to relay any message he received
from Uncle Agrios to him in Utah.

He hurried from the kitchen into the street and stared
across the roofs of Greek Town toward the mountains, the
great ranges running westward to Utah. He inhaled deeply,
feeling his lungs filling with breath and joy for the first time in
all those oppressive months. Then he walked back inside the
lunchroom to tell Skountzos he would be leaving.

CHAPTER ELEVEN

Stellios

On the night that Stellios first walked into the house of the priest in Snowmass, Utah, and saw Father Basil's young daughter Alexandra, his soul churned and the earth trembled beneath his feet. The girl's slender body, glossy dark hair and great dark eyes made her the most stunning vision he had ever seen. Shortly after the dance ended, miners gathered around him and, for the rest of the evening, he didn't get a chance to see her again. But the memory of her loveliness haunted him.

In the days that followed, as he met with the Cretan miners and listened to their grievances, a vision of the girl kept returning to him. He thought of her during the day, in the final moments before he slept at night in his rooming-house bed, the instant he opened his eyes in the morning. Her misted beauty also appeared to him in his dreams.

When he caught a glimpse of her in church or walking in the town with her mother, another aspect of her loveliness was revealed. He had first noticed her beauty and grace as she danced. Later he was caught by her beguiling smile, which seemed to warm the space around her. Young as she was, she revealed a poise beyond her years.

They finally met, in church on his second Sunday in Snowmass, when Alexandra was introduced to him by Santilis. Surrounded as they were by men in the crowded narthex of the church, her eyes struck like arrows into his body. As he murmured the familiar words used in greetings, he felt once again that strange, bewildering bond between them he'd experienced the first night he'd seen her.

But the powerful attraction she had for him was also disconcerting. He had come to Snowmass to organize the miners into the union and to dissuade them from any precipitous action against the padrone and the mine owners. These tasks required all his energy and whatever conciliatory skills he had acquired while organizing miners in a score of towns. He hadn't time to daydream about a dark-haired beauty who had burst like a flower upon his barren heart.

He tried to discourage his longings by admitting they were hopeless. Despite her mature appearance, he knew the girl was still very young. He was penniless, without any possessions beyond the shabby clothing on his back. The girl herself, innocent and protected in the sanctuary of her family, might be repelled by him. Her parents would find him roughhewn from a life of disorder and violence. The most sensible thing he could do to end his lunacy was to finish his work in Snowmass and move on.

After all these reasonings, the vision of Alexandra brought a softness into his spirit. In the gray mill town, desolate as all the mining communities he had known, he was drawn suddenly to the song of a bird, a wind at twilight carrying the scent of flowers, the summer stars strewn like jewels in a midnight sky.

Finally, with an awe and reverence unlike any feeling he had ever experienced, he understood that for the first time in his life he was in love.

The summer continued through a series of warm days followed by a cooling at twilight. When dark clouds swirled over the mountains and rain fell, for a while the grittiness of the air was cleared, but the pall of dust quickly returned. Even after they scrubbed themselves, the dust smeared men's hands and faces like rust.

Stellios worked hours each day with small groups of miners to make them understand how the union might help them gain better housing and sanitation, and safer conditions in the pits. While the men listened to him and seemed to trust him, they were resentful of discipline and suspicious of any curb on their individual freedom. In Crete, a man settled his own grievances with fists or a gun or he wasn't a man. Unions and other associations were signs of weakness. Frustrated by their stubbornness, Stellios understood their temper and adamant pride, because he remembered how much he had once been like them.

He had to be cautious, because his meetings had to be kept small and held in secret. He hadn't any wish to be caught by the Coal and Iron Police again. The last time he'd been beaten by company deputies had left him with three broken ribs and passing blood in his urine for a month. Afterward they'd thrown him into a freight car and ridden him out of town. He didn't want that to happen again. He wanted to stay in Snowmass and finish his work. He also knew he wanted to remain because of Alexandra.

In the middle of July, the mine whistle screeching near noon signaled an accident in the tunnels. Stellios ran to join the crowd around the shaft entrance. He volunteered to join the first rescue crew to descend in the cage. They worked underground all day and at twilight had carried to the surface

nine injured men and the blanketed bodies of two dead
miners.

The funeral held for them in the Snowmass church was less
mournful than angry. The pine coffins of the dead miners
were ringed by several hundred grim young men, some
openly brandishing pistols, which were illegal.

After the funeral, the miners held a stormy meeting in the
church. Several men called for a strike, blaming the injuries
and deaths on faulty timbering in the mine. A few more militant Cretans supported an armed assault against the houses of
the mine managers to "teach the dogs a lesson!"

Stellios argued earnestly against either action. They weren't
yet strong enough to make a strike effective, he warned them,
and violence would only bring violent reprisals against them
by police or soldiers. He asked them to wait, making their
grievances about safety conditions part of a protest to include
their meager wages, short-weighing at the scales, and the unfair power of the padrone. When he finished, a young miner
spoke bitterly against him.

"I think this man, this legend in the coalfields, hasn't anything to say to us! He prattles that we should stay patient
while our friends are injured and killed! I thought he came
here to lead us in a war we know must be fought if we're ever
going to hold up our heads like men! Now I find that isn't
true! So to hell with his cursed union, and I will never again
attend any meeting he calls!"

When he finished his tirade, the young miner, followed by a
few of his friends, strode in fury from the church. The men
who remained muttered uneasily. Then Father Basil rose to
speak. In his black cassock he stood before them, a somber
and paternal figure.

"I haven't known Petros any longer than the rest of you,"
he said quietly, "but I know he isn't afraid of wars and bat-
tles. His wounds and scars are proof of what he has suffered

to help other miners. And he was among the first men down into the mine to bring up our boys. No, that isn't the action of a timid man. If he preaches restraint and patience now, it is because he has learned that that is the only way to achieve the reforms you need. So I beg you to curb your passions, my sons. Violence will not bring Kostakis and Demetri back to us. So listen to Petros. His counsel would be my counsel. Help him to help us all."

The men quieted down then and in a while dispersed. As they left the church, Stellios passed close to the priest, who waited by the door. For an instant their glances met and Stellios nodded his gratitude and thanks. The priest smiled faintly, affirming their comradeship and bond.

From that day, Stellios was emboldened to spend more time at the priest's house. He'd bring the Papadia a chicken, a brace of rabbits he had trapped, a few eggs someone had given him as a gift. When she protested that he was depriving himself of these provisions, he reassured her his needs were few, while she had to feed a family. In the beginning of his visits he sensed some distrust in her attitude toward him, and he wondered uneasily if she had divined his interest in her daughter. After a while she seemed pleased to see him. He tried to strengthen his acceptance by performing chores for her. He repaired items of furniture and built new ones. He made a cabinet for Andreas and a hope chest for Soula. He didn't trust himself to build anything for Alexandra.

He grew fonder of the family and wished it were his own. He understood why the young miners loved the Papadia. In addition to her daily hospital visits, she never turned a visitor away. She and her daughters served a flow of sweets and tea. The clay oven outside their house, reminiscent to Stellios of the ovens outside the houses in the villages of Crete, always smoked with the aroma of baking pastries.

In addition to serving the miners, she brought some of the

breaker boys from their tents and shacks so she could wash their hair in the large tub in the yard. She also mended their stockings and washed their clothing, which often crawled with lice.

"They are so young to live so wretchedly," she lamented to Stellios one day. "They are little more than children, who should still be in school or at play."

"They need to work to live, Papadia," Stellios said. "No one will feed them if they don't. And the mine managers can hire them for a fraction of the wage they pay a grown man. Our union wants to correct these abuses and help them."

"Father Basil tells me you preach a peaceful doctrine, Petros," she said. "Can these abuses be corrected peacefully?"

"I will preach peace until the men are united in a strong union," Stellios said. "Then we'll demand an end to the abuses. The owners will decide whether that is done peacefully or by war."

"If it is war, then will you lead the men?"

"That leadership will be up to wiser men than me," Stellios said. "I am an organizer, an ordinary worker with a task assigned to me. There are other organizers like me throughout the mines."

"I know nothing about unions and strikes"—the Papadia shook her head slowly—"but I know you're not an ordinary man, Petros. That much is evident not only to me but to others in our house."

"After such encouragement, Papadia"—Stellios turned aside to conceal the flush he felt in his cheeks—"I will return to building your new kitchen table with even greater zest."

Each of his visits to the priest's house was made with the fervent hope of seeing Alexandra. Most of the time, there were others present with her as well: family friends or her brother and sister. Though he yearned to be alone with her, on those rare occasions when that occurred, he was hesitant and nervous about what to say to her.

On an afternoon at the beginning of August, Stellios carried chairs from the Papadia's kitchen outside under a tree to scrub them with a wire brush and limewater. He had been at work only a short while when Alexandra emerged from the house. His pulse beat faster, but he continued scrubbing the wood vigorously.

She left the porch and walked slowly toward him. He was conscious of the flow of air between them altering, becoming warmer and more turbulent the closer she came. When she reached him, he could not resist looking at her. She was dressed in a simple cotton frock, her slender legs bare, her flesh glistening in the sunlight that filtered through the branches of the tree.

"Can I help you, Petros?"

He shook his head. "This won't take me long. Besides, this isn't proper work for you."

"What is proper for me?" Her voice flared with defiance. "Shall I sit demurely in the parlor, my hands folded in my lap obediently, until some man issues me a command?"

He stared at her in surprise. "I didn't mean that, Alexandra," he said. "I meant only that you'd soil your dress."

She watched him in silence for a moment and then stepped forward to pick up the brush he had put down. She bent and scrubbed the wooden seat of one of the chairs, her arm sweeping vigorously back and forth, while she ignored the suds that splashed her dress. When she straightened up, he nodded at her contritely.

"You are as good a chair scrubber as any man," he said.

She accepted his apology gravely. He felt restless under the level gaze of her dark eyes.

"You come here to see us almost every day," she said

quietly. "You always bring something or you build chests and tables and wash chairs. Why are you so good to us?"

He frowned at the brush. "As I explained to your mother, I don't have a family and my needs are few and I have time . . ."

"I know what you've told my mother," she said. "Is there anything else you want to tell me?"

The directness of her question rattled him. He tried to answer, but the words tangled on his tongue.

"I think sometimes you might be coming to see me," she said softly. "But you pay less attention to me than any of the rest of my family. I might just be another piece of furniture."

"Alexandra! How can you say such a thing?"

"Because I've been waiting for weeks for you to say something to me or to my parents," she said. "Every time you leave, I have the feeling that something has been left unspoken."

He watched her, his heart hanging on her words.

"I may be young, Petros," she said, "but there are things between men and women that even a young girl understands. I see the way you look at me when I enter or leave the room. I would be a foolish child if I didn't notice that or the way you watch me sometimes when you think I'm not looking at you."

"Alexandra! I haven't meant to offend you! Forgive me!"

"You haven't offended me, Petros," she said gravely. "If you are eager to come to our house, I'm pleased to have you here. I felt those feelings the first night you entered our house, on my birthday."

He had dreamed of her so often that for a shaken, bewildered moment, he thought her words might be part of the dream.

"You may think me a shameless girl for saying these things," she said, and for the first time her voice trembled, "and you may never want to see me again. If that's true and you never return to our house, I will mourn you as I would someone dear I have lost, and I will understand that a girl must never talk this way to a man. But if you feel the way I think you feel about me, Petros, then please, I beg you, speak to my father."

She finished and waited, giving him a chance to speak. He absorbed her words and their meaning. He drew a deep breath and tried to choose his own words with care.

"God help me, Alexandra"—his own voice trembled—"I haven't dared to speak because you're young and lovely and because I have nothing! No property, not a single horse or sheep, not a solitary fruit tree so we might be assured of an orange or a peach for dinner. I don't feel worthy of touching the hem of your skirt, and your father would be right to horsewhip me for daring to think about you. If this were Crete, your brother would shoot me for the way I looked at you!"

"We're not in Crete," she said firmly. "This is America. Men and women have more freedom here. My brother wouldn't have any right to shoot you for feeling the same things I feel."

He found it hard to curb his jubilation. "All right, Alexandra," he said. "This is America. And since you tell me you don't think I'm a lunatic, I will talk to your father! He may not be as kind as you, but, yes, Alexandra, I will talk to him!"

"Good," she said quietly. "Good." She turned then and started walking back to the house. After crossing a short distance, she turned back. She raised her hand and waved to him, a gesture so gentle and bewitching that he felt as if her fingers caressed his face. Then she hurried into the house.

Stellios tossed sleeplessly that night and rose before dawn to walk to the church. A score of men were already there to see the priest, and he reconciled himself to waiting several hours in the line. He didn't mind waiting, except that it provided him time to consider the outrage of the priest when Stellios told him what he wanted.

A few moments later, Father Basil emerged from the nave with one of the men and saw Stellios. The priest asked the next man to wait and motioned Stellios inside.

"I'll be glad to wait my turn, Father," Stellios whispered to him.

The priest shook his head. "The others are here almost every day," he said. "But I've never seen you in line before. Come in, my son."

They walked through the silent, incense-scented church to stand in the sacristy beneath the stern saints in the icons.

Stellios began to speak in a low, tense voice. "Father, I've been thinking all night of ways to make sensible what I wish to ask you," he said ruefully, "but there isn't any way. So I will ask first for your forgiveness, and then this fool would like to ask permission to call on your daughter Alexandra."

His words rang hollow and absurd in the silent church. He waited in suspense for the priest to answer.

"You're not a fool, Petros," the priest said gently. "You've been discreet and proper in our home, but your admiration for our Alexandra has been evident to the Papadia and me." He paused. "She is still quite young, but she's also mature in some ways. The Papadia was like that when she was Alexandra's age."

"If she didn't want my attentions or if she preferred someone else," Stellios said, "I'd never bother her again."

"I don't think that will happen," the priest said. "She looks on you favorably too, Petros, so even if I were to forbid you seeing her, she has a rebel's spirit in the tradition of our island that has bred so many great rebels." He paused again as if hesitant how to continue. "No, Alexandra will accept you, I think, because you are a good, courageous man respected by other men. The Papadia and I have grown to respect and care for you too, but I must tell you, candidly, some things I fear. You are a man with a mission. You've been hounded by the police, jailed and beaten. You'll be beaten again, perhaps seriously injured. God help us, if you are injured seriously or jailed for a long time, Petros, what will become of your wife someday? What will become of your children?"

Stellios nodded, accepting the justice of the priest's concern. "I believe in my work, Father," he said gravely, "and cannot give it up. There is danger in it, I know, but if I'd remained a miner and was married to Alexandra, there would also be danger of my injury and death, as other young men have been entombed in those mines. As none of us can know our fate, I do not know mine. All I can pledge is that while I live I'll protect and love Alexandra as you and the Papadia have done up to now."

The priest did not speak again for what seemed to Stellios a long time. The flames from the candles in the sacristy shone on his troubled face. For a desperate moment, Stellios feared he might refuse his plea.

"You have my permission to call on Alexandra, my son," the priest said finally.

"Thank you, Father." Stellios tried to speak quietly, but he was sure the leaping in his blood betrayed his voice. He bent and quickly kissed the priest's hand, feeling his fingers moist and trembling. Afterward Father Basil embraced him.

"God bless you, my son, and keep you safe," he said softly, "for the miners, for Alexandra, and for us."

In the days that followed his visit with the priest, Stellios rose zestfully each morning to do his work with renewed resolve. The miners winked slyly at one another about the reason for his rejuvenation.

He spent as many hours as he could spare from his activities in the house of the priest. Each time he entered the door and Alexandra ran to greet him, he was overwhelmed by her beauty and his good fortune. Nothing in his life made him believe he deserved such a bounty.

Although he had a new status as a suitor, producing wry glances and some giggling from Andreas, Stellios still had scant time alone with Alexandra. Because they were often in the company of family and friends, their contacts were confined to covert glances, quick smiles, a few fleeting words.

Sometimes as he was leaving, at the end of the evening, the Papadia took mercy on them and allowed them the last few minutes alone. On one such night as they stood obscured in the shadows outside the door, they kissed for the first time. For hours afterward Stellios tasted a fragrance of honey on his tongue.

In that month of August, the family discussed their intention to marry. Father Basil and Papadia Cristina wished for them to wait until the spring. Although Stellios agreed to the delay, Alexandra was insistent about being married in the following month.

"Why should we have to wait?" Alexandra asked fervently. "We know we love each other! Then, let us start our lives together! I wish to be married before the winter begins!"

Her parents wavered and she pleaded with them. They finally agreed. The priest smiled wryly at Stellios.

"I told you she was a rebel," he said. "Once she sets her mind, she moves like an earthquake."

"Only in matters of love and marriage, Papa," Alexandra said.

The following Sunday, after mass, Father Basil announced the impending marriage and invited everyone in Greek Town to the wedding and reception. The miners couldn't resist cheering, and outside the church, they surged about Stellios and Alexandra to offer their best wishes and congratulations. Stellios sympathized with the men, who envied him, and once again he wondered why he had been chosen for such a singular reward.

On an afternoon about a week after the announcement of their engagement, he sat having tea in the kitchen with the Papadia, Alexandra, Soula and Andreas. In addition they were joined by the old healer, Barba Sotiris, and the circuit-riding midwife, Kyra Aspasia, who had stopped briefly on her way through Snowmass to bring Alexandra and Stellios a small wedding gift. She was a robust woman of uncertain age who delivered Italian, Japanese, and Slav as well as Greek babies in mining settlements all over Carbon County. She was also a fortune-teller, famed for her canny divinations.

She regaled them for almost an hour with dramatic stories of last-minute deliveries. She was unsparing in her descriptions and appraisals.

"In the end, all babies come out the same," she told them, "shriveled little pullets streaked in slime and blood and bawling because they have to leave the warm nest of the womb for this wicked world."

"Kyra Aspasia is right about that much," Barba Sotiris said. "Birth and death are the only moments when the mystery is intelligible."

"God be praised!" the midwife exclaimed and made her cross. "For once, this fashioner of poultices and setter of bones makes sense! Memorialize this moment, Papadia!"

"We'll remember it, Kyra Aspasia." Papadia Cristina smiled. "Would you like more tea and another piece of baklava?"

"I must be on my way," Kyra Aspasia said. "There is a

woman in Provo who is nearing her labor. Thank you any-way." She pushed back her chair to rise.

"Kyra Aspasia, please tell my fortune before you go!" Andreas pleaded.

"And mine!" Soula said.

"You're both too young yet," Kyra Aspasia said brusquely. "Your characters and destiny are still unformed."

"Then, how about Barba Sotiris?" Andreas motioned at the old praktikos. "He has to be old enough."

"He's too old for me to bother with," Kyra Aspasia scoffed. "Whatever is going to happen to him has happened already."

"I'm grateful to be spared your nonsense," Barba Sotiris grumbled.

"Then, tell Mama's fortune!" Soula said.

"Your mama knows her fortune." Kyra Aspasia grinned. "Being the wife of a parish priest decrees her fate. That's God's domain and I don't interfere."

"Since they won't let you go until you tell someone's for-tune, Kyra Aspasia," Alexandra said, "please tell mine." She smiled across the table at Stellios.

"All right, Alexandra," the midwife said. "You're only a breath older than these two, but you have the glow of a woman on the threshold of a new adventure. I'll tell your for-tune." She motioned to Soula and Andreas. "Bring me a dish with three spoons of honey," she said, "three almonds, a spoon of olive oil, and a raw egg."

Soula and Andreas hurried to bring the items Kyra Aspasia requested. As the old woman assembled them before her and motioned to Alexandra to sit closer, Stellios felt an uneasiness chill his flesh.

Kyra Aspasia dropped the almonds into the honey and added a few drops of oil.

"Stir it now," she said to Alexandra. "Make sure all your fingers and your thumb are moistened."

Alexandra grimaced as she dipped her fingers into the liquid. She stirred it for a moment and then withdrew her hand. Kyra Aspasia quickly broke the egg into the dish. The yolk floated on the surface, while the white infiltrated the honey and oil, creating tributaries dominated by a sun and a triad of stars. Everyone fell silent as the midwife stared intently into the design.

"You will become even more beautiful . . ." she began.

"Listen to the woman!" Barba Sotiris snickered. "Anyone with eyes can see the girl is a beauty now! How's that for fortune-telling?"

The midwife ignored him. "Two will become one . . ." she said in a low voice.

"Of course!" Alexandra clapped her hands in delight. "When two people marry, they become one!"

Stellios wished to believe that was the link the midwife foresaw, but the cold foraged deeper through his bones.

"I see mountains, trees, rocks," the midwife said. "There is a bird . . . larger than a fox . . . larger than a sheep . . ."

"This gets more fantastic every minute!" Barba Sotiris whispered. "Andreas, my boy, look out the window. Above the mountains, rocks, and trees, which are clearly visible, look for a flying unicorn!"

Kyra Aspasia did not seem to hear him. She stared intently into the liquid, the veins in her temples pulsing with the effort of her concentration. For an instant, Stellios thought a shudder swept her body. Then she pushed the dish aside roughly, spilling honey over the rim.

"There are cynical spirits at this table!" she snapped, and glared at the old man. "For that reason I cannot see the girl's destiny clearly."

"Simply your fading eyesight, Kyra!" Barba Sotiris cackled. "Keep on delivering babies and leave the fortune-telling to the Gypsies!" He nodded knowingly at Stellios, as if the midwife's failure confirmed that she dealt in nonsense.

Kyra Aspasia rose from the table to exchange farewells. Before she left the kitchen, Stellios caught the midwife staring at him. He saw her expression only fleetingly, but that was long enough to discern her grim, mournful face.

Soon after her departure, Stellios left the house himself. He needed the darkness and solitude so he might unravel the ominous revelation he had witnessed in her face. The more he thought about it, the more certain he became that she had glimpsed his blood-stained past. He had been living an illusion, imagining he might keep his baneful past hidden. As the midwife sought to foretell the future of Alexandra, she had divined his murder of Aleko in Crete, the hanging of his brother, Mitsos, the deception behind his name. Her aborted prophecy was a warning that he mustn't marry Alexandra until he had first told her the truth.

But, in the burdened, gloomy days that followed, he also understood that his confession might lose him Alexandra. That prospect filled him with despair and, wrestling with the dilemma, he avoided seeing her until they met in church the following Sunday morning. He found her anxious and puzzled about the reason for his absence. After the liturgy had finished, realizing a decision to speak couldn't be postponed any longer, he borrowed a horse and buggy from Santilis. He asked permission from Papadia Cristina to take Alexandra for a ride and, when she consented, he and Alexandra rode away from the church along the path that led up the foothills of the mountain.

They rode in near silence for an hour, absorbing the blooming summer. They paused, finally, in a small clearing surrounded by fragrant pine trees and clusters of wildflowers. Farther up the mountain, a stream surged water across the rocks, that bubbling, spraying sound mingling with the cries of birds that wheeled and soared above the peaks of trees.

Stellios tethered the horse to a tree and spread a blanket from the buggy beneath a pine tree. Alexandra sat down close to him, smoothing her dress, watching him. Her cheeks were flushed and warm, her black, glossy hair glinting with flecks of blossoms blown from the flowers. His breath caught in his throat before her beauty.

"Alexandra," he said quietly, "there are some things I must tell you. Promise, my darling, to let me finish before you speak."

She stared at him uneasily and then nodded slowly. He struggled to begin, his attention suddenly caught by a monarch butterfly, its colorful, delicate wings skimming the air. He followed the butterfly until it had disappeared into the foliage, and then he began to speak.

Haltingly at first, he told Alexandra about his past, beginning with his rough and brutish youth in Crete, his envy of Aleko and his rage. With his voice singed by shame, he confessed the murder of Aleko, his flight with Mitsos to America, their labor in the camp at Crow Mountain. He told her about the steadfast Buzis, the battle with Mishima and how he and Mitsos had fled, and the pursuers with their hounds who caught them. When he came to the death of his brother and his own miraculous escape, she didn't speak but slowly raised her hand to fumble beneath his beard so she might feel the scar the noose had left around his throat. When her fingers touched the ridged, leathery flesh, she cried out at how close he had come to death.

After finishing he braced himself for her bitterness or anger. He wasn't prepared for the way she flung herself into his arms. She held him fiercely, crying with what he came in wonder to understand were compassionate and forgiving tears. He was touched and thankful, but he also felt a strange exhaustion that came of his purged heart.

She remained in his arms in silence for a while. The movement of sunlight through the pine trees altered the patchwork of shadows around them.

"My dearest," she said quietly, "how much you've suffered."

"I made others suffer more," Stellios said. "Aleko's family, the little Buzis, my poor brother, Mitsos. I was guilty and they were not."

"But you have made amends in your life," Alexandra said earnestly. "You have repented, changed your ways, and now you help others. God will forgive you."

"None of us can speak for God, Alexandra."

"He is merciful! I know He is! He has forgiven you; otherwise, why would He bring us together?"

"He is merciful, but He is also just," Stellios said quietly. "As long as I live, my crime cannot be erased. Whatever retribution He chooses for me will be deserved."

"No!" she cried. "I won't let you be punished! I will intercede for you with God! Our love will prove we deserve His mercy!"

"Our love will help, I know," Stellios said. "But one thing only might have saved me."

"What is that?"

"To have Aleko still alive."

"But that isn't possible!"

"I know," he said, his voice low and resigned. "God help me, I know."

They sat quietly while he felt her fingers padding lightly across his cheeks, caressing his temples, gently stroking his beard.

"Do you think I'm wicked for touching you?" she asked softly.

"No, my darling," he said. "You're not wicked, but you're young and don't understand how touch can court fire."

"I am young, yes!" she said defiantly. "But I am also in love! And a woman in love is ageless, whether she is sixteen or sixty! And here, my beloved, on the mountain in this nest of flowers, I want us to make love!"

Her words caused a tension in his limbs, while the scents of flowers made him dizzy.

"In Crete men are killed for touching a girl's head-scarf," he said.

"Are you afraid, if we make love, that my father would kill you?"

"A hundred men would gladly do it for him." He shook his head. "But that's not what I fear. Your father and mother trusted me to take you alone on the mountain. I don't want to violate their trust."

Even as he spoke of obligations, he couldn't suppress a curious longing that assailed his body. Making an effort to restrain himself, he tried to break free of her and rise.

"Listen to me, dearest!" she whispered. "I'm not a child and I want us to make love now. In a few weeks we'll be married and share our wedding bed for as long as we live. But I want this moment when you confessed everything to me to be sealed forever between us!"

There was desire in her voice, but there was also a fear, a woman's premonition of something he couldn't understand.

"Alexandra . . . you listen to me . . ."

"No!" She shook her head. "No!" She clung to him tightly and he felt the beat of her heart, a pulse that traveled from her flesh to his body. Looking into her great, sensitive eyes, which endowed her face with an almost unearthly radiance, he began to caress her, gently, tenderly, in a way he had never caressed any woman before. At the same instant, he wanted to cry out to the sky and the mountain to bear witness to the purity of his love.

Their bodies seemed adrift among flowers, the pine needles fell across her cheeks, her skin glowed in the specklings of sun. He moved closer to her, their lips whispering endearments. In their caresses her bodice was loosened and he saw the flawless mound and nipple of her virginal breast. He felt his heart burst open and all his years of wretchedness and grief take flight.

Once, in that passage of time, she cried out in pain, but also in delight. Afterward she bled and, remorseful, he paused, but she came urgently into his arms once more. When their bodies finally came to rest, deeper shadows encircled the trees. He plucked the pine needles from her hair, moving his body to protect her against the coolness. He felt her breath warm and moist on his cheek and lips.

"Now we have made a baby," she said quietly.

She spoke so gravely, he couldn't resist smiling.

"Babies are not made that easily."

"That's how little you know," she said. "A baby is created when a woman feels so much love that the union between her and her lover becomes sacred. That is the way I feel now."

He was touched by her words and hugged her again.

"We better start back," he said. "It will be getting dark soon."

They rode in the buggy down the mountain, listening to the trilling of cicadas, watching the arc of the sun's descent. Alexandra held his hand and, from time to time, turned her head to kiss his shoulder. Beyond the sun, the faint outline of the moon became visible. He could never remember seeing sun and moon in such convergence, as if they were journeying on an earth removed from the one he had known.

They entered the pall of smoke over the mining settlement and passed the church. When they reached the priest's house, he jumped down from the seat and helped Alexandra descend. Soula burst from the front door and ran to the buggy.

"I've been waiting for you for hours!" she cried excitedly to her sister. "He's here! He came while you were gone! Come inside quickly!"

"Who is here?" Alexandra asked. Soula didn't wait to reply but hurried back inside the house.

"You go inside," Stellios said. "I'll take the horse around to the stable." He didn't tell her that he wanted a few moments alone to compose himself before he confronted her father and mother. As if she understood, she stretched on her toes and kissed him lightly.

As Alexandra walked into the house, he led the horse around the back and tied him to a rack beside a trough of oats. Moving to the door, he passed a window and saw the family clustered inside. Pausing to see who else was with them, he felt suddenly as if a knife had plunged into his belly to pierce his entrails. He stepped forward, pressing his face against the glass, uncaring that they might see him staring in like a madman at the face of Aleko. Then he realized it wasn't Aleko, but his brother, Manolis, who had been on the wagon with Aleko the day of the murder.

For an instant, he wavered at the edge of the earth. He understood that all that had transpired on the mountain was simply a prelude for this moment of revelation. A name could be changed, an identity concealed, an ocean and a continent spanned. But, from the time of the Furies, an ancient law decreed that a man must take vengeance on the slayer of his brother. Only then could the curse be torn from the blood and the dead find their rest.

Stellios knew that Manolis had pursued him to kill him for the murder of his brother. Even as he weighed the merciless, irrevocable justice of that mission, panic and terror seized him and he ran like a coward into the night.

CHAPTER TWELVE

Manolis

When Manolis had arrived by train in Salt Lake City, he made arrangements to travel on to Snowmass in a wagon hauling freight to mining towns. He began his journey at dawn on Sunday, sitting on the seat beside the driver.

They rode for hours through a landscape of huge rocks shaped by erosion into strange looming forms. He stared at them in awe, thinking of the Titans in legend. This was a terrain marked for valorous men and heroic deeds, reinforcing his conviction that he was entering a new, fruitful period of his life.

By late afternoon, they had arrived in the outskirts of Snowmass. The wagoneer dropped him on a path below the Greek church, and he hurried toward it, his canvas bag slung across his shoulder. Passing the graveyard, he quickly made his cross, and then beyond the church he saw the house Soula had described to him in her letters. Tears moistened his eyes, and he hastily wiped them away.

A group of young men smoking outside the house stared at him curiously. When he entered the front door, he saw more men inside, and he was disappointed the family wasn't alone. Then he caught sight of the small, slender figure of Papadia

Cristina, almost hidden within a ring of tall men. He called her name and hurried to greet her. She embraced him warmly, and their jubilant greeting brought Father Basil from an adjoining room. Manolis bent to kiss his hand, but the priest pulled him into his arms and hugged him. Andreas joined them, taller and bigger than Manolis remembered. Finally, he saw Soula and couldn't believe she was the slim child he'd last seen the day their ship landed at Ellis Island. She had grown much taller; only her pale face and large, dark eyes resembling the girl he'd remembered. She started shyly to extend her hand to him and then moved impulsively to kiss him quickly on the cheek. He caught a scent of flower blossoms in her hair.

After he had met a number of the young miners, the Papadia took him to the kitchen and served him a plate of okra with a glass of wine. While he ate, Soula sat on a nearby stool. From time to time, he looked at her. She smiled, and then averted her eyes. Once again he found it hard to believe how much she had changed.

Later in the evening, after most of the young miners had departed, Alexandra and her fiancé returned from their ride up the mountain. When they heard the buggy, Soula ran out to tell her sister the news of Manolis' arrival. A few moments later, Alexandra entered the kitchen. If he was surprised at the changes in Soula, he was stunned at Alexandra. She was, he had to admit, even more beautiful than her lovely younger sister, but, in addition, she evidenced a radiance that seemed to light the darkest corners of the room. As she hugged him, she told him how delighted she was that he'd be present for her wedding.

"I don't know what's taking Petros so long." She peered out the window. "Andreas, will you please go and tell him to hurry?"

She turned again to Manolis.

"You would never guess who our best man will be."

"I guess I wouldn't," Manolis laughed.

"Tall-as-a-star Starkas from our ship," she said. "Remember? He and my Petros have become dear friends."

Manolis was cheered that he'd see his companion of the voyage again. "We'll all be reunited once more," he said.

Andreas returned to the kitchen to tell them he couldn't find Petros.

"Maybe he's returning the horse and buggy to Mr. Santilis," Papadia Cristina said.

"The horse and buggy are outside," Andreas said.

"Then, some of the miners have carried him off," Father Basil said. "Several were asking about him earlier. They take their problems to him as often as they come to me." He smiled at Alexandra. "Manolis will meet your Petros tomorrow. Take the horse and buggy back to Mr. Santilis, Andreas."

They sat and talked for the next few hours, until everyone grew drowsy. When the family had retired upstairs, the Papadia spread blankets for Manolis before the small fire that burned in the fireplace.

"Sleep well, Manolis," she said. She stretched on her toes to kiss him goodnight, and he thought of his mother in their village so far away.

The Papadia walked upstairs, and he removed his shoes and breeches and slipped between the blankets. He was listening to the embers crackling and sighing when he heard someone quietly descending the stairs. Soula appeared, pausing on the final step. In the flickering firelight, he saw that she wore a flannel nightgown that hung to her ankles. Her pale face glowed in the shadows.

"Manolis?" She whispered his name.

He made a sign to her that he was awake.

"I only came down to tell you how glad I am that you're here," she said softly.

She hurried back up the stairs. When the voices and movement in the rooms above him grew quiet, he heard the wind wailing beneath the eaves. Feeling nested and secure among people he loved who loved him, he slipped finally into a restful sleep.

For a few days he remained with the priest and his family. Then he located lodgings in town in the boardinghouse where Mr. Krokas lived. When the man learned of his aptitude at reading and writing, he offered Manolis a position as a clerk in his notary office. Manolis worked there through the day and, at the insistence of the Papadia, continued to eat his meals with the family.

"We have, at the very least, five persons at our table," she told him, "and often a good many more. There will always be a place for you, Manolis. Besides, Soula and I are determined to add more meat to your tall, lean frame."

He was delighted to accept her invitation and looked forward to the dinner each evening and to sharing the lively banter at the table. Yet the real pleasure of the evenings for him were being with Soula. She bewildered him at how swiftly she alternated between the roles of child and young woman. When her brother teased her, she made bizarre faces back at him or, despite her mother's admonition, stuck out her small, pink tongue. At other times, when she listened to her father talking about the plight of the miners, a pensiveness settled in her face, an expression of such sympathy that Manolis felt she listened with her soul.

Although during that first week Manolis heard the miners in the coffeehouse speaking with admiration and affection of

the man Alexandra was going to marry, he hadn't yet met
Petros. The morning after Manolis arrived in Snowmass,
Petros had sent Alexandra a note telling her that union business was taking him to Salt Lake City and he'd return as soon
as he could. Alexandra's distress at their separation confirmed
to Manolis that she loved Petros dearly.

On Sunday morning, Manolis attended church with the
family. When the mass ended, he followed Papadia Cristina
and the girls from church. Alexandra walked a few feet ahead
of him, and as she passed through the doors into the sunlight,
she cried out. When Manolis emerged from the church, he
saw her embracing a tall, bearded man. She led him back to
them. Papadia Cristina and Soula greeted him warmly.

"This is my Petros," Alexandra said to Manolis, and her
face shone with joy. "Petros, this is our dear friend who
crossed the ocean with us."

The first impression he had of Petros was of a big man of
leonine strength. Even the tangle of his black, thick hair,
curling into a beard that concealed most of his face, evoked
power. There were scars on his temples, and the ridge of his
nose had been broken and mended crookedly. All the scars
and blemishes suggested he had suffered.

But it was the man's eyes that most affected Manolis.
Looking into them, he seemed to be staring at a shadowed
veil masking something he had seen before. Because Petros
was a stranger, he found that flutter of recognition bewildering. As they shook hands, he felt his fingers trembling. That,
too, was unsettling.

Miners came to greet Petros, and in a few minutes he and
Alexandra were engulfed in a crowd. When Papadia Cristina
cheerfully invited everyone who wished, to come to the house,
Manolis walked back with Soula and Andreas. Inside the
house, Petros continued to be surrounded by others. Once

or twice when it seemed that Petros noticed him staring, Manolis felt the dark enigma of his eyes.

Later that night, when he returned to his rooming house and went to bed, he had difficulty falling asleep. He felt as if his brain would split apart, because it held some knowledge it couldn't transmit to his senses.

All through the following day his uneasiness continued. When he asked Mr. Krokas, in the notary office, about Petros, the businessman couldn't tell him any more than he already knew. Petros was a union organizer, respected and admired by the miners and loved deeply by Alexandra and her family.

"When did he come to America from Crete, Mr. Krokas?"

"I don't know, my boy."

"Do you know the village he came from?"

Krokas shook his head.

"Has he spoken of his family?"

"He must have a family," Krokas said. "All men have. But I know nothing about his relations." He paused. "Why so many questions, Manolis?"

"He reminds me of someone," Manolis said in a low, flustered voice.

"A friend?"

"I don't know," Manolis said.

That evening, Petros wasn't with them at dinner but came soon afterward. He sat in a corner, drinking a glass of wine and smoking his pipe, which exuded a thin trail of smoke. Manolis couldn't keep from staring at him, feeling a tension almost more than flesh and blood could bear. The others must have noticed his nervousness, because he caught the priest and the Papadia watching him with concern. He told them he wasn't feeling well and left.

He followed the path that ran from the house to the church, grateful to be free in the clear night. A partial moon was visible above the steeple of the church, casting light across the trees and the path. From the direction of the town, he heard the strains of music.

He had reached the graveyard when he heard his name. He turned and saw that Petros had followed him. He paused a few feet from Manolis, the beam of the moon revealing his scarred, bearded face.

"I know that in an hour, or a day, you will remember, Manolis," Petros said quietly. "I didn't want that memory to return for you while we were with the family. This moment of reckoning belongs to the two of us."

The night around them was suddenly, totally still, as if the earth itself were holding its breath.

"When I saw you through the kitchen window last Sunday night," Petros said, "I ran in panic and, for a week, hid on the mountain. Then I understood I couldn't remain hidden. What fate has written in black ink, even the sun cannot whiten." His voice faltered, became somber and low. "I am Stellios Trombakis, Manolis. I am the killer of your brother."

The words burst in Manolis' head like a dark wind, storming through his blood, shattering his senses.

"I won't plead for mercy, Manolis." Stellios made a resigned gesture. "Nor will I raise my hand against you. God knows I deserve to die for that brutal, unforgiving act. Punish me, then, so the living and the dead can find their rest."

Manolis felt a trembling shake his body, a rage so consuming that if he had had to destroy the world to kill Stellios, he would have done it then.

"I came after you to kill you!" he said hoarsely. "I swore on Aleko's grave that I would kill you!"

"Kill me, then!" Stellios said earnestly. "I told you I won't resist you!" He fumbled in his jacket. "Here is my gun! Do it now!" He flung the weapon so that it landed on the ground at Manolis' feet.

"You goddam murderer! You deserve to die!"

"Yes, I deserve to die! Then, kill me, Manolis! Pick up the gun and do it now! They'll think the company police shot me! Or if you fear punishment, tomorrow we'll go together up the mountain. You can kill me there by pushing me off a cliff. They'd call it an accident! You'll not be blamed!"

Manolis rejected the scheming words. The man's nature was crafty, evil, treacherous. Even offering his weapon was a clever ruse. Manolis bent and picked up the gun, his blood crying out for blood.

"Petros!" They heard Alexandra's voice on the path from the house. Neither of them moved until she reached them. "Petros," she said anxiously. "Why did you leave like that?"

She saw Manolis and must have felt some of the tension and rage that besieged the air around them. She stepped closer to Stellios, her face shaken with a sudden fear.

"It's all right, my dearest." Stellios moved to shield her body with his own. "Manolis and I were just talking about a problem he asked me to help him solve." His voice pleaded for Manolis not to say anything before Alexandra. "We can settle it tomorrow, Manolis," he said earnestly. "I'll be at the Arcadian coffeehouse first thing in the morning."

As Stellios waited for him to answer, a cloud obscured the moon, darkening the earth. For a moment both of them seemed to Manolis to resemble hooded figures in mourning.

"All right," he said. "I'll meet you in the morning. We'll settle it then."

Sitting in his room, the gleaming gun on the bed beside him, he considered the incalculable twistings of fate that

had brought him and Stellios to meet in Utah. He hadn't
found Stellios, Stellios had found him. That meant Manolis
needn't wait any longer for word from his uncle Agrios. The
mission was now his alone to fulfill.

But vengeance wasn't any longer a clear, simple punishment for a murderer. There were others involved—like Father Basil and Papadia Cristina, who had treated him as if he
were their son. There was Alexandra, who was betrothed to
Stellios, their marriage only a few weeks away. Finally, there
was Soula, who might someday become his wife. If he
fulfilled his vow and killed Stellios, he would bring them grief
and sorrow, and would destroy his own chance for happiness.

But neither could he bear the thought of Stellios living un-
punished. That would betray Aleko, publicly humiliate his
family in the village, and disgrace those men of his family
who had not failed their stern obligations. He remembered
the stories he had heard, as a child, of the man from another
village who had killed his great-uncle Lefteris, the murderer's
knife broken off in his uncle's body. Five years later, in a distant part of Crete, his great-uncle Stratis had killed the murderer with the broken-off half of that blade. That was the way
vengeance should be fulfilled.

All night long, he agonized over the dilemma. When dawn
spread a gray shroud across his window, he hadn't yet slept.
But through the anguished hours he felt his resolve harden-
ing, his heart resisting temptations to mercy, pity or love.
He decided that if he did not kill Stellios, he'd never be born
into manhood.

With his decision made, he walked from his room to the
coffeehouse, the cold weight of the gun in his belt pressed
against his belly. He sat at a table in the corner, watching the
door. Men entered the crowded, smoky room, but Stellios
didn't appear. True to his treacherous nature, his promise had

been a deception. For the first time, Manolis thought with dark joy of his revenge.

Later in the morning, he rose to leave the coffeehouse in search of Stellios. At that moment, several excited miners rushed in the door. One man stepped up on a chair so he was visible to everyone in the room and shouted for silence.

"The Coal and Iron Police have arrested Petros!" he cried hoarsely. "We saw him with our own eyes, bound in chains, being dragged by the bastards to jail!"

In the stunned silence that followed his words, men looked at one another in dismay, huddling to speak in somber tones. A number of them surrounded the men who had brought the tidings.

The news embittered Manolis, because his vengeance would have to wait. For a moment, he was uncertain what to do, and then he decided to find Father Basil. The priest would know when Stellios was released.

He left the coffeehouse, hurrying past the transient hotels and boardinghouses toward the church. The news about Stellios had spread rapidly through Greek Town, and groups of grim-faced men gathered on street corners. Some of them had come straight from their shifts in the mine with their faces blackened and the pit lamps still fixed to their caps.

At the church, Manolis found Father Basil assembled with Santilis and about a dozen miners. The distraught priest came to speak to him.

"We are planning to meet with the town officials and the chief of police," the priest said. "Krokas has sent a wire to the governor asking protection for Petros." He shook his head in resignation. "I'm afraid these measures will be futile."

"Can I do anything for you, Father?"

"There's nothing you can do here, my boy," the priest said. "But can you go and stay with my family at the house? Alexandra will be grateful to have you there."

Manolis nodded, and the priest returned to his meeting, his black cassock swirling about his ankles.

At the priest's house, Manolis found a dozen somber miners standing outside like sentries. For the first time since his arrival, he saw men carrying rifles, with revolvers stuck in their belts. Andreas was with them, his face flushed with excitement and anger.

"I wanted to go to town," he said bitterly to Manolis, "but my father has told me to stay here. Have you heard anything? Have they broken Petros out of jail?"

"They're trying to do that peacefully, Andreas," Manolis said. Andreas shook his head in disgust and turned away.

Soula opened the door for Manolis. She came gratefully into his arms, and he felt her slim body trembling. When he greeted Alexandra, he sensed the terror beneath her apparent calm.

"Petros will be returned safely to us, Manolis." Papadia Cristina spoke earnestly, as if to reassure herself. "We have prayed to God and we must believe that He will be merciful and anwer our prayers."

Manolis waited with them in the silent, mournful house while the morning dragged into afternoon. In the yard, venting his temper, Andreas began chopping wood, striking the ax loudly against the logs. When the Papadia and Soula served lemonade to the men outside, Manolis drank tea with Alexandra. She had spent the hours walking restlessly from room to room until weariness made her sit down.

Seeing her dark, haunted eyes and her cheeks drained of blood, Manolis felt remorse and shame. He was there in the guise of a friend, when he had been ready to cause her a greater sorrow. Now her misery foreshadowed for him what her mourning would be like if Stellios were dead.

"Have you ever been in love, Manolis?" she asked him suddenly.

"I'm not sure," he said. He didn't think it was the time to tell her he loved Soula.

"You'll know love when it happens," she said softly. "As if, when we're born, we're only half of what we should be. When I saw Petros, for the first time, I felt myself whole and complete. Do you understand, Manolis?"

She asked the question gravely, as if she were the teacher and he the child. He nodded mutely, staring at the window that was darkening with the fall of twilight.

"You can't know how he's suffered, Manolis," Alexandra said. "You've seen the scars on his face from beatings, but he has a terrible scar around his throat. Evil men hanged his brother and him. His brother died but, by a miracle, Petros was saved and brought to me." She stared at her hands, her voice tightened by an effort not to cry. "Now they've taken him from me again."

So Mitsos was dead, he thought grimly, and Stellios had almost died. If both brothers had been hanged, he'd have been spared the act of vengeance.

His wavering and remorse made him angry with himself. He didn't want to listen anymore to Alexandra talking about her love for Stellios. He was grateful when Papadia Cristina entered the kitchen and asked him to kindle a fire in the fireplace.

Later in the evening, Father Basil returned home. When he entered the house with Santilis and a few miners, Alexandra rushed to him.

"Did you see him, Papa? Have they hurt him? Is he well?"

"They wouldn't allow any of us to see him, not even your

father," Santilis said gravely. "They say he is being held for trial."

"We mustn't give up hope, my darling," Father Basil said quickly. "We'll try again tomorrow. And by then, we may also hear from the governor." He motioned to the Papadia. "Cristina, could we have tea and perhaps some bread and cheese? None of the men have eaten."

When Cristina and the girls had left the room to prepare a snack, a tall miner Manolis knew as Leonidas spoke.

"There's little reason to hope, Father, and we all know it," Leonidas said bitterly. "Petros is in mortal danger. Those trumped-up charges of conspiracy and the shooting of those deputies in Silver City are an excuse. They know how important he is to the union and they won't let him live to stand trial. He'll be shot, they'll say while trying to escape."

"They wouldn't dare do such a thing!" Father Basil said in shock.

"They have before and they will again!" Leonidas said fiercely. "We mustn't give them the chance with Petros! I ask you again, Let us do it our way. In an hour I'll have a hundred armed men to storm the jail! We'll break him free!"

"That's the only way, Papa!" Andreas said. "They'll kill Petros if we don't!" The boy's face glowed with fervor. His father gave him a reproving look.

"We mustn't free him that way, Leonidas," the priest said quietly. "If you storm the jail, men will be shot and killed. Petros wouldn't wish that to happen."

"Father Basil is right," Santilis said somberly. "I recall once when some miners were quarreling and about to settle their dispute with guns, Petros calmed their anger. I thought then he was a man who abhorred violence."

But that isn't the man I remember, Manolis thought bitterly. He has lied and deceived them and concealed the truth that he is a murderer and a brute.

He slept again that night by the fire. He slept fitfully, waking several times, once thinking he heard someone upstairs crying. He considered again the strange sequence of events that had begun when he arrived in Snowmass.

A loud knocking at the door awakened him in the morning. Papadia Cristina and Father Basil were already in the kitchen, and when Manolis had joined them, he was delighted to see the giant Starkas. The big man grabbed Manolis in so robust a hug he felt his ribs groaning.

"So we meet again, boy!" Starkas said. "When there is trouble, good Cretans show up to have a share!"

When Alexandra, Soula and Andreas entered the kitchen, a moment later, Starkas hugged them all within the span of his broad arms. Manolis noticed how the sturdy, commanding Cretan buoyed the family's spirits.

"I've got good news!" Starkas said and grinned. "The day shift of miners refused to go down to the pits. They vow not to work until Petros has been released."

"Who authorized such a strike?" Father Basil asked in surprise.

"The men decided for themselves"—Starkas winked—"with a little help from here and there."

"What are the authorities doing?"

"They've filled the streets with deputies and police," Starkas sneered. "The mine managers are blustering and making threats."

"They'll be sorry if they tangle with our boys!" Andreas said.

"You're right, my boy!" Starkas said. "Our Cretans know about slavery and imprisonment and how to strike for free-

dom!" He paused. "But something even more important than
the strike is taking place," he said, an excitement trembling
his voice. "Miners from other towns who've heard of the ar-
rest of Petros are coming into Snowmass. They've been arriving all night from Price and Provo, from Springfield and
Spanish Fork!" He laughed vigorously. "You know old Cleon
Kezios, from Helper? He brought his four sons and twenty
more armed men!"

"God help us!" the priest said. "We'll end up with a full-
scale war!"

"Maybe a war won't be necessary," Starkas said brusquely.
"If they see we mean to have Petros out, one way or another,
they could back down." He gestured at the priest. "Anyway,
Father, we have a meeting scheduled with the mine managers
and we'd like you there."

"Papa!" Andreas pleaded. "Let me come with you!"

"No!" his mother said.

"You stay here and look after your sisters," Starkas said.

"Manolis can look after them!"

"I want Manolis with me!" Starkas said sternly. "I'm in
command now and I order you to remain here."

"Don't worry, Andreas," Manolis consoled the boy, "I'll re-
port to you on everything I see and hear."

"Be careful, Manolis, please!" Soula cried the warning so
fervently that everyone looked at her. She turned away
quickly, leaving Manolis touched and grateful for her concern.

When Father Basil, Starkas and Manolis arrived in town,
they found miners thronging the streets and filling the coffeehouses and lobbies of the hotels. Other men clustered on bal-
conies or leaned out of windows. Though it was illegal to
wear arms, men brandished them openly. Everywhere the
mood was tense, impatient and angry.

In a great demonstration, at noon, a thousand men marched from Greek Town across the tracks through the neat, clean shopping areas of Old Snowmass. Starkas linked arms with Manolis in the front rank of marchers carrying Greek and American flags, ragtail pennants, and signs demanding freedom for the imprisoned.

The greatly outnumbered deputies and police formed a ragged, uneasy cordon before the shops. About half a hundred of them nervously guarded the jail where Stellios was being held. As the marchers neared the jail, their leaders kept them moving to avoid clashing with the police. But word spread through the ranks for the men to roar.

"Let Petros hear us!" Starkas bellowed. "Let the coal and iron lackeys hear us too!"

The roars from the throats of a thousand men reverberated and thundered like a bombardment through the town.

When the marchers returned to Greek Town and dispersed again into the coffeehouses, Manolis walked through the crowds, catching a flurry of rumors that more miners would be arriving, including a contingent of a hundred Sfakian fighters who were marching from Salt Lake City. They were expected to reach Snowmass by the following morning. There was also a rumor that the famed labor organizer Mother Jones was on her way to the town. There were other reports that the mine owners had asked the governor to send in the militia.

Whatever the truth of those rumors, all afternoon and into the evening more miners kept arriving in town. Like an army assembling, Manolis thought with awe, a militant host prepared to fight and die for the freedom of a solitary man.

There were incidents of violence. A dozen fights broke out between miners and deputies that produced some torn knuckles and bloodied heads. Then, at twilight, it appeared the war might have begun when a flurry of shots erupted from the freight yards. That skirmish resulted when a detachment of deputies and police occupied the rail yards and the railroad station. In retaliation, Starkas sent a hundred armed miners to take strategic positions in the rocks above the town. From that high point, if violence broke out, they could have poured a heavy fire down on the shops and houses in Old Snowmass.

All that night the watchfires of those men burned on the mountain, giving the occupants of the town a feeling that an army had them under siege.

Then, as quickly as the confrontation began, the crisis was over. Fearing their houses and shops would be burned and destroyed by the growing numbers of armed men, the mine managers and police capitulated. Early in the morning, Starkas emerged from a meeting to proclaim that Stellios was being released.

As word of their victory spread through the crowds, the tumult and thunder of gunshots spread from street to street, mounting in volume. A delegation of miners escorted Stellios from the jail, while hundreds of others lined the route he would walk from Greek Town to the Church, where Father Basil would offer a mass of thanksgiving.

Manolis waited in the crowd until Stellios appeared in a phalanx of men, hundreds following in his wake. The firing and shouting became deafening. As Stellios passed not far from him, Manolis saw he had not escaped unscathed. He was bedraggled, with blood on his clothing and face, but he walked in the procession like a hero, men reaching out to touch him with their hands as he passed.

Moving with the throng toward the church, Manolis was bewildered at the outpouring of affection and devotion. He had known Stellios as a primitive man, uncaring about any other human being. The loyalty and tribute he was receiving was reserved for truly noble men, the adulation Aleko would have earned had he lived and come to America. Men would surely have cheered Aleko as they cheered Stellios now.

And then a thought possessed Manolis, a revelation like an explosion in his body. He sensed that in some inexplicable, mystical way, the murdered and the murderer had been merged. Whether by remorse and repentance, or by the divine justice of God, Stellios had absorbed the soul of Aleko. In the moment of his triumph, tall and strong, black eyes glowing, radiating heroism and a valiant heart, Stellios even resembled Aleko. For Manolis to kill him would have been to murder Aleko a second time.

As he flung away the vow he had taken to avenge his brother, a great freedom burst the knots of his heart. He drew breath more freely than he had breathed in years, feeling in a redemptive way that he had also been released from a prison, more terrible than any jail devised by men.

In the final weeks before the marriage of Stellios and Alexandra, Manolis was at the priest's house daily to witness the men bringing small gifts for the bride and groom. These presents were often beloved mementos they had carried with them from Crete. They stayed long enough to drink a cup of tea and inquire anxiously whether the bridal gown being sewn by the seamstress in Salt Lake City would be ready in time.

Hundreds of men prepared for the wedding and celebration to follow as if they were the bridegrooms. They washed and patched their best clothing, bartering with friends for a shirt or a pair of breeches. Those who still had the treasured boots, polished and repolished them to a lustrous shine. While, all night long, the lyra and bouzouki players practiced their dancing and drinking songs.

Inside the house, the Papadia and her daughters baked from morning until dark. After delivering flour and sugar to them from town, Manolis loved to linger in the warm, fragrant kitchen, admiring Soula with her flushed cheeks and apron smudged with flour. As the Papadia briskly kneaded the dough, she lamented that the wedding couldn't have taken place in Crete.

"For weeks before my own wedding," she said wistfully to her daughters and Manolis, "there were twenty women baking with my mother. I remember the laughter and gossip and, from every room in the house, the shrieks of playing children. I wish you could have had that too."

"That's all right, Mama," Alexandra reassured her. "Stellios and I love each other. We're lucky too, because hundreds of men wish us happiness."

Manolis told himself that he, too, helped nourish their happiness. While he had never explained to Stellios the reasons he had renounced his vow of vengeance, soon after Stellios had been released from jail, Manolis returned his gun. For a few moments then, his eyes moist, Stellios struggled to speak.

"I don't deserve your mercy and forgiveness," he said finally, "but I accept it thankfully, for Alexandra and for myself. I'll try to be worthy of it and, I swear to God, Manolis, that for as long as I live I'll try to be your brother."

The secret remained sealed between them, neither man speaking of it after that day. When Manolis felt a trepidation about someday having to explain and justify his decision to his uncle Agrios and his family in Crete, Alexandra's joy appeased his distress.

By late September the summer seemed over. Twilight fell earlier and, during the night, frost glazed the earth. The chilly days hinted at an early and cold winter.

But the morning of the wedding dawned like a balmy day in August. As the sun rose higher in the sky, the fading greenery gained a resurgent sparkle. For a single day, the earth seemed to muster a renewed florescence for Stellios and Alexandra.

The Snowmass mine was shut down for the day, but the miners were not idle. In preparation for the celebration, men dug the pits to roast the lambs on the spit. Casks of wine were hauled by wagon from the town to the long tables set up outside the house. There were a hundred loaves of crisp-crusted bread and casks of cheese and olives.

Hours before the start of the wedding, the church was jammed with men, while an overflow crowd gathered outside. They milled impatiently until the horse and buggy carrying Alexandra, Soula and the Papadia arrived at the church. During the night, the men had decorated the buggy with streamers and bunting. Even the harness of the horse was garlanded with flowers, so when a proud, strutting Andreas drove up, horse and buggy shone with the grandeur of a royal carriage.

Manolis found himself jostled aside by a score of other men, who offered their hands to Soula and Papadia Cristina. When Alexandra stood up in the buggy, even the men at the perimeters of the crowd must have had their eyes seared by the spellbinding vision of her beauty. From the diaphanous veil that graced her black hair to her flowing white bridal gown, she must have reminded them of the weddings of sisters and friends they had seen in Crete.

Shortly after the women entered the church, a pair of horsemen galloped up. As the men broke into lusty cheers for the groom and the best man, Stellios leaped to the ground. He was clad in the finery of a Cretan chieftain, with wide-sleeved shirt, fringed tasseled vest, dark breeches and black glistening boots. Starkas, whose assorted garments resembled the plumage of a peacock, waved gaily to the throng and walked into the church.

When Manolis entered the narthex, the Papadia, with the

bride and Soula, who was her bridesmaid, were concealed in an alcove. Stellios, Starkas and Andreas had walked to join the three priests waiting before the altar table. In addition to Father Basil, there was Father Foundakis, from the church in Salt Lake City, and the swarthy circuit-riding priest, Father Grivas. Above their vestment-clad figures loomed the icons of the austere saints, the floating mists of incense, the myriad candles with flames like molten gold rising from their wicks.

In a moment, Papadia Cristina came from the alcove with the bride and Soula. Alexandra looked nervously at the crowded church. Soula smiled at Manolis, and then she also hesitated before the tremor of anticipation from the assembly. Men twisted and stretched to catch a glimpse of them. As the bride and Soula entered the nave, walking in a slow processional up the aisle, the Papadia watched beside Manolis. She was crying, while, all around them, he saw men with tears in their eyes.

Father Basil descended the steps to take his daughter's arm. He led her slowly to Stellios, who bent and kissed his hand. Bride and groom took their place before the altar table.

Manolis led the Papadia to the front of the church below the altar as Father Basil began the ceremony by exchanging the rings three times on the fingers of Stellios and Alexandra.

Father Foundakis raised the Book of Gospels into the air. "O God most pure, the Creator of every living thing, who didst transform the rib of our forefather Adam into a wife and didst bless them, and say unto them, increase and multiply and have dominion over the earth . . ."

The circuit-riding priest raised his own voice, hoarsely honed by prayers chanted in lonely hamlets and threadbare huts. "Grant them of the fruit of their bodies, fair children, concord of soul . . . Exalt them like the cedars of Lebanon, like a luxuriant vine. Give them seed in number like unto the full ears of grain, that they may shine like the stars of heaven in thee, our God."

The flames of the candles flickered, trails of incense rising and vanishing beneath the dome. A holy mist permeated the church, inflaming the air. The priests chanted and prayed.

Father Basil raised the twin crowns of orange blossoms joined by a satin ribbon and placed them gently upon the heads of Stellios and Alexandra. "Be thou exalted, O Bridegroom, like unto Abraham, and be thou blessed, like unto Isaac, and do thou multiply like unto Jacob, walking in peace and keeping the commandments of God in righteousness."

With the crown of blossoms gleaming in Stellios' thick, black hair, Manolis felt suddenly that if the bridegroom turned around he'd see Aleko standing beside Alexandra. The vision stung his heart and eyes.

"And thou, O Bride, be thou exalted like unto Sarah, like unto Rebecca, and do thou multiply, like unto Rachel . . . and rejoice thou in thy husband, fulfilling the conditions of the law, for so is it well pleasing to God."

When the priests led the bride and groom three times around the table in the slow, measured ritual dance to God, Starkas followed them, gingerly holding the crowns on their heads.

Manolis heard the Papadia whispering a prayer, and he echoed her prayer, staring at Soula, wondering if they would someday circle the altar table together.

Near the end of the service, the bride and groom drank from the chalice, as they would forever after share the cup of life. Then the priests joined their voices in the benediction. "May the Father and the Son and the Holy Spirit, the all-holy and life-giving Trinity, bless you and keep you unto your length of days . . . Amen."

A great sigh like a wind swept through the church. Stellios turned to Alexandra and slowly, so slowly raised her veil. Manolis saw her glistening, exquisite face as Stellios bent and placed a light, chaste kiss upon her lips. The crowd responded with a heartfelt murmur of delight.

Afterward Father Basil kissed each of them, and Father Foundakis and Father Grivas kissed them. Soula kissed them, and Starkas hugged them together in his robust arms. They turned and started down the aisle, pausing before the Papadia and Manolis. They kissed her, and Alexandra kissed Manolis. For a moment, he smelled blossoms and the molten wax of candles about her. Then Stellios extended his hand to him, and Manolis saw the naked emotion in the bridegroom's eyes. He hesitated only an instant and then reached out to clasp the other man's hand. The strangeness of grasping the hand of a man he had once sworn to kill sent a heat coursing through his body.

Holding the Papadia and Soula by the arm, Manolis led them from the church toward the noisy, jubilant mass of men waiting outside. As Stellios and Alexandra emerged into the sunlight, a volley of gunfire split the air, one rumbling detonation following another. At the same time, they were deluged with a rain of rice and blossoms, a grinning Andreas leading the assault. Stellios, laughing and dodging, tried to shield Alexandra. When the tall Starkas emerged from the church, his height caught the brunt of the shower of rice. He staggered about, trying to protect his head and eyes.

Paced by the thunder of the guns, Stellios hurried Alexandra toward the buggy at the base of the steps. Men leaped forward to shake his hand and pound his shoulders. Some reached out to touch his sleeve or to fleetingly touch a fold of the bride's gown as if hoping to wrest a measure of good fortune into their own lives.

Following with the Papadia and Soula a short distance behind them in the midst of the crowd, Manolis noticed a man standing beside the buggy. He was taller than any of the men around him, wearing a dusty windbreaker and a battered, wide-brimmed hat that concealed his face. There was a tension in the way he waited, a wariness in the way he stood, that did not belong to the celebration. Without being certain why the sight of the man alarmed him, Manolis began pushing through the crowd toward the buggy. His shout to Stellios was lost in the thundering volleys of guns.

As Stellios and Alexandra reached the buggy, the tall man stepped calmly into their path. Stellios reached for his hand as well. The tall man raised his head, sunlight exposing his face. For a stunned instant Manolis thought he was seeing the ghost of his brother, and then he recognized the countenance from an old photograph in his house in Crete. He did not hear the shots he knew were fired, but he saw Stellios stagger and then fall. Then Uncle Agrios raised the gun above his head, brandishing it for an instant in a fierce and defiant gesture before the crowd. Afterward he ran around the buggy to one of the horses the groom had ridden to the church. He leaped on the animal's back and spurred it swiftly away, racing along the path that led toward the mountain.

The men closest to the buggy were the first to see what had taken place. They stared at the fallen Stellios in a stricken, bewildered silence that spread from man to man, the voices and laughter fading, the last gunshots exploding crisply in the air until they, too, fell silent. The earth grew still, so muffled and hushed that the distant, plaintive cry of a bird trailed from the sky.

When Manolis reached the buggy, joining the men who crouched about Stellios, Alexandra knelt on the ground beside him. Below the white bride's veil lay her husband's dead face. And in that moment, from her lips came a scream that tore the stillness into shreds, a lament of such anguish that Manolis would hear it again and again until the hour of his own death.

AMERICA
1912

Father Basil

All day long, the midwife, Kyra Aspasia, had been at their house attending Alexandra, who had begun her labor at dawn. Now, in the twilight of what had been one of the longest days of his life, Father Basil had made the trip between his house and the church a dozen times until, finally, Cristina had pleaded with him to wait at the church, promising they'd send for him as soon as the baby was born.

He walked outside once again to stare toward the lamp-bright windows of his house, imagining his beloved daughter in pain and struggle. In a way, he was secretly grateful to have been spared the distress of her labor. Although he had willed himself to be near Cristina when their children were born, he had always felt that childbirth was a sacred ritual men had no right to witness.

He was grateful that Alexandra's baby wasn't being born during the desolate, cold winter. All around them now were the stirrings of spring. Only the day before, he had noticed the first greening of the leaf-bearing trees on the slopes of the mountain. While, in that moment, in the darkness around him, he could smell the wind carrying the earth's resurgence across a sky with stars so huge and bright he felt if he reached up he could snare one with his hand.

Yet, he thought sadly as he reentered the church, no matter how many seasons passed, none of them would recover from the agony of his daughter's wedding day. The murder had burst upon their celebration like a thunderbolt hurled from some demon who could not abide their happiness.

A few months short of a year had passed since that day, and there were still moments when he found it hard to accept that Petros was dead. He had loomed among other men not only because of his physical strength but for his compassion and greatness of spirit. Even after death, such a man remained an exemplary image of human life.

For a day and a night while his flower-garlanded coffin rested in state in the church, a thousand mourners filed past, men bending to kiss his hand or his cheek in a gesture of homage that would be remembered in the coalfields forever. After his funeral, fearing desecration of his grave, the throng refused to allow him to be buried in the graveyard beside the church. A band of men, led by Starkas, carried his coffin into the mountains. There were rumors they had buried him in a cave and sealed the entrance with an avalanche of rock. Other men whispered in awe that a dam had been built to divert the flow of a mountain stream and Petros was buried in a grave in the riverbed. Then the dam was broken, the water rushing down to flood the earth over the grave so no man would ever tread the ground where Petros was buried.

Father Basil didn't know which story might be true. He did know that his daughter's terrible mourning for her bridegroom was unlike any sorrow he had ever witnessed. For several months she rarely spoke and couldn't keep what small quantity of food and drink she consumed in her stomach. She grew listless, her large eyes receding into the black, curved hollows. Cristina and he were frightened that she'd pine away until death reunited her with Petros once more.

But then a miracle had taken place, the marvel of the seed of life in her body. Although Father Basil understood that the child had been conceived before they married, in violation of church canons and shocking many of the young men in the parish, he and Papadia Cristina were finally grateful for that union, because it provided their daughter a faithful link to life. With the knowledge that she carried the child of Petros in her body, her heart and spirit mended. If she still mourned her lost love, there were also times when Father Basil saw her clasping her swelling belly with a soft, secret contentment. He was reassured then that she would live and that she would prevail.

That dreadful winter, he had also endured a disabling melancholy. Many nights, he experienced the loneliness of the sleepless who feel themselves disembodied ghosts wandering the earth while others are at rest. In the silence of those afflicted hours, he relived the nightmare of what had taken place.

He would have remained ignorant of any purpose behind the killing if it had not been for Manolis, who, soon after the murder, confessed to him about the vendetta. The young man was driven to speak by his feelings of remorse and guilt, because the killer had been his uncle and because he himself once had planned to murder Petros. The priest tried to console him, praising his decision to be merciful and forgiving and explaining that God would not hold him culpable for the baleful deed of another.

In his solitary moments, the priest pondered the journeys that had brought Petros and Manolis together in his house. Every action in their lives from the time of the murder of Aleko Manousakis, in Crete, had led with a relentless inevita-

bility toward the confrontation. He himself had contributed to
it by helping Manolis with his brother's ticket in the steamship office in Rethymnon. Then Petros had met and loved
Alexandra, and the chef in Chicago had lied to Manolis and
sent him West . . . on and on through the siftings of chance,
their paths converged.

Yet, whatever circuitous journeys the two men made were
overshadowed by the savage, secret stalking of the one who
finally killed Petros. Manolis had not spoken to or seen his
uncle Agrios since arriving in America. He didn't know how
Agrios had tracked Petros or whether he had had a chance to
kill him before. Perhaps he had found him earlier, the priest
thought, and with the implacable cruelty inherent in the vendetta, bided his time for that moment when Petros seemed
happy and most anxious to live.

In the end, the meaning of why Petros should have been allowed to struggle and ascend from brutishness to humanity
only to be murdered, would remain a mystery, one of the par-
adoxes in which the contradictions tangle like weeds. Expla-
nations and reasonings were the feeble efforts of man to
probe those unsolvable enigmas. All that mortals were destined to know, as Heraclitus had written, was that out of life
came death and out of death life, out of the young the old
and out of the old the young, out of waking sleep, and out of
sleep waking, the streams of creation and dissolution never
ending.

The interior of the church had grown black as pitch, and
he rose and lit a cluster of candles. As their flickering wicks
cast trails of light through the darkness, he knelt before the
Sanctuary and prayed. He prayed for his daughter Alexandra,
struggling now to bring life from her womb. He prayed for his
daughter Soula and for Manolis, in the dew and vigor of their
youth, that they might redeem his guilt and find their love to-

gether someday. He prayed for his sturdy son, Andreas, that he might never succumb to the unyielding and obdurate passion that drove men to murder. He prayed for his beloved Cristina, faithful through all their travail, lending him comfort and strength. From the great repository of her woman's heart, she warmed and nourished them all. He prayed for the hundreds of young men laboring in the dark, wet tunnels beneath the earth, that they might remain safe and, someday, be bound in love to wives and children. Finally, he prayed for himself, for the frail vessel of his heart and the fragile container of his spirit, that by his labors in the vineyard of the Lord he might earn his death someday.

Into the murmur of his prayers, a sound intruded. He raised his head quickly and then rose and walked from the church into the night to listen. He heard the sound again, a startled cry, a thin, shocked wail rising from his house, whirling across the darkness, joining the wind, soaring beneath the stars.

And with the cry that he knew was the birth song of his grandchild, he felt his sorrow and melancholy dispelled. If the anguished questions could never be answered and if the compulsion to murder lurked in every mortal heart, the promise of humanity went on as well, each birth reaffirming the magical, revelatory nature of life.

In that moment, he made his cross for what the solitude and the night had given him to understand. He longed suddenly to look upon that squirming, naked and still untainted child born of the love of Petros and his Alexandra.

Whispering and singing his prayers, he hurried through the darkness toward his house.